My Greek Summer

My Big Greek Summer

SUE ROBERTS

Bookouture

Published by Bookouture in 2018

An imprint of StoryFire Ltd.

Carmelite House
50 Victoria Embankment
London EC4Y 0DZ

www.bookouture.com

ISBN: 978-1-78681-363-3
eBook ISBN: 978-1-78681-362-6

To my daughters Rachel and Vicki.
Life is for living. Follow your dreams.

CHAPTER ONE

It's funny how we make assumptions about people, isn't it? You might be surprised to learn that the grey-haired couple in the pub, who you thought were still holding hands after a lifetime together, had actually met on an Internet dating site three months ago. Or that tattooed leather-clad biker on the next table, sipping a pint of real ale… you would never guess that he had spent his younger years as a trained dancer and now teaches salsa dancing at the local community centre to supplement his courier wage. We do it all the time. I mean, the customers who see my cheery pink-lipped smile as I serve them food and drinks at the Pig and Whistle would never guess that I'm an emotional mess inside.

'Would you like any side orders with that?' I chirp as I punch their food orders into the till, even though my stomach churns at the thought of eating a single morsel.

I've lost twelve pounds in the last three weeks, a fact I would normally shout from the rooftops, had it not been heartbreak weight loss, aka the divorce diet. It's better than Slender World, Weight Controllers, or any other diet out there, and the best part of it is you don't even have to try. The heartache causes an instant loss of appetite, ensuring that you never gain a pound.

I thought that me and Danny Davis would last forever. We started going out together at school when we were both fifteen years old and bona fide members of the A team. We were the good-looking, popular ones who sneered at anyone who actually did any studying at school. We pitied those poor inky swots who were destined to live a life of greyness and boredom in their neat suburban semis, whereas us dudes would be travelling the world in a camper van. The boys in the A team rocked up at school on purple metallic mopeds as soon as they had reached their sixteenth birthdays, staking their place as masters of groove, while the bespectacled book-laden geeks could only look on in envy. Oh yes, school was all about planning the next disco and lying on the grass at breaktime, discussing such topics as whether shaving your legs did actually make the hair grow back thicker. Look where that got me though. Almost thirteen years down the line I'm working in a local pub and Danny Davis has just broken my heart.

I must stop daydreaming. There's an empty beer glass and wine glass on a nearby table that need removing and I don't want Brian, the kindly pub manager, to think I'm slacking. The last thing I need now is to lose my job, as it's the thing that makes me get up in the mornings.

I like working at the Pig and Whistle. If you're going to work in a pub restaurant then this place is as good as it gets. 'The Whistle', as it's known locally, is a sprawling pub with a maze of alcoves, situated six miles from Liverpool city centre in the Knowsley countryside. It attracts a variety of clientele, its biggest pull being the fact that it is an independent pub with its own microbrewery; it also has an outstanding chef called Darren, who came runner up in a Young Chef of the Year competition two years ago.

It's bright and cheery, with grey flagstone floors and chunky wooden tables and chairs. It's a mix of modern and homely, with chrome fixtures and fittings alongside stone walls bearing old farmland photographs. It has several log fires that roar into life during the winter months, and five different types of hand-pulled cask ales. The oak wood bar is slightly horseshoe-shaped and offers every alcoholic beverage known to man with the exception of absinthe, after an unfortunate event involving a man stripping naked at a pensioners' club lunch.

I have such a great view of everybody from behind this bar that it's like being a captain at the helm of a ship. There aren't too many locals that drink here, although there are a few that inhabit the terraced cottages near farmland just a couple of hundred yards away. There's Geoff, the ruddy-faced pig farmer, who exudes an interesting scent; Bill and Dot, married for forty years and still holding hands; and two young couples, one being me and Danny, who have bought our cottages seeking an idyllic location. It's semi-rural with a twice-hourly bus that goes into Liverpool city centre.

The rest of the pub clientele is made up of passing trade, parties celebrating special occasions, and Christmas nights out when the pub features tribute acts. These acts are generally very good, apart from last year's singer who was more Bruce Forsyth than Bruce Springsteen.

My job has been my salvation here these past weeks. People-watching just happens to be my hobby and observing the comings and goings of the pub clientele has made me realise I'm not the only one going through a tough time. Arranging a funeral-party buffet last week should have put everything in perspective really, yet my heart still aches for Danny.

The couple just leaving the table with the two empty glasses on it are having an affair. I can spot the signs a mile off. There were the furtive glances around the pub interior as they walked through the door, and the intermittent entwining of hands throughout lunch. Plus, the slender young woman looks more like the daughter of the slightly portly, well-heeled gent she's with. It makes me think of Danny and how he was able to hide his little affair with such ease. You think you know someone, but I didn't have a clue…

A group of young women arrive for lunch but Jack, one of our waiters, has disappeared. He's probably sneaked out for another cigarette. He's going to have to go. Jack's a student who's half-hearted about his job, and thinks he can get by because of his Brad Pitt (in his younger days) looks, but the pub has an enviable reputation for service that must be upheld.

I'm about to show the women's group to a table when Jack reappears, exuding his usual charm, so I resume my place behind the bar. Then my heart stops. A guy who is the image of Danny has just walked through the door. He has the same tall, slender build and brown, slightly curly hair. He strolls towards the bar, where I notice he has brown eyes rather than the aquamarine of Danny's. He smiles a slightly lopsided smile, revealing sparkling white teeth.

'What can I get you?' I beam, even though my heart is hammering at being in front of someone so remarkably similar to my husband.

'A pint of your best bitter and your phone number, please.' He grins.

'You're a bit forward, aren't you?' I reply, as I pull him a pint of Magpie bitter, a current favourite.

'Saves time.' He laughs. 'Gets the rejection out of the way quicker.' He feigns a sad expression.

We chat for a few minutes before I serve another customer. I should feel happy that I am being flirted with, and there is no doubt he is attractive, but I'm not interested. He's probably got an unsuspecting wife or girlfriend somewhere anyway.

I'm distracted by another group of people entering the pub and ask Lyndsey, a waitress, to watch the bar as I show a slim, glossy-haired businesswoman, with an expensive woollen coat, to a table with her group.

Jack is actually doing some work now, taking food orders from the party of young women who are flirting outrageously with him. Strands of blonde hair have tumbled down from my neat and tidy bun and attached themselves to my face in this unexpected heatwave towards the end of May. I am trying to cover the ketchup stains on my white blouse, which the toddler on the next table has just deposited on me with his sticky hands, as I plonk some menus down onto the wooden table and tell everyone about the blackboard specials, which are pork-and-cider casserole or sea bass with steamed asparagus.

The woman in the woollen coat has success oozing from her pores and I briefly consider that she must be around my age. She must have been the type that worked hard at school; someone who focused. I feel a brief stab of regret that I didn't do the same thing.

I don't dislike my job, in fact I love it, but I dreamed of becoming a journalist. That's all I did though. Dream. I never actually *worked* hard enough to achieve it. I was far more interested in boys, shopping, nightclubs, and anything that involved having fun.

I was the one who would round up all my friends to take taxis into neon-lit thoroughfares in different towns for nights out. I shudder when I think of how my best friend Hayley and I once hitch-hiked to London with a bearded trucker, who remained menacingly silent throughout the whole journey. We checked into a youth hostel in Holland Park, where we spent the next three nights exploring the city, only returning home when our money ran out. I can't recall the last time I had any sort of adventure, although maybe that's exactly what I need right now.

The woman with the copper-coloured highlights eases herself out of her blue woollen coat before handing it to me. It smells of Miss Dior. 'Be a doll and hang this up for me would you, Mandy,' she says, giving me a wry and very satisfied smile.

CHAPTER TWO

I take the woman's coat and stare; she looks vaguely familiar. It can't be, can it? She looks so slim and, well, sexy. Janet Dobson and sexy would never have been said in the same sentence. I'm flabbergasted.

Alice-band wearer and all-round overachiever Janet Dobson, who we dubbed 'the Persil girl' (as her PE kit was still mysteriously whiter than white even when we had run across muddy fields in cross country), tried to join our circle at school but we wouldn't let her. It was the *Grease* movie all over, Janet being Patty Simcox – always being on the periphery of the circle looking in, and I'm ashamed to say that we used her mercilessly. Her uncle had a newsagent's shop near school and we used to get her to steal the odd packet of cigarettes and chocolate bars in exchange for the privilege of hanging round with us.

Our final encounter was on the Leeds and Liverpool Canal, where I was instrumental in knocking her off her bike and sending her sprawling into the murky depths of the canal. (Accidentally, obviously. Long story.) Even then I swear her red shorts and white polo shirt combo were still sparkling when we dredged her out.

Had she not spoken just now, I would never in a million years have recognised her, but it was the voice. She never did have the easily identifiable Liverpool accent the rest of us had, but it was the tone of her voice that gave her away. It was a sort of cross between a newsreader and a singer.

'Janet?' I splutter, as the penny finally drops.

'Hello, Mandy,' she sings, revealing a set of expensive, cosmetically enhanced teeth.

'How are you?' I manage to say while handing her a red leather menu.

'Ve-ry well,' she says, drawing out the words with great emphasis. 'Ve-ry well indeed. So, this is where you work then?' she says, raising an eyebrow and casting her perfectly made-up eyes around the place. 'Not bad. I mean if bar work is all you can get, it might as well be a nice pub.'

Her little group give tight smiles before burying their heads in the menus.

'I'm bar manager here,' I retort, trying to keep the irritation out of my voice. Then I'm irritated with myself for letting her get to me. I shouldn't be trying to impress Janet bloody Dobson. I would be proud to be the cleaner in a place like this, as Joyce our cleaner is. We're one big happy family.

'Well done,' Janet says in such a patronising tone that I want to shove her menu where the sun doesn't shine. But I'm a professional.

'Drinks?' I beam. 'Then I'll be back shortly to take your food order.'

I note down what Janet requests before taking the order to the bar.

When the drinks (bottled water and two bottles of Sauvignon Blanc) have been despatched and the food order sent to the kitchen, I take my place back behind the bar, pretending to be busy at the till, and scrutinise Janet's table from afar. There is a young bohemian-style girl wearing a colourful maxi skirt and a denim jacket. She has a tie-dye scarf looped across her hair bandana style and several silver earrings in each ear. She appears to be scribbling notes. Seated next to her is a thirty-something attractive woman with red hair, wearing office-type uniform of black pencil skirt and crisp white blouse. Finally, there is Janet, in an elegant black shift dress with a pink cashmere cardigan. I wonder what kind of business they are in and why they haven't been in the pub before to conduct one of their meetings.

'Table Four!' comes the shout from the kitchen, shaking me from my thoughts. It is the food for Janet's table.

A young waitress called Lucy abandons filling the fridge with mixers and steps into the kitchen to take the plates, but I intercept her.

'I'll take this one, Lucy.' She shrugs and goes back to her bottled soft drinks, which make a very rainbow-like display as every flavour from orange to blackberry stand side by side in the tall black and silver fridge.

'There you go,' I say brightly, depositing two pork cider casseroles and a blackboard special of sea bass onto the chunky wooden table. 'Enjoy your meals; can I get you any sauces?'

I'm dying to find out what line of business Janet is in, but I don't want to ask. I'm slowly placing the tartar sauce onto the table with the speed of a sedated snail, but their conversation appears to have dried up as they sip their drinks.

'I must say,' Janet says, finally, in between mouthfuls of fragrant sea bass. 'This really is very good. I can't think why we haven't been here before.'

'Where do you normally go?' I enquire casually.

'Oh, all over really. Up and down the country and often out of the country as well. It's easy to forget just how good some of our English country pubs are.'

Janet smiles a genuine smile and the rest of the party nod in unison as they tuck in to their food. I'm about to ask them what takes them all over the country, when I hear an almighty bang from the kitchen, followed by a piercing scream.

I dash to the kitchen and discover that a microwave has blown up. We only ever use them to reheat things, but it seems that Sally, one of the new kitchen assistants, decided to heat a pudding in a foil tray and, after a colourful display of Northern Lights proportions, the door flew open and deposited sticky toffee pudding all over the facing white wall. Sally is crying her eyes out, Darren is standing there open-mouthed and Lyndsey is laughing hysterically.

Lyndsey always laughs when something terrible happens. It's a nervous reaction but try explaining that to the wife of the gentleman who was choking to death in one of the alcoves last week, while Lyndsey laughed like a drain. One Heimlich manoeuvre later, and a ride home in an ambulance, and everything was OK… Apart from the wife vowing never to return to a pub where they employ 'a lunatic bitch'.

Lyndsey is such a fantastic waitress that her inappropriate laughter is forgiven. She is speedy and efficient and so striking – with her slender, olive-skinned figure and pretty face – that she generates amazing tips, which she is happy to put into the shared tip jar.

Janet's group finish their meals and leave a generous tip, before gathering their coats to leave. *Well, Janet*, I think to myself, *you've had your moment of glory, and if I'm honest I hope you enjoyed it – I was a complete cow to you at school.*

'Bye, Mandy,' Janet says, smiling. I'm finding it hard to decide whether her smile is genuine. 'Here's my business card,' she says, handing me a black card with gold lettering, 'should you ever wish to partake of my services.'

As the party disappeared into the car park I thought that would be the last I'd ever see of Janet Dobson.

CHAPTER THREE

I started going out with Danny Davis when he came to my rescue outside the local community centre disco when we were both fifteen years old. A group of us had sneaked outside for a cigarette, when super sleaze and Billy-no-mates Gary Smith snatched my silver clip-on earrings from my ears and proceeded to put them down his underpants. They belonged to my sixteen-year-old neighbour, who would have murdered me if I hadn't returned home with them. 'You know where they are.' He smirked, pointing to his groin. Seconds later he was frogmarched round a corner, before returning with a bloody nose; my friend's earrings, which I retrieved with a tissue, were on Danny's outstretched palm.

I didn't really know Danny that well, even though he was part of my wider circle of friends, but a week after the earrings incident he turned up at a school disco, looking gorgeous in an aquamarine-coloured shirt that matched his eyes. After a few sneaky ciders and a slow dance to a George Michael song, I was smitten. We broke up after a year together, as I decided I was too young to be tied down and Danny pretty much thought the same. I had lots of fun with my girlfriends in the years that followed but, five years later, not long after my twenty-first birthday, we were back together again.

It was hard to believe how quickly the intervening years had passed. Danny made it harder for me to forget him during that time, as he would occasionally frequent the same places I did. He would walk me home at the end of the evening and we'd kiss. That was the pattern of my life for a while. I was so besotted with him I could never resist.

I hadn't seen Danny around for some time, when I walked into a pub on New Year's Eve and there he was. He looked gorgeous in a grey suit with a white shirt underneath that enhanced a light tan acquired from a recent lads' holiday in the sun. At midnight, when he took me by the hand and led me round the back of the pub for a 'proper kiss', I knew he had stolen my heart again...

I can still recall my mother's reaction to the news of our wedding plans all those years ago. I was standing in the kitchen of my family home, drying some dishes with a striped tea towel and chatting to Mum as she hummed along to a song on Radio 2.

'You're getting *what?*' my mother exclaimed when I told her of my impending nuptials.

'Mum, we've known each other for years. Danny is definitely the one.'

She briefly stopped beating the eggs into a Yorkshire pudding mix and frowned slightly. 'Well, I know that, love, but you're so *young.*'

Mum was wearing a grey tracksuit that she'd bought with the intention of regularly attending the gym. (She'd been twice in the previous two months.) Her fair hair was tied back in a ponytail and she wasn't wearing any make-up. She's still the only person I know who looks years younger without it...

'Mum, I'm twenty-one. Yes, it is young, but you and Dad weren't much older when you got married and you're still happy together, aren't you?'

She didn't answer as she carried on beating the eggs. I knew she was just worried.

I got the impression many times over the years that my mum wished she hadn't got married so young. Oh, she was happy enough with my dad in her own way, but I know she often thought about how she could have been a nurse at Walton Hospital. She could have been a matron or a ward sister at the very least, but she sacrificed her career to look after me and my dad. She is a bright lady, my mum. Our terraced house in Liverpool has always been spotless and nicely decorated, but she isn't really a terraced house sort of person. At the very least Mum should have a semi-detached house in Southport, with a conservatory.

Once again, I feel a twinge of regret that I didn't work harder at school. Maybe Mum would have been proud of my achievements, which might have eased her own unfulfilled ambition?

'Mum,' I remember saying that day, as I tried to allay any fears she may have had. 'Danny and me are good together. And it's not as if we're going to get bogged down with kids or anything. We both want to have some fun, travel a bit and go out every weekend.'

She wasn't convinced.

'But you won't have the money to do all that once you've paid your mortgage and everything, Mandy.' Mum sighed. 'When money troubles present themselves, love flies out of the window.'

She's full of these sayings, my mum.

'Well, you can always come home if things don't work out,' she said firmly. 'Home is where the heart is.'

My dad sat rolling his eyes affectionately in the background, as he often did…

Now, as I watch my mother in the kitchen, I remember the conversation so well, although it all feels like such a long time ago.

Mum takes a shepherd's pie out of the oven and the delicious aroma makes my stomach rumble. One thing I've missed about living at home is my mum's cooking. Even the simplest of dishes taste amazing when my mum makes them. She's like a Marks & Spencer ad: 'This is not just egg and chips; this is Mrs Evans's egg and chips.'

I cross the room and hug her. She wipes her hand on her apron and hugs me back. She smells of Sunflowers perfume and garlic, which immediately transports me back to a holiday to France on a school trip. It was memorable in more ways than one, because there was a forest fire that swept along the back of the youth hostel and we had to be evicted in our nightclothes to another site an hour's drive away; one that had no facilities apart from outdoor chess and boules.

Unbelievably, it was the second forest fire I'd witnessed on a holiday. My dad had a pay rise one year, when I was around nine years old and we went to Rhodes in Greece. I adored it. I never forgot the twinkling of the Mediterranean Sea and the long beaches with sand so hot it burnt your feet. I loved Christakis beach taverna and their homemade milkshakes, topped off with vanilla ice cream and a fresh strawberry.

It had been particularly hot the year we went to Greece and the sight of helicopters depositing water onto a small forest fire several miles away had frightened my mum sufficiently to never set foot in a hot country again, so the following year it was back to Wales – 'No chance of a forest fire there!' – Llandudno to be precise, where, to be fair, we always had a brilliant time.

I'm an only child so I was allowed to take my friend Hayley along so I was never alone. Hayley and I were thirteen when we experimented with self-tanning wipes on one of those holidays. We applied them before we went to bed and woke up the next morning looking like streaky Oompa Loompas, not to mention ruining the sheets.

Mum cuts the shepherd's pie into huge slabs before warming some peas up in a saucepan, the smell bringing me back to reality, yet evoking something so comforting and familiar.

Thoughts of holidays transport me back to Rhodes in Greece.

I remind Mum about that holiday as she switches a fan on in the kitchen in an attempt to cool the stifling air.

'Nothing could be as hot as that holiday in Rhodes, eh, Mum?'

'Ooh, yes, I remember, love. I just about coped with that heat, didn't I? Could you imagine me being there now with these night sweats? I'd literally melt. You'd find a pool of water in the morning where I once slept.' She chuckles.

I will never forget that holiday. I loved every minute of it. My memories of cooling off with endless ice creams and dips in the turquoise sea will stay with me forever. And who knows? One day I may even get the chance to return. In fact, maybe now is the perfect time to take a little holiday. And there's nobody to stand in my way.

CHAPTER FOUR

I'm emptying my clutch bag at home when I find the little black business card.

Entertainment Express
Catering for every musical event
Contact Janet on 0845 677543
janet@entertainmentexpress.com

Events organiser? Well, you could knock me down with a feather. I would have put money on Janet being an accountant or lawyer, or some other sober-suited professional. I would never have had her down as an events organiser, it seemed far too glamorous, although I have to grudgingly admit that she has changed a lot. Gone are the slightly chubby cheeks, and there is no sign of an acrylic Alice band stretched across her head, but rather an expensively highlighted head of copper-coloured hair.

I put the card back into my bag and pour myself a large glass of white wine. It's become a little bit of a habit; I never drink while I'm at work so I have a large (-ish) glass when I go home, but only the one. I still expect to hear the sound of Danny's car door slamming outside as he returns home, and a tear rolls down my cheek.

We'd been married almost eight years and everything was going just fine – or so I thought. We'd made our cosy terraced cottage into a real home, with its cream walls, dark wooden floor, and an exposed brick fireplace. There were always lots of flowers displayed around the house. I love fresh flowers but I knew Danny wasn't so keen, so the fact that he often brought a bunch home for me made their scent even sweeter.

When I was over at Mum's one day, she was at pains to point out that this was the time when things could go wrong, if they were going to, as it's the 'seven-year itch' phase. Little did I know how prophetic her words would turn out to be.

There's a bunch of assorted chrysanthemums in a clear glass vase on the fireplace, which I bought myself from Tesco. I pour myself another drink as the tears roll freely down my face now. It's been six weeks since Danny left and I still feel as though a rug has been pulled from under my feet.

I glance at the framed wedding photo of us on the wall and remember my wedding day with affection. We got married at St Chad's Church in Liverpool, an imposing nineteenth century building, in front of eighty guests, with a reception at a local hotel afterwards. We tried to keep the gathering small but my dad's extended family is so big it would have been impossible to do that without leaving someone out. Dad paid a large share of the costs; such was his insistence not to offend anyone.

I go to the drawer in the lounge cupboard and begin to flick through my wedding album. The day was without doubt the best day of my life. Danny had never looked more handsome in his grey three-piece suit and I felt like a queen in my pearl-encrusted ivory silk gown. My three bridesmaids, including my best friend Hayley, wore dusky pink gowns and carried cream floral bouquets. I wonder what I should do with this album full of happy memories now?

Hayley has been my best friend since primary school. We had a rather dubious start when we both selected the same jigsaw to do on our first day, and she grabbed it and wouldn't let go. I managed to hide one of the pieces when she wasn't looking, such was my anger, and she spent half the morning looking under tables and everywhere for it. I told her about it in Year 6, when we were revealing secrets about each other at our leavers' assembly.

The wedding reception went like a dream, with humorous speeches, fantastic music from the DJ and a bunch of very merry, but well-behaved guests. Everybody had a ball. Not a hitch, which in a small way disappointed me slightly as I wanted at least one funny story to recall in years to come. My neighbour Jane's wedding the previous year had seen two fainters; the best man split his trousers; an uninvited dog slip through a side door when someone was having a smoke and destroy half the buffet table; and a fist fight between two ancient aunts drunk on home-made lethal punch.

I loved being married to Danny and expected that it would be that way forever. We'd stopped going out as much, owing to our working patterns, as by the time I'd finished my shifts at the pub and he'd done his long day at the garage, we were both shattered. But we still loved each other. We had been a part of each other's lives for so long. We had cosy evenings in with takeaways; the nearby Bengal Kitchen had never had so much business before we moved here. We had pretty much worked our way through the menu, a fact that my trousers digging into me one evening when I bent down to lift a box of mixers bore testament to.

Now I lift the waistband out on my trousers with several inches to spare and I'm reminded of how much weight I have lost in just six weeks. I don't carry extra weight well as I'm rather short (although I do have a nice figure). Short, blonde and bubbly would probably normally be an accurate description of me, although short, blonde and confused would be a more fitting description right now.

'Don't be letting yourself go now that you've got a ring on your finger,' my mum had warned.

I wonder why I never listened to my mum's words of wisdom.

I flick my phone on to check for any messages and, once again, I recall the night I had my first suspicion that there was something not quite right in my marriage. It was a Thursday night and I realised it was going to be a late one as there was a fiftieth birthday party in full swing at the Pig and Whistle with no sign of winding down soon. The birthday girl must have had a hard life, as she looked sixty if she was a day. She was dressed in a cream tube mini dress and her hair was an alarming shade of pink, giving her the appearance of a matchstick.

There's always something to celebrate and, despite some of the horrible things going on in people's lives, they always share the joys. Only last weekend we had a party in celebrating their son's twenty-first birthday. They lost their other son four years ago, the mother confided to me when I helped her get a red-wine stain off her peach dress. They wanted their eldest son to have a lovely time despite the deceased son's birthday being only four days earlier, when they had been to a local beauty spot to release balloons in his memory.

Anyway, that Thursday night, my stomach rumbled as I realised I'd been so busy I'd hardly had time for a break that evening. I remember matchstick woman raising her arm and asking for another bottle of Pinot Grigio. I was amazed that she could even lift her arm as she seemed to have consumed her own body weight in white wine. I was exhausted but hungry, so I texted Danny and asked him to order me a lamb bhuna for when I got home. And that was the evening I wish I could rewind.

CHAPTER FIVE

It was 12.30 when I finally arrived home on that dreadful evening and I was surprised to find Danny still sitting up and nursing a bottle of beer. He has an early start on weekdays as the garage he works for is just outside Liverpool city centre and he likes to leave early to avoid the traffic.

He works for one of these huge car-repair chains that offer breakdown service and doorstep recovery at very reasonable prices. He loves his job and is lucky enough to have always known what he wanted to do for a living and has worked hard to achieve it. From an early age, he was tinkering around with old cars at his uncle's garage, and then followed the formal path of study to ensure he got offered employment.

'You're up late, babe,' I said, before shovelling tender pieces of lamb bhuna and fragrant pilau rice into my mouth as if I hadn't eaten in a month. I undid the waistband on my trousers and flopped back onto the cream leather sofa, balancing my tray of food and bottle of beer precariously as I did so.

'Couldn't sleep,' Danny said, taking another sip of his beer. 'Work was a bit quiet today so I'm not overly tired. How was your day?'

I looked at my handsome husband with his aquamarine eyes, which everyone comments on, and suddenly realised that it'd been a while since we'd had sex… but I was shattered.

I launched into stories of the bar and told him about matchstick woman, who amazingly walked in a straight line out of the pub after drinking three bottles of Pinot Grigio that evening, but I got the impression that he wasn't really listening, his thoughts elsewhere.

God, the curry was to die for…

I couldn't imagine any takeaway anywhere ever being as good as the Bengal Kitchen's. We're on first-name terms with the owners, who even send us Christmas cards, which I happen to know is a rarity. The building is a grotty little ex-transport café, and they have spent little on giving it more kerb appeal, but the food is simply divine. There is a constant queue of cars outside the place at the weekend and the midweek specials they offer have people coming back for more – especially me.

'Have you had your supper?' I asked Danny that night, as I pushed some naan bread and onion bhajis across the coffee table towards him.

'Nah, I've eaten loads in work today. Sarah in the office is doing Slimming World, not that she needs to though. She's been bringing huge containers of food into work. The vegetable lasagne and chickpea curry are amazing,' he said with a satisfied grin on his face.

'Oh,' is all I could manage, suddenly feeling like an overstuffed sausage as I surveyed the empty plate in front of me. I looked at my husband's slender frame. He's tall and naturally thin so can eat what he likes without putting on weight.

He flicked on the TV as *Lethal Weapon 4* was about to start.

'Decent film, this,' he said before going into the kitchen for another beer. I was a bit puzzled by this as it was a work night.

'Aren't you in work tomorrow?' I asked, glancing at the clock.

'Thought I'd have a day's holiday,' Danny replied casually.

I felt slightly aggrieved that he hadn't mentioned this. He normally only ever booked a day off to coincide with mine so that we could do something together, otherwise we were like ships that passed in the night.

'Have you got any plans?' I said almost accusingly, but he just shrugged and said he would see how the mood took him.

I was absolutely done in and dying for my bed. Yet, somehow, I felt like we needed to talk.

'Is there anything wrong?' I asked tentatively.

Danny took a long time to answer before assuring me that no, there was nothing wrong. I put his strange mood down to tiredness, but then remembered that he'd said he wasn't tired because he hadn't had a very busy day. Somewhere in the back of mind I felt uneasy. I couldn't put my finger on why, but I just did.

I changed into my pink pyjamas and settled on the sofa with a cup of tea and a Freddo chocolate bar. I always feel like something sweet after a spicy curry and a Freddo is just enough. Danny cast a quick, disapproving glance as I screwed the wrapper up and tossed it into the bin.

Danny Glover was just about to burst through a door for a shoot-out in *Lethal Weapon 4*, when my Danny turned to me with a serious expression on his face.

'Mandy… are you happy?' he asked.

I was thrown by the completely unexpected question and found myself momentarily floundering with a response.

'Err, yeah, why wouldn't I be?'

'I dunno. I was just thinking… All those plans we had. Nearly eight years married now, and I'm not sure we've fulfilled many of them.' He took another swig of his beer.

'Well, if you mean having kids, I'm not sure we could fit them in with our working schedules. Plus, we're still paying the car loan off.'

My mum's words were suddenly in my ears again, telling me that there wouldn't be much spare money once we'd got ourselves a mortgage.

'No, not so much kids, there's plenty of time for that, but we're nearly twenty-nine and sometimes I feel about fifty. We don't seem to have any fun any more.'

I realised I didn't want to have this conversation, because it was something that I had buried deep in my own subconscious. What he was saying was that we had got into a rut and I was foolish enough to think he wouldn't notice, yet too exhausted to do anything about it. Oh, we still went out once in a while, but it was with the same people and to the same pub. The Collier's Arms with Hayley and her latest boyfriend for the quiz nights, or round to Mum's for Sunday lunch on the weekends when I wasn't working. Occasionally we managed a trip to the cinema on a Wednesday evening, if either of us could be bothered.

I suddenly got an image of all the old gang at school in Year 11. Some of our crowd decided to actually *do* some studying after failing to do any at school, enrolling at the local college and completing courses.

Angela Turner went to work as a nanny in Spain and ended up marrying her single-parent male employer. She was now living in a stunning, whitewashed, terracotta-roof-tiled villa just outside Madrid. Mike Dee worked his way up to head chef at a top restaurant in Cheshire (with a two-month waiting list for a table), having discovered a flair for cooking on a catering course and 'wild boy' Barry Barker now ran a successful breaker's yard in Southport.

I thought of all the hopes and dreams we'd had, in particular driving off into the distance in a genuine 1960s Volkswagen camper van, not knowing exactly where we were heading. We would go grape-picking in France or tend bars in Spain, anything that would earn us some money before rocking up at the next unknown location.

Instead we'd bought a silver Vauxhall Astra diesel because it was economical to run, which we drive as far as the Lake District or Scotland for our annual holiday.

I didn't want to talk to Danny any more. I didn't want the foundations of my cosy home and comfortable relationship shaken. We did alright.

I said a weary good night as he stayed downstairs to watch the rest of the film. I was aching with tiredness, but sleep wouldn't come. I wondered who this Sarah woman was. Danny had never mentioned her before, but he'd obviously noticed her figure as he said she didn't need to diet. I wondered why he had asked me if I was happy. But, more importantly, why had I been so afraid to ask him the very same question?

CHAPTER SIX

One thing I've learned from working in a pub over the years is never to judge a book by its cover. Just like the silver-haired Internet big daters, Big Dave the salsa dancer, and never more so than Leonard Walker.

I first encountered him several years ago when he first began to frequent the Pig and Whistle. He was hovering around outside at about eleven forty-five in the morning and asking what time we opened, as I fumbled with the keys. I felt slightly unsettled by him. He had the dishevelled appearance of a vagrant, with his unshaven skin and old Barbour waxed jacket, and was showing several of his teeth missing when he smiled.

It turned out that he and his Jack Russell had walked three miles from his country pile to have a spot of lunch. He had been suitably impressed by the food and the variety of single malt whiskies, of which he partook of three, together with a toasted brie sandwich, before reading the *Guardian*. Then, just after two o'clock, he tipped his hat and set off to walk the three miles home.

Leonard became a regular visitor after that, calling in at the pub a couple of times a week and always at the same time. As he perched himself on a stool at the corner of the bar, I noticed the look on some of the customers' faces, clearly making assumptions about him just like I had done. When it became apparent, throughout several conversations, that he was *seriously* rich, I had dared to ask him why he had never thought of getting his teeth fixed.

'I don't like dentists,' Leonard had replied simply, sipping his large single malt whisky that cost five pounds a pop. 'Or hairdressers.' He'd smiled, stroking a bedraggled strand of grey hair that had escaped from his tweed cap. 'Oh, I know it would be easier to look the part of a rich country gent,' he'd continued, 'but the fact is I'm not interested. I'm not out to impress anybody; not like those fools who have the latest model of a car on finance, or a mortgage that takes almost every penny of their earnings. What way is that to live? Where's the fun?'

'Hmm... Easy to say if you've got piles of money,' I'd suggested, as I'd keyed in some meals for a family of four. I remember wondering how the already excited children would be after their feast of pizza, chips and full sugar Coke.

'I'm simply saying that many people place value on the wrong things,' Leonard told me.

I've learned from our conversations that Leonard lost his beloved wife to breast cancer five years ago. He has a son in Australia, who he sees several times a year, but he now lives alone in his six-bedroomed Georgian home. He has a housekeeper called Gloria, who looks after him. When he showed me a photo of his home one day when we were chatting at the bar, I recognised it immediately. I must have walked past it several times in the past, often wondering who lived in such a grand house.

I've grown very fond of Leonard. He is very wise and intelligent and people could learn a lot from him. That is if they bothered to get close enough, when they would realise that despite his weathered appearance, he is spotlessly clean and smells of classic woody aftershave with a hint of citrus.

I also love how Leonard puts people in their place with such eloquence. I listened with interest the previous week as a middle-class snob was sitting at the bar telling whoever would listen that he would never go on a package holiday. No, he booked everything independently as he was a 'traveller'.

'Do you have your own plane then?' Leonard had enquired, sipping his Scotch. 'Because if you don't, then the likelihood is you will be sharing the same plane as the peasants who booked the package holiday. Ditto the hotel or apartments, unless of course you have booked a private villa, in which case there is a reasonable chance that it will have previously been occupied by a professional. But, of course, you never can tell these days. Ordinary working-class people have now discovered that they can afford and are entitled to the same holidays as everyone else. Fancy that.'

I could have jumped across the bar and kissed Leonard. The pompous bore had been pissing me off for weeks, but after Leonard's calm little speech he didn't come into the pub much again.

Leonard's father was a jeweller, from humble beginnings, who ended up owning a chain of shops and making a fortune. As a teenager, Leonard had travelled around the world with his parents, something I envied him for.

'It's never too late to travel,' he told me once. 'The world is different now, far easier to get cheap flights over the Internet. In my parents' day, there was a lot of toing and froing to travel agents with the airlines charging exorbitant prices. We would never have travelled the world had my father not been extremely wealthy.'

I suppose it's true. One of the customers at the pub bought a round-the-world air ticket after her fiancé had jilted her just before the wedding. It only cost a few grand and after three months away she arrived back home briefly, before jetting off to live in Ibiza.

I don't think I'd have the courage to do such a thing and the realisation startles me. In my teens, I was the one who wanted to travel the world, climb Mount Everest and swim with dolphins, none of which I have done. I'm not even thirty years old yet and it's not as if I have the responsibilities of a family. I don't know when exactly my adventurous streak disappeared, but I just became content. I could never see the point of constantly filling up a diary with things to do, dashing around all weekend cramming stuff in before returning to work on a Monday morning. I had thought Danny was content, too, but I was to discover that I was way off the mark with that one.

I was jolted back into the present by the arrival of a large party of travellers who have just arrived for dinner. They always pitched up in a field just off the motorway and would call in here before they were moved on. They are a polite enough bunch and leave decent tips, although they do take dozens of the little sachets of sauces, salt and sugar when they depart – Oh, and toilet rolls. I noticed Lyndsey surreptitiously removing the cutlery tray to take it into the kitchen.

It's normally my afternoon shift but I've agreed to work late tonight, as I dread going home since Danny left. I've invited Hayley over later, as tomorrow's her day off from the bank where she works as a cashier. We're going to have a couple of bottles of white wine, but if she fancies a curry later I might just manage a small one. I suppose this is how my life has become now, but I can't help wondering: *Is this as good as it's going to get?*

CHAPTER SEVEN

I had exactly three days off work in April, when my marriage ended. Danny had gone on a work's leaving do in Liverpool and stayed out all night. He'd rung me at one o'clock in the morning, saying he was going to crash with one of the lads who had a flat in town, as he was far too drunk to make his way home. Looking back, I should have realised that he hadn't *sounded* that drunk, and his refusal to accept a lift home from me should have rung alarm bells. But you never think, do you? I was just touched by his thoughtfulness when he said, 'Don't disturb yourself, babe, coming out in the cold and dark. I'll be back early in the morning, go back to sleep.'

Danny never came home early in the morning, but early in the afternoon, skulking like a dog that had just eaten the family roast chicken. His hand kept on stroking his neck involuntarily as he tried unsuccessfully to hide the love bite on his neck.

I remember little of the rest of that afternoon as I calmly asked him to leave. He was as white as a sheet, but he did as I asked. He left me. Just like that. There was no explanation. No fight, drama or anything. He simply walked away... and I hated him for it.

I was a complete mess and found myself walking through the countryside sobbing uncontrollably. It began to rain, and the huge drops mixing with my salty tears and blurring my path added insult to injury, but I walked on. I walked through bracken and nettles, which scratched at my legs, but I never felt a thing. I must have looked a right sight when I turned up at Leonard's red-brick Georgian house and stood in front of the huge, wrought-iron gates, which had secure entry.

An unfamiliar voice on the intercom asked me to announce myself.

'It's Mandy,' I almost whispered into the machine. 'I'm a friend of Leonard's.'

After a few minutes, the gates swung open and I made my way pathetically up the long driveway towards the front door. I was wet through and my blonde hair hung like rats' tails. I had nothing apart from the clothes I stood up in and my purse. I always remember to take my purse wherever I go; it contains money, bank card and front-door key, which is pretty much everything you need.

A woman in her late fifties, with a kindly face and an auburn-coloured bob, ushered me inside, before going to a cupboard and handing me a towel for my dripping hair. She then led me into a vast kitchen, where the smell of baking bread enveloped me. It was a beautiful space with solid cream units and thick, dark oak work surfaces. There was a Belfast sink and a huge blue Aga, which dominated the far wall. A Victorian drying rack hung overhead with bunches of dried herbs and lavender hanging from it.

The lady, who had introduced herself as Gloria, planted a cup of tea and a huge scone with jam and clotted cream in front of me, just as Leonard appeared at the side door of the kitchen followed by Ted the Jack Russell, who wagged his tail furiously as he bounded towards me.

'Now then, this is an unexpected pleasure,' Leonard beamed, before noting my sorry expression. He removed his wellingtons and outer coat and placed them in a separate boot room.

I choked back tears as I explained what had happened, and Leonard just listened. He didn't interrupt or pass comment, he just listened and beckoned his housekeeper Gloria to bring more tea over, to which he added a generous slug of brandy from a bottle on the kitchen counter.

'You're very welcome to stay for a few days. I have one or two guest rooms,' he said, smiling at me.

I felt relief wash over me. I didn't want to go home to my mum's as I couldn't even face telling her.

After a while, Gloria offered me some vegetable soup that was simmering on the stove in a large Le Creuset pan, but I wasn't hungry. Even the home-made crusty loaf that she removed from the oven failed to whet my appetite. I just wanted to lie down. The long walk to the house, along with the brandy in my tea, had made me feel suddenly sleepy. Leonard, as if reading my thoughts, instructed Gloria to show me to 'one of the back bedrooms that overlook the garden'.

It was beautiful room, but I would have expected nothing less, as on my way upstairs I had seen that the whole house was tastefully decorated and immaculately kept by Gloria. I could just imagine the look on some of the regular customers' faces at the Pig and Whistle if they could see this place.

The bedroom, which overlooked a vast garden, had buttermilk walls with countryside prints and primrose-coloured cotton bedding. The furniture, which consisted of a double wardrobe and chest of drawers, was dark wood. There was a gold-coloured chandelier in the centre of the room, which cast flecks of light along the deep cream carpet as a watery sunlight streamed through the window. At least that depressing downpour had ceased.

I flopped down onto the bed and wondered what the hell I was doing there. Earlier in the day, I'd thought my marriage was fine. But here I was lying on a bed in the guest room of one of the pub customers. I bet that when he'd offered me a spare room, if I ever needed it, Leonard had never imagined that I would really take him up on his offer.

I undressed before taking a shower and slipping into a floral cotton dressing gown that Gloria had kindly laid out for me. It made me think of my own dressing gown, which was hanging on the back of the bedroom door alongside Danny's, and I stifled a sob.

I suddenly wanted to punch him. Why had I left my lovely home? When did I turn into this drip of a female? I should be hammering the vodka with Hayley now, while she insulted Danny with her colourful vocabulary. But I just couldn't face being with anyone close. Not yet.

I climbed into the high bed and ran my hands along the white sheets, which were of the highest quality. They were superior Egyptian cotton, not like the ones I'd bought from the market, which were probably as Egyptian as a McDonald's in Cairo.

I checked my mobile phone for messages. Nothing. No missed calls or texts. I couldn't believe Danny would do this to me. I knew that I was the one who'd asked him to leave, but I'd had every reason to.

The conversation when he'd asked me if I was happy played over and over in my mind. Why the hell did he ask me that? He clearly wasn't happy himself and yet I'd avoided asking him if *he* was unhappy. Maybe we could have talked it through and avoided this mess?

I could hardly breathe. I felt a sickness to the pit of my stomach as I considered the possibility that Danny might never come home. He was the only man I had ever loved and I just didn't know what I would do without him.

I took a large swig from the silver hip flask that Leonard had pushed into my hand before I'd come upstairs, and then leaned back into the feather pillows that wrapped themselves around my head like a giant marshmallow.

Tomorrow would be another day. Tonight I needed to sleep. It wasn't too long before the brandy relaxed my weary bones and I was snoring gently into my tear-sodden pillow.

CHAPTER EIGHT

It was like cliché overdrive when I finally went to my parents' house a week later and told them about Danny leaving. Dad just enveloped me in a huge bear hug and told me everything would be alright and that Danny was 'a bloody fool'.

Mum, after she had gotten over her initial shock, told me that there were 'plenty more fish in the sea', as she served up fish, chips and peas for tea. Suddenly I wasn't hungry. I was a little taken aback by how insensitive she was being. I thought she liked Danny. Maybe I was wrong.

My dad is shaking his head in the background, telling Mum that it's just a rough patch and that every marriage goes through them. It made me think about my parents' marriage, which I believed was really happy. I wondered if they ever had a rough patch? Would I even have known if they did? Good parents always protect their children from personal problems, don't they? If they did go through a bad patch, then they must have come through it OK as they've been married for thirty-two years and adore each other.

'I did tell you marriage isn't a bed of roses,' Mum said as she buttered some bread and plonked a heavy brown teapot onto the table.

I was dreading leaving Leonard's glorious home, and not just because of the kindness I was shown. No, I was dreading coming home to my parents' house as I feel like a failure. Ridiculous, I know, as I'm not the one who has broken our marriage vows, but even so I feel an irrational sense of shame. We both stood in the church in front of all our family and friends and declared our love for each other on our wedding day. *Till death us do part.* But what was the point?

I wasn't sure I could take much more of Mum's fussing. She meant well, of course, and I love her to bits, but she was driving me mad. I think she was trying to kill me with food. She placed a home-made Victoria sponge on the table and cut me a generous slice. The half-eaten fish and chips were on the plate next to me but she persisted with the cake.

I got a sudden memory of my friends knocking for me in the morning to walk to school, whereupon my mum would pounce on them and ask if they had eaten any breakfast. They quickly learned to say yes, even if it wasn't the truth, otherwise they would be tied to the chair with their striped school ties and force-fed buttered toast. Or near enough. I never forget Hayley putting her hand in her blazer pocket, while looking for a pen during a science lesson, and pulling out a handful of crumbs from a Scotch pancake that my mum had slipped into her pocket.

I'd been at my parents' house for three days when my thoughts turned to returning home. I was dreading walking through the front door, but I knew I must. There had still been no message from Danny, but maybe he had written me a letter? We used to write each other lots of little notes in the early days. Little Post-it notes on the fridge, in the bathroom cabinet and on the headboard of the bed. I can't remember when we stopped doing that, but somewhere along the line the notes stopped, replaced by an occasional text. I knew I needed to talk to him, but I couldn't bring myself to ring him.

My thoughts would swing between wanting to strangle him and wanting to fall into his arms. Why should I bloody well be the one to contact *him*? He was the one who just left without a fight.

I was in my old bedroom when the tears began to stream down my face . I looked around the room, which had barely changed, apart from a lick of paint and a new, pale blue butterfly-print duvet set. It's used as a guest room now but I never expected to be the guest.

I kept hoping I would wake up and it had all been a bad dream. How could my marriage have just fallen apart and I didn't have a clue it was happening?

I managed a smile as I had a sudden recollection of the time we first went to a nice restaurant together, during one of our brief reunions Danny had picked up his first month's wages from the garage at the age of seventeen, splashing out on a designer shirt and booking us a table at Luigi's Italian in town. The waitress must have assumed we were over eighteen when she showed us the wine list and Danny ordered a bottle of Merlot. Things were going great and we were just finishing the delicious pasta, when I over-gesticulated with my arms (something I have a tendency to do) and my glass of red wine went all over Danny, completely covering his brand-new white shirt. The waitress appeared with the dessert menu at that moment and lifted the menu to her face in an attempt to stifle her giggles.

We quickly got the bill and headed to a late-night department store across the road to buy a new shirt before heading off to a bar. I was determined the night wouldn't be ruined, but Danny was more annoyed that he never got to have his tiramisu, which he was looking forward to. 'And that wine cost eighteen quid a bottle,' he'd moaned.

We'd laughed about it in the pub later on after a few beers. I'd told him that pink wasn't his colour and that he should never, ever buy a pink shirt.

I suppose I'm fortunate enough to have so many happy memories to look back on though. Some people never have those in a whole lifetime.

CHAPTER NINE

It's been a crap day so far. I had a call last night from Danny saying we needed to talk and I swear I heard a woman's voice in the background. He said it was the woman on *News at Ten* but I find it unlikely that she would be saying to her co-presenter 'are you coming back to bed, babe?' The phone went suspiciously crackly at his end, then he terminated the call saying he would text me to meet up and 'talk things through'.

It took me hours to get to sleep. I just tossed and turned as my mind went into overdrive trying to figure out how the hell things had come to this.

It was clearly no one-night stand, as Danny would hardly just up sticks and run off with somebody he hardly knew. And I still ponder the woman in the background, who Danny explained away as a news reporter. No, this was something that had obviously been brewing and they got together on that work's night out. Maybe it was that Sarah woman from the office at work. Perhaps it had been going on for months? How would I know? With my irregular shifts at the pub, Danny could have been running a harem from our front lounge and I would have been none the wiser.

He'd stopped coming to the pub as regularly this past year or so. In the early days, he would perch himself at the corner of the bar for the last hour or two before walking me home, sometimes stopping for a snog in the woods en route. I can't remember the last time anything like that happened. They say that the initial urgent passion in a relationship fades after a while, but I think that depends on the couple. We once had a barmaid at the pub who used to go home at lunchtime to have sex with her husband, before he started work in the afternoon, and they'd been married for twenty-five years.

It was two o'clock in the morning, with me tossing and turning and being unable to sleep, when I went downstairs and made myself a hot-chocolate drink, to which I added a large slug of Tia Maria. It tasted so good that I had another. Then another. By four o'clock in the morning I'd drunk half a bottle and was sobbing into our wedding album once more. I was conscious of work the next morning, so somehow I managed to crawl upstairs and get back into bed but I hardly slept a wink.

When the alarm clock went off in the morning I had the headache from hell, yet, somehow, I managed to drag myself into work early to do a stocktake.

Things had pretty much gone downhill from the minute I walked into the pub and skidded across the floor on a squashed grape, before falling on my arse.

Joyce the cleaner arrived half an hour later and began to sweep the floor with her red brush.

'Are you late?' I bitched, as I rubbed my bruised backside and Joyce swept the grape, along with other debris into the matching red dustpan.

'No, you're early,' she fired back, hand on hip.

Of course I was. It wasn't her fault, and I told her so and apologised immediately. She came over to me then and wrapped me in a bear hug.

'You look like shit,' she said, as she released me from her grip and studied me at arm's length. ''Ere, I know what you need, get this down yer neck.' She poured a large brandy from behind the bar and handed it to me.

I wanted to throw up.

'Hair of the dog, love. Works every time, but I'll go and put the kettle on if you'd prefer a nice cup of tea.' She winked as she bustled off to the kitchen.

I love Joyce. She's a glamorous sixty-two-year-old who looks at least a decade younger. She wears her black hair loosely piled up on the top of her head, and does her cleaning in figure-hugging clothes and running shoes. She has a great figure for her age, which she puts down to yoga, cleaning and twice-weekly classes at Big Dave's salsa class.

She lost her husband suddenly to a heart attack four years ago, but has resolutely continued to live her life to the full. She is such an inspiration. 'You never know how long you've got on this earth, love,' she says. 'Do what makes you happy. Life's for living.' She is currently in training to run the Liverpool half-marathon for the British Heart Foundation later in the year.

I keep thinking about the conversation with Danny. I was sure I heard a woman's voice in the background, but maybe it was the television. I just don't know any more.

I try to busy myself with the stocktake, noticing that flavoured vodkas are very popular at the moment, as is gin. People seem to drink lots of shots these days, too. I don't know how they do it. Some of the young people have several shots just as a 'warm up' before they disappear into town for the evening. It makes me wonder what happened to the crazy party girl who is currently suffering a hangover after a few Tia Marias in hot chocolate.

After the lunchtime rush, I'm so tired I don't know if I can stay awake until 3 p.m., when I'm due to finish. I've made one or two mistakes, which Lyndsey points out to me as she quickly retrieves a vodka and Coke from a child who is just about to take a sip. She steers me by the elbow into a quiet alcove, before telling me to take a break.

'Mandy, you nearly gave that kid vodka; you put chilli sauce instead of ketchup on another child's fish and chips; and almost served the man on table three chicken satay instead of chicken salad.'

'Where's the harm in that last one?' I venture with a grin, but Lyndsey is not smiling.

'Peanut allergy,' she says, with a serious expression. 'They've been in before and the dad always orders something without nuts. Don't you remember?'

I do indeed remember them now, and I'm ashamed at my stupidity. I'm exhausted and emotional and I know I shouldn't be here, but work has been my salvation these past few weeks. I am sitting down in a chair, as Lyndsey kindly goes off to fetch me a coffee, when out of the corner of my eye I spot Brian, the manager of the pub.

Brian spends most of his time in the microbrewery next door, experimenting with and 'sampling' new flavours, so his appearance in the restaurant makes me feel uneasy.

Brian is sandy-haired, red-cheeked, and seems to be morphing into one of the beer barrels, such is the protrusion of his stomach.

I could just imagine him sitting on the floor in the cellar with a tap on his mouth and a sign saying: 'Brian's Brew'. I stifle a giggle.

He saunters over before taking a packet of salted peanuts from a card and pouring the entire packet into his mouth.

No peanut allergy there then.

I have a flashback to when my best friend Hayley first discovered her pineapple allergy. It happened at primary school when she took a bite of a pineapple upside-down pudding. Within seconds her face had turned beetroot, and her lips would have been the envy of any trout-pouted modern-day female. She was OK, thankfully, but had to endure taunts of being called Mick Jagger for the rest of the week.

'Mandy,' Brian says, smiling at me before placing his bulk on a wooden chair opposite me. 'How are you feeling?'

I like Brian. He is the kind of boss you can talk to and he generally listens. He appreciates ideas and input from his staff, but he also runs a tight ship. I realise this and can't help wondering what's coming next.

'Not too bad, just a bit tired today,' I say, wishing I wasn't having this conversation.

'The thing is,' he says, placing his chubby hand on top of mine like a concerned father, 'I know things are tough for you at the moment, especially as you and Danny had been together so long.'

The mention of Danny's name makes my heart heavy.

'But,' he continued, 'even though I have every sympathy for you, some of your mistakes have not gone unnoticed. I have to take my responsibilities as a manager seriously, as you must appreciate. So, I'm going to suggest you take a break.'

'Do you think so? No, honestly, I'm alright really. Just tired, I suppose. I haven't been sleeping too good lately. Funny, though, Lyndsey said the same thing. I'm having a break now, actually – she's just gone to get me a coffee.'

Brian twiddled a beer mat between his fingers. 'I mean a proper break. A couple of weeks, maybe. I'm sorry, love, but I have to think of the customers. It's my job.'

I know he's right, of course, and there is no doubt a proper rest will do me good, but I feel so guilty bringing my private life into the workplace.

'Lyndsey can run the bar in your absence, she's more than capable.'

I agree with this. Even if I don't, I get the distinct feeling the decision had already been made. It's a comfort to know my job will be left in such safe hands though.

My phone suddenly buzzes into life with a text message from Danny, asking if we can meet at the house tomorrow. My stomach turns over as I text back arranging to meet him. And depending on the outcome of the meeting I may or may not take a long holiday in the sun.

CHAPTER TEN

I've arranged to meet Danny at a coffee shop in town, as I don't want him walking out of our home for a second time. There's a slight drizzle coming from a miserable grey sky, which reflects my mood perfectly. I don't quite know what I'm expecting as I walk along with the hood pulled up on my black parka.

I pass Luigi's Diner on Bold Street, which became a regular haunt for me and Danny, in our first throes of love. More recently it was for other people's celebrations. I love Bold Street with its artisan shops and independent little restaurants and coffee shops facing each other across a cobbled street. I notice a new Jamaican restaurant and wonder how long it will last. Luigi's Diner and Café Latino have been around for decades, while some of the newer eateries have shut up shop a year or two after opening.

I used to spend hours wandering up and down here with my Auntie Betty when I was a kid. She was an art student and used take me with her to Bents art store, where we'd browse the tubes of paints lined up in their boxes like little rows of soldiers. I used to stroke the horse-hair brushes and marvel at the assortment of frames, pictures and watercolour paintings displayed on the white walls. Now, I stare into the art deco coloured-glass windows of the building as the memories come flooding back.

When we had finished our shopping, my aunt would take me to Pier Head, where we would have hot chocolate and doughnuts from a mobile-caravan café that overlooked the River Mersey. Occasionally, on fine days, we would take a ferry across the Mersey to New Brighton and spend an hour at the funfair. I have such happy memories of my aunt, who is now a successful artist living in London. I still receive beautifully hand-painted cards from her at Christmas and birthdays.

Every milestone birthday on both sides of the family was celebrated at Luigi's Diner on Bold Street. Luigi would join us at the end of the night to enjoy a glass of red wine and have a 'sneaky cigarette' in the flagged courtyard, when his wife had left. I notice the red checked tablecloths and fake flowers in the little bud vases, and a wave of nostalgia washes over me.

I feel sick to my stomach. How did I mistake a crisis for a comfort-able rut? Admittedly I had piled some weight on, but doesn't true love go deeper than the physically perfect exterior? The questions go round and round in my mind, until I am finally standing hesitantly outside Starbucks. A quick glance through the window reveals that Danny hasn't arrived yet. I have a sudden urge to walk off and dive into the nearest pub for a swift vodka and Coke, when I spot him walking towards me.

My heart begins to race. He looks different in a pair of plum-coloured jeans and a black denim jacket over a white T-shirt. Not his usual attire. I also note that his hair has been restyled into a side part, which if I'm honest doesn't suit him at all. And it seems suspiciously straight. *Please don't tell me he's started using hair straighteners.*

We smile nervously and say hi before finding a small wooden table after ordering coffees (latte for me, Americano for him).

I'm the first one to speak. 'So, what now then?' I say stupidly, taking a large glug of my drink and almost scalding my tongue.

He's gazing into his Americano as he stirs it round and round. 'I don't know,' he replies quietly.

'What do you mean, you don't know? At the very least you owe me an explanation. You just bloody upped and left without any warning.'

Danny lifts his blue eyes and meets my gaze properly for the first time in forever.

'Are you trying to tell me you thought everything was OK?' he asks, almost in surprise.

'Well, yeah, we were alright. Comfortable, I suppose, just like any other couple in a long relationship.'

'Yeah, if you're fifty or something. We're not even thirty yet. Christ, my mum and dad have more fun than us – and they're in their sixties.' He takes a drink of his coffee. 'Do you want a muffin or something?' Danny suddenly interjects, as if we're out on a shopping trip or something.

'Err, no, thanks. I've lost some weight lately so I might as well try and keep it off.'

'I had noticed. You look good.'

This irritates the hell out of me. 'So you notice when I've lost weight or put it on? Is that all that bloody matters to you? I thought we had a bit more going for us.'

'So did I, Mandy, but you seemed to lose interest in our marriage, spending half your life in that pub.' He almost spits the words out. 'There were plenty of times when I suggested doing something a bit different, but you were never available. You were always covering someone or other's shift so that *they* could have a life, while your own marriage was going down the toilet.'

I'm taken aback. It's like a slap in the face.

'Bloody workaholic you are,' Danny mutters, before draining his coffee and heading to the counter to order another.

I suppose I did neglect our marriage... I recall with shame that Danny had indeed tried to suggest some activities for us to do together, which I never seemed to have time for. He suggested archery once and I laughed at the suggestion, reminding him how rubbish I was at darts. On another occasion, he booked a surprise weekend away to Chester, and I couldn't go at short notice as I was covering for someone else who was on holiday.

I'm feeling a bit guilty about this, before remembering that *he* was the one who left the marital home. And, besides, the surprises were always something that Danny was more interested in than I was. Take archery, for example. He'd been banging on for months about how he would like to give it a try, so it was hardly a grand romantic gesture. The same goes for the Chester break. It wouldn't have been sightseeing and romantic dinner dates, but standing on the terraces of the racecourse watching the horse racing. Each and every sporting event that Danny fancied attending came under the guise of a day out for 'us', and he has the cheek to say I was uninterested in his efforts.

'So, where are you living now?' I say as brightly as I can.

'Err, I'm staying with a workmate for now,' he says, staring into his coffee again.

I'm worried about the future. He's paid half the mortgage this month, as usual, but I need to know what's going to happen going forward. He reassures me that this will continue until 'we've sorted something out'. I don't feel as though we've sorted a single thing yet.

I look at my handsome husband's face and feel an urge to touch it, when his phone bleeps a text message. I notice, before he scoops the phone up, that it is from someone called Sarah. I hope he will ignore it and feel that our meeting is more important, but he doesn't. He reads the message and his face breaks into a smile, before he tells me that he's just nipping to the toilet.

I decide to go to the counter to order a blueberry muffin after all, as I skipped breakfast, when I notice him. He's on the phone outside the café and I can see his face. He's chatting and looking relaxed.

I suddenly remember the name 'Sarah' as someone he works with. *Slimming World Sarah.*

Danny chats animatedly then throws his head back and laughs. He looks so alive and happy. I haven't seen that expression on my husband's face in a long time. In that moment, I realise something. I think my marriage may really be over.

CHAPTER ELEVEN

I really don't feel like taking a holiday, but my mind clearly isn't on my job properly despite my best efforts. This scares the hell out of me, as it's the one thing in my life I am always firmly in control of. I know it's for the best that I'm not at the pub, and I shudder at my recent mistakes, but the truth is I don't want to be alone. I'm lucky enough to work with friends who are like family to me. Even the customers are like my extended family, fanning out like peacock feathers all around me and making me feel secure. I feel rudderless at the thought of being without the warmth of the Pig and Whistle, even if it is for a week or two.

I'm sat at home watching TV and nursing a glass of Sauvignon Blanc, when my phone rings. It's my mum and, much as I love her, I'm not in the mood to have a chat. She'll only be ringing to see if I'm eating properly. There's probably a gallon of home-made pea-and-ham soup en route by 'Big Dave', the courier, at this very moment. My mum swears that her pea-and-ham soup is a cure-all for everything and hauls it out at gatherings on a regular basis. When she proclaimed its cure-all properties recently, at a neighbour's funeral, the deceased woman's widower said it was a pity she hadn't given his wife some a bit sooner. My mother had sniffed at the remark and told me that her neighbour had probably died of boredom living with 'that miserable old bugger who wouldn't laugh if he saw a chair walk'.

I let the call go to voicemail and after a few tuts and mutterings she finally leaves a message:

'Oh, sorry, love. Think I was pressing the wrong buttons. You know what I'm like with technology [chuckles]. *Anyway, give me a ring. There's a new lady started work at the box office. She's a retired nurse and does Botox injections. She thinks I should try it and I just wondered what you thought? Maybe you could have some? It might make you feel better. Anyway, love, give us a ring.'*

I refill my glass and let out a long sigh. Does my mum really think that having a frozen face would cheer me up? I'm not against it. I think it looks great on other people but, knowing my luck, I would probably end up looking like Jack Nicholson when he played the Joker in the *Batman* movie. I'm thinking that maybe my mum should consider it though. She's a very good-looking woman, but she's been looking a bit tired lately. Maybe it would give her a boost.

I'm channel-flicking when I come across *A Place in the Sun: Home or Away*. It's a choice between Rhodes in Greece and Folkestone in Kent, as the couple are both beach lovers. It soon becomes clear that the presenter has his work cut out trying to persuade the wife that Rhodes is the better choice, as her heart is clearly set on Folkestone. She has found fault with every single Rhodes property that presenter Jonnie Irwin has shown her: kitchen too small in property one, veranda too small in property two (a stunning two-bedroomed house with mountain views). The third and fourth properties are 'too remote', even though they are only a fifteen-minute walk from a vibrant village.

The husband is wearing the blank expression of someone who learned many years ago not to have an opinion about anything, and, after enthusing over the first two properties, he gives up, knowing full well they will be moving to Folkestone.

I'm drawn in by the beauty of Rhodes. I'd forgotten just how picturesque it is, with its beautiful long beaches flanked by pine forests and mountains, and my childhood memories come rushing back.

Back in Folkestone, wife Joan is grinning from ear to ear as they are viewing a property with a large garden, which means she can grow vegetables and keep chickens. You can almost hear hubby Doug thinking of how much bigger his beetroots would be in Rhodes.

When the programme finishes I'm so inspired by the Greek landscape that I start to think I may use my holiday and have a little break, like Brian suggested. I've never really travelled alone, but I tell myself firmly that it's time to get a grip and man up. I always dreamed of being an intrepid traveller, so maybe this is my chance. It's just a shame that Hayley doesn't have any annual holidays left at the bank or I'd ask her to join me. Lyndsey at the pub is another good friend who would be an ideal holiday companion, but she'll be covering me in my absence.

Buoyed by the TV programme (and several glasses of Sauvignon Blanc) I fire up my laptop and decide to trawl the internet for holidays. I view every type of accommodation in Thakos, before settling on some apartments 'a stone's throw' away from the sea. I'm not even sure how much the village has changed since I last visited, but at least it will seem a little familiar.

I shouldn't really be spending money now that I'm newly single, but my generous dad deposited several hundred pounds into my account recently, in case I needed 'a little break'. I drain my wine and enter my card details into the holiday search engine. A few minutes later it's done – Sea View Apartments for ten days. I'm going on holiday to Greece! And I'm going alone!

CHAPTER TWELVE

The airport is surprisingly busy with families, considering it's only June. Families who must be risking huge fines for taking their children on cheaper holidays outside the statutory school-holiday dates. Someone at the pub told me that parents have started to lie to schools, feigning illnesses for their children. I can't help thinking it's a tough call. They are giving their kids the chance to travel the world yet teaching them that it's OK to flout the rules.

I'm sat in the departure lounge reading a new novel, but my brain can't process a single word. I must have read Chapter Six several times, but I can't take it in. I feel a mixture of nerves and excitement as I'm about to embark upon my lone adventure. I consider buying a large vodka from the nearest bar, but it's heaving with tattooed blokes going on a lads' holiday to Faliraki.

I wonder if Danny will start going on lads' holidays again? Or will he drift into another relationship? Why couldn't we fix what *we* had? I'm exhausted with all of the questions going round and round in my head. My mum always says, 'If it's meant to be it will be.' I wish that saying could be of some comfort to me right now.

The call for boarding comes across the tannoy, but I decide to stay in my seat. I have a seat number, so there's no need to stand in an endless queue. Plus, I can use my phone a bit longer here before I have to put it in airplane mode. I check my phone for text messages for the umpteenth time but there's nothing. I don't know what I'm expecting really. Maybe I imagine Danny running through Departures, shouting my name and carrying a giant bunch of red roses just as the gate has closed. Hardly. And it's not as if I'm never coming back. It's only a ten day break. Or maybe it won't be. Maybe I'll do a sodding Shirley Valentine and stay there. I could get a job in a restaurant just like she did.

I exhale slowly as I join the tail end of the queue. The Faliraki boys step in line behind me, having quickly sunk another pint before the last call for boarding. One of the group, a tall blonde bloke, who looks like Owen Wilson, flashes a smile at me and engages me in light-hearted chat. I hear his mates saying, 'What's he like? He hasn't even left the airport yet.' I chat politely until minutes later we are through Gate 15 to board Flight R3490 to Rhodes International Airport. My heart is hammering in my chest. What am I doing leaving my support network behind to go off on my own? I calm myself down as I remember that Brian has told me to take some time off from the pub, so my days would probably only be spent at home alone, with constant calls from my mum.

I can do this. I take a deep breath and cast a backward glance to the departure lounge where I see no one but a cleaner in a blue uniform pushing her trolley. I think of the drinks trolley on the plane. Suddenly I'm exhausted and desperate for my seat and a large vodka. There's no going back now, although I realise, to my surprise, that I'm ready to see what adventures lie ahead.

CHAPTER THIRTEEN

The sweltering heat wafts across my face as I disembark from the plane. That exciting, indefinable smell of a foreign country assaults my senses as I inhale deeply. Tall cypress trees wave gently in the breeze, and I smile to myself as my mood is lifted. I'm here and suddenly I feel joyous at the prospect of rediscovering the holiday village I came to as a child. I travelled by myself, which is, I realise, the bravest thing I've done in a long time.

The arrivals lounge at Rhodes airport is in chaos. There are lone travellers with backpacks, loved-up couples holding hands and families with restless children, who are running around like animals released from a cage after their long plane journey. Babies in buggies are straining to get out, while their weary parents try to placate them with toys.

After yet another queue at the ladies' toilets, I'm at the carousel waiting for my suitcase, when I suddenly feel a vague glimmer of excitement. In less than half an hour I'll be at the little village of Thakos, lounging by the hotel pool. I spent hours perusing the apartments online, to make sure I chose exactly the right place, and came across the little village I visited as a child with my parents. I think about Christakis beach taverna again and the Zoo Bar where the DJ looked and dressed like Timmy Mallett in his heyday.

I didn't want some party place with throbbing nightlife. I couldn't face that yet. I recall the neon lights of Faliraki on a girls' holiday; going to bed at five in the morning and sleeping on the beach all day after a full English breakfast. No thanks. Thakos sounded ideal, with its 'clean beach and a sprinkling of friendly tavernas, it's a place to relax and recharge the batteries'. Perfect.

As I heave my huge pink patterned suitcase off the carousel, with sweat beads forming on my head, my phone bleeps a text message. It's from Danny. *I don't believe it.* It simply reads: *R U OK?*

What the hell does that mean? Of course I'm not bloody OK, he's my husband and he's just sodded off, what does he expect me to say? Part of me wants to reply, but the sensible part of me thinks, *He's got a cheek, and why does he want to know how I am? Why now, when I'm coming away to think things through? Feelings of guilt, no doubt.*

I delete his message and head for the taxi rank. It's only around a ten-minute drive to the village, where I will get myself a much-needed stiff drink. I don't want to think about anything over these next ten days, especially Danny. I want to take one day at a time and just enjoy the sunshine. It's been a miserable summer so far in England and it's mid-June now and there is a clear blue sky with a sweltering sun in Rhodes. The season is in full swing so I intend to make the most of it.

I'm about to get into a taxi when I see the Faliraki boys loading their cases into a silver mini bus. Owen Wilson waves and calls over to me, wishing me a good holiday, accompanied by a wink. I smile to myself – perhaps there is life after Danny after all?

My taxi speeds along the dusty road. Time is money for these taxi drivers, who I imagine are desperate to get back to the airport for the next fare. I'm sure the driver raised an eyebrow when I told him where I was heading, before shrugging and saying, 'OK, lady.'

Fifteen minutes later, and feeling slightly car sick, having slid and bounced along the black-leather seat all the way, we arrive at the village of Thakos, where the driver deposits me on a dusty road. There are two children playing with a ball, and a fruit and vegetable cart, where an old Greek lady dressed in black is buying a watermelon, as dusk gently falls.

'Your 'otel is there,' the driver says, pointing to an apartment building up a slight hill that has no road access. 'I go no further.'

I pay him and he speeds off into the distance.

The old lady at the fruit cart proffers a ripe peach and smiles a gappy-toothed smile. I purchase four peaches, which she places into a brown paper bag before showing me a bottle of water. It's slightly lukewarm but I suppose I can put it into the fridge at the apartments. I hand over three euros and she smiles gratefully.

After checking my map again, I trudge my suitcase up the incline, wondering if he's left me in the wrong place, as the photograph of Sea View Apartments looked stunning and not at all like the building I eventually arrive at. I am greeted by the sight of a tired-looking hotel and a stray ginger cat that is being chased by a barking dog. There's a moustachioed fifty-something man in a vest sitting on a white plastic chair and smoking a cigarette, who stands up to greet me.

'Welcome, lady,' he says, smiling warmly before leading me into a small, old-fashioned reception area. 'I hope you have a good journey. Welcome to Sea View.'

There's a noticeboard pinned with photographs of party revellers, which look as though they are a few decades old, and an assortment of statues of the Virgin Mary stand on a shelf that's attached to a wood-panelled wall. An elaborate fake-flower display sets off the 1990s homage, although it does all seem spotlessly clean.

The owner, who tells me he is called Andreas, checks me in and gives me a room key. I notice a small bar and lounge area with not a single person in sight. My Greek dream is beginning to feel like a Greek tragedy.

After checking in, I order a large vodka and Coke at the bar, which I almost down in one, the ice-cold drink cooling me immediately.

'So,' I say brightly. 'Where's the pool?'

'The pool?' Andreas frowns, scratching his head and avoiding eye contact with me.

'Err, yes, the swimming pool?'

'We have no pool. But it's OK, you can use the pool at Paradise Apartments. The owner, he is my friend.'

He puffs a cloud of cigarette smoke into the dingy bar. This is not looking good. I scrutinise the Internet printout of the apartments again and sure enough there is a picture of a sparkling blue pool. I thrust it under his nose.

'What about this picture then?' I demand huffily.

'Yes.' Andreas smiles. 'That is Paradise Apartment pool. Very nice, yes?'

I scrutinise the small print and realise, to my dismay, it does say patrons of Sea View Apartments are 'welcome to use the pool at the nearby Paradise Apartments'.

I order another large drink, which I decide to take up to my apartment. Suddenly I feel exhausted. The owner registers my expression.

'Don't worry,' he says, placing a bowl of salted peanuts in front of me. 'The sea is so close. Sea view,' he boasts enthusiastically. 'You don't need any pool.'

I can't agree. I like lounging by the pool, but feel too tired to argue. And as I climb the stairs to my apartment, with Andreas ahead of me carrying my luggage, I can't help wondering whether I should have booked that holiday in Faliraki after all.

CHAPTER FOURTEEN

The next morning, I open my curtains and I'm greeted with the most stunning view of a shimmering turquoise sea. The spacious apartment, with its whitewashed walls, beach prints and pine furniture, looks fresh and clean in the bright daylight, and not at all like the dark tunnel that I stumbled into the night before. There's a large blue and white tiled bathroom which looks spotlessly clean (although the white plastic shower and the flimsy fish-patterned shower curtain look very dated). In the small kitchen I have a fridge, a kettle, some complimentary sachets of Nescafé and a two-ring electric cooker. There's crockery in the cupboard and cutlery in the drawer, as well as a corkscrew. Everything I need to prepare a Greek salad or enjoy a take-away, as I don't intend doing any cooking.

I make a coffee and take it outside. I'm at the end of the building and the branches of a tall lemon tree slightly overhang my balcony. I sit on one of the white plastic chairs and just stare at the sparkling sea, which seems as though it is almost a touch away. Andreas, the owner, was right about the view. In the distance towards the end of the beach I can see a large hotel, which is probably the all-inclusive hotel I read about during my online search.

I dare to think that it might not be so bad here after all. I've had a good night's sleep in a comfortable bed and I'm planning to explore the village after breakfast.

I'm surprised to find that there are several other guests having breakfast on a shaded veranda overlooking an olive grove. The place looked completely deserted last night when I arrived, but perhaps I judged it too hastily. One English couple smile and say good morning while enjoying their full English breakfast. Another couple nod and continue with their fruit and Greek yoghurt. They are dressed in shorts and walking shoes, as if ready to go exploring the footpaths and mountains. Their muscular, bronzed bodies suggest years of outdoor exercise. I decide on coffee, apple juice and scrambled eggs on toast to start the day.

Andreas brings the food to me with a wide smile. 'So, you have a good sleep, yes?'

'Yes – and you were right about the view,' I concede, while sipping strong, almost unpalatable coffee. The eggs were a different story though. Delicious, yellow, free-range eggs, scrambled to perfection. I noticed the hens on some enclosed land to the right of the hotel, which I can just about see from my balcony. Earlier this morning a young man was gathering some eggs into a basket, before disappearing into the distance on a moped.

I remembered that almost everyone gets about on mopeds on the Greek islands. Women calling in at the shops, draping their striped plastic bags over the handlebars, young workers zipping in and out of hotels on errands, and even people with young children seated on their knees, precariously, I think, but it is second nature to them as they grow up with it.

The walkers finish their breakfast and head off. It's only nine thirty and the temperature is already in the seventies. I hope they have plenty of water with them, and then realise that thoughts like that will turn me into my mother.

Andreas returns with the coffee pot to offer me some more, which I politely decline.

'No, thanks. I'll have a little look around the village then go to Paradise Apartments pool. Is it next door?'

Andreas looks slightly uncomfortable. 'Not exactly next door. Would you like some more apple juice?'

'So where exactly then?'

'No more than a ten-minute walk, I promise. But you have beach. Three minutes' walk.'

'*Ten minutes?* I'll be exhausted before I even get there, especially in this heat. Is there a bus or anything?'

Andreas sits down. 'There was once a bus that used to come down this street every half-hour, but the people stopped coming here on holiday. The bus service is only every two hours now, and you've just missed one. But I will take you,' he says, with such a warm, genuine smile that I feel bad about complaining. It's not his fault that the numbers of tourists to the small hotels have dropped dramatically, favouring the all-inclusive hotels. I've never seen the appeal of all-inclusive hotels personally. I like to explore my surroundings and eat in various restaurants throughout my holiday. I suppose it makes sense if you have kids who want a pool and an endless supply of drinks and ice cream, though.

I'm pondering my next move, when the egg collector walks in. He's like a younger, slimmer version of Andreas, with his olive skin and dark brown hair and eyes. He's attractive, I can't help noticing. No one could deny that Andreas must be his father, surely? He glances around the breakfast area before taking a note from Andreas, who introduces us briefly – he is indeed Andreas's son, and his name is Costas – then zooms off up the road on his moped once more.

I suddenly get an image of Danny and my heart sinks. The feeling of sadness still comes and goes and I wonder how long it will be before I wake up in the morning and he is not my first thought.

After breakfast, I change into a pair of white linen shorts and black vest and decide to walk to Paradise Apartments before it gets too hot. Andreas has told me to ring him and he will come and collect me, but I think I will watch out for the bus. I plait my blonde hair and place some sun cream and a towel in my beach bag. I put my sunglasses on, buy a bottle of cold water from the bar, and I'm ready to go.

As I walk along the dusty road, flanked by olive trees and fig trees, I realise the extent of the lack of tourism in this village. There are several boarded-up restaurants and the few remaining ones have a slightly run-down appearance. I feel sad that a place of such stunning beauty could be reduced to this. There is a peaceful drone of crickets in the background as I make my way along the quiet road; a sudden smell of figs as I walk over some that have been trodden underfoot on the pathway. I pass lemon trees and lime trees as I stroll past a ceramic shop, displaying colourful Greek bowls and plates outside. An elderly man in the doorway, wearing a white vest and brown cap, says good morning and beckons me in. I promise to call in the following day. There's a young woman with long dark hair sat on a plastic chair reading a magazine. She lifts her head and smiles.

Before too long, I arrive at the Paradise Apartments and discover, to my surprise, that the pool area is surprisingly full. It's a cheerful building, painted a pale yellow with bright yellow-and-white canopies over the windows. Vibrant pink bougainvillea are dotted about the immaculately kept gardens, where a young hotel worker is watering the plants. The receptionist, a young Greek lady, welcomes me warmly before showing me to the pool and taking a drinks order. I choose a sunbed in a quiet corner with a large parasol and sit myself down.

Very soon I have applied more sun cream and am settled down with my novel and a large cold beer. This is the first day of my holiday and I want to try to relax a little, as I can still feel the knots in my stomach and the tension in my shoulders. I slide further down my sunbed and hope that this place can work its magic and, as I close my eyes and surrender to the massaging effect of the warm sun, I wish I could stay here forever.

CHAPTER FIFTEEN

I wake because someone is gently shaking my arm. As I open my eyes I realise it's the girl from reception.

'Madam,' she says apologetically. 'I am sorry to wake you, but the sun is very strong. You have been sleeping directly in it for a while. That is not good on your first day.'

She hands me a bottle of water before dragging the parasol over to cover more of me.

'I must have dozed off for a minute, I didn't realise I was so tired.'

'You slept for two hours. This is why I wake you.'

I sit bolt upright. '*Two hours!*'

I can already see my legs taking on the appearance of a lobster with a white rectangular patch where my book has fallen onto my leg. *Dear God.*

There's a young boy sitting on the sunlounger next to me, eating an ice cream and staring at me. He's wearing flippers and Spider-Man swimming shorts.

'You were snoring,' he says, in between licks of strawberry ice cream. 'And making funny noises.'

Oh no. I know how I sound when I dream. I make this ghostly wailing sound as if I'm haunting a graveyard. No wonder all the sunbeds that were close to me are suddenly empty and people have moved to the opposite side of the pool.

I sit up and my head hurts. I sip some of the water. Maybe I should go inside, into the cool marble lobby. I gather my things and hobble slightly into the inside of the hotel, where the air conditioning blasts a welcome coolness all over me. A few seconds later, the barman has appeared with a large tumbler of water filled with ice, before the receptionist reappears and asks how I am feeling.

'You won't be the last person to fall asleep in the sun. It was just rather a long time and some of the guests said you were... erm... sleeping deeply.'

I want to die of embarrassment. I'd been feeling so stressed that my body just gave out to the soothing effects of the sun. Thank goodness I'm not staying here as I wouldn't want to face the other holiday-makers over breakfast the next morning. I thank the receptionist, whose name is Delia, and wonder what would have happened to me had she not woken me. I could have ended up in hospital with serious dehydration.

When I finish my drink, I stand up and immediately sit back down again as I feel slightly dizzy. This is not good. Delia beckons to a passing hotel worker, a young man in his early twenties, and engages in a brief conversation with him before coming over to me.

'This is Dimitri,' Delia says, smiling. 'He will take you back to your hotel whenever you are ready. Stay in your room. Plenty of water, air conditioning on and apply aftersun cream,' she sensibly advises.

I'm sure she's seen it all before. Brits abroad toasting themselves on the first day and ruining the rest of their holiday, but I'm not usually one of those people. I could kick myself as I'm going to have to stay in the shade for a couple of days now. Oh well, I'll have to sit under the pergola back at the apartments, and I have my book, which is very enjoyable. It's the story of a man who goes on holiday to Turkey, then finds himself marooned there.

I think about how I would feel if I could not get home from here, and at this moment in time I wouldn't mind. Well, maybe not forever, but I just can't face putting the key in the door of my cottage knowing I am going to be living a single life there without my husband. I still can't get my head around it as it all seemed so sudden; once again I wonder how I never noticed the problems in our relationship.

I'm making my way across reception, when a middle-aged lady, with a canvas beach bag bearing the logo 'I love Rhodes', smiles sympathetically as she notices my bright red legs.

'Ooh, love, are you alright? Try some yoghurt on that. It's supposed to take away the sting,' she says sympathetically.

'Oh right, thanks, I might give that a try later. It's my own fault for sleeping so long in the sun. I've been a bit stressed lately.'

'Really? Well, never you mind, love. If you can't relax here then you can't relax anywhere. I think the Greek islands are a little bit magical.' She winks.

I hope she's right.

I thank Dimitri as he drops me off outside my holiday accommodation and I am grateful that there is no one at reception as I make my way upstairs to my apartment. I take a cool shower before changing into a floaty dress and sitting in a shady part of the balcony. There is one couple having a Greek salad lunch on the veranda, which overlooks the olive trees. The silver-haired lady looks much older than her dark-haired dining partner, who she touches affectionately on the arm throughout their lunch. They have a stunning view of the bejewelled sea, which might bring out the romance in anyone.

It seems such a far cry from the Liverpool street that I grew up in, a stone's throw away from the docks; the wild Irish Sea there contrasting with the aquamarine Mediterranean here, in my mind. The boys in our street used to run down to the docks to watch the huge container ships coming in from around the world. They would play on the piles of corn at the corn works, returning home to a clip round the ear from their mothers, who could never get the smell out of their clothes. I went down there once, with some of the other kids, but a mouse ran across my foot and I never went again.

Worse than the mice were the rats, though. I never forget my next-door neighbour finding a brown rat curled up in her Pyrex casserole dish in the cupboard under the sink; we could hear her screams through the thin terraced walls. Happy days!

I imagine a childhood in a place like this, then consider that in many ways it wouldn't be too different from my own. We had Crosby Beach and the glorious sand dunes, which were like mountains to us. We would climb them and slide down giggling with the marram grass scratching at our legs. We didn't have the same amount of sunshine as Rhodes, although my mind always recalls long sultry days during the school holidays, listening out for the familiar tune of the ice-cream van.

Rhodes has three hundred days of sunshine a year and families eat outdoors together late into the evening, chatting and drinking, as children play happily at their feet. The sun seems to cast a magical power over everything and I'm absolutely gutted that I won't be able to lie outside and enjoy it for at least a couple more days.

CHAPTER SIXTEEN

I come back inside the apartment and plug my phone into the phone charger and it beeps into life immediately. Hayley has sent me ten text messages over the last twenty-four hours. The last one reads:

Have U vanished off the face of the earth? Let me know UR OK. Getting worried. xxxxxx

Shit. I had forgotten I'd promised to text her as soon as I arrived, which, I realise, was a day and a half ago. I tossed my phone into my bag after the text from Danny at the airport and the battery had died. I'll let it charge up a bit and text her later.

My skin is beginning to sting a bit so I apply another liberal coating of aloe vera aftersun, which soothes me temporarily. Cheap as chips (it costs under a fiver) and the only thing that really does the job. I spent ages at the beauty counter of Mason's department store before I came away, as an assistant tried to flog me some aftersun lotion that cost thirty quid a bottle. When I asked her what was so special about it, she seemed a bit flummoxed.

'Well, it has special ingredients to soothe and soften the skin after being in the sun.'

No shit, Sherlock.

'Yes, but *what* exactly,' I persisted, examining the ingredients and trying to discover the secret elixir.

'Well, there is aloe vera to soothe, and rose oil and seaweed,' she announced, after reading the ingredients on the bottle just as I had done.

'But there's nothing there to justify that price. The very same ingredients are in this,' I said, fishing out my tube of aftersun from Supersaver chemist over the road.

'You get what you pay for,' she replied huffily, before snatching the tester tube and putting it back on the counter.

'Not if it's got the same stuff in it,' I countered. I realise I do like to have the last word; something that drove Danny mad. But I only do this if I know I'm right. 'Maybe you should get to know your product properly before you try to push it onto unsuspecting customers.'

I could see her over-made-up face begin to flush red with anger, so I decided she must be pretty mad. I think I upset her further when I asked for and succeeded in obtaining lots of free make-up samples from the young assistant on the next counter, who was only too keen to please.

I still can't believe I fell asleep in the sun. I didn't even realise I was so stressed, but I suppose my body told me otherwise. Let's hope my Supersaver aftersun soothes my skin.

I do think it's important to know your product and I know every single thing about the drinks in the bar as well as the effect they have on the customers. I know that vodka makes people lose their inhibitions. Bottled beer is for trendy young men or older guys pacing themselves on a long night out. Hand-pulled ales are usually drunk in alcoves by men engaging in meaningful conversation, and white wine is the staple for the girls' night out, with a few shots thrown in, which are usually regretted the next morning. Jäger Bombs are the worst thing for getting a hangover, Bacardi is the best for avoiding them, and wine and beer should never be mixed. I can advise anyone about any type of alcohol. I take customer service very seriously and believe that whether you work in a bank or a bar it makes no difference. My dedication and eye for detail had me promoted from a casual waitress to bar manager within twelve months, with responsibility for a budget and selecting new drinks for the pub.

I wonder whether I took my job a little too seriously? Maybe Danny was right. Maybe I was too concerned with work, making sure everything was just perfect, while all the time my marriage was anything but.

My phone begins to ring and I notice it's my mother. I'd better take it or she'll be worried. Hayley has probably convinced my mother that I've been sold to the sex industry or something.

'Hi, Mum, how are you?'

'Oh, I'm fine, love, how are you? Are you warm enough? I hope you've packed a cardigan and not just a lot of skimpy vests and dresses. It can get quite cool in the evenings near the sea.'

'Mum, I'm in Greece. It's about twenty-seven degrees outside.'

'Oh, is it really hot then?'

'Well, yes, it's pretty hot. Hot enough to get sunburnt.' I regret saying the words as soon as they have left my lips.

'Oh, no, have you got sunburnt? I hope you have plenty of after- sun, and if that doesn't work try yoghurt. That Greek yoghurt should do the trick.'

Greek yoghurt sounds really medicinal. I wonder if anyone actually eats it.

'I'm fine, Mum, really. The apartment is lovely [*small lie*] and the village is brilliant [*bigger lie*]. It's just how I remember it.' [*Big fat porky-pie. It's nothing like how I remember.*]

I remember a bustling main street overflowing with tourists seated outside heaving restaurants, and local children playing in the village square, mingling with the tourists until the sun went down. Now there are long-forgotten establishments alongside apartments and tavernas that are just scraping a living, while the all-inclusive hotel across the water on a private beach waves its flags of all nations in triumph. The patrons of the hotel must spend all their time inside, where everything is laid on, or lounging around the hotel pool, as you never see them outside the all-inclusive complex. I suppose it makes perfect sense if you have kids but it's putting all the little Greek tavernas out of business.

'When you say hot,' Mum continues, sounding slightly worried, 'you don't think it's hot enough for a forest fire, do you? Are there many trees around your hotel?'

'No, Mum,' I lie, as I stare at the lemon tree, its branches practically touching my window.

My mum has always been a bit of worrier, but since the menopause it's reached a whole new level. She worries about anything and everyone. When she started escorting the twelve-year-old who lived next door to the bus stop in the morning 'because it was still dark', I persuaded her to see the doctor, who suggested some antidepressants for anxiety, but she was having none of it.

'Well, I'm up early anyway and her mother doesn't open her curtains until about ten o'clock,' she sniffed. 'And I think Amy quite liked our little chats.'

Amy didn't. She had to endure the taunts of her friends who wondered why a fifty-four-year-old woman, who wasn't her grandmother, was walking her to the bus stop every morning.

My mum reluctantly tried HRT in the end, after her obsession with thinking she had left electrical appliances plugged in became draining. She had to return home from work several times a week to check she hadn't left irons or hair straighteners plugged in, even though she hadn't. It was hormones, the doctor said. The post-menopause drop in oestrogen was responsible. So Mum tried some HRT and never looked back. It's not perfect, of course. She still occasionally lapses into irrational states of anxiety (like now), but mainly she's fine.

'No, Mum, no trees too close and certainly not hot enough for a fire. It's only June now and the temperatures don't reach their peak until mid-August. Relax.'

'Well, alright,' she says eventually. 'Just be careful. And don't forget to send me a postcard. Bye, love.'

I'm not even sure I'll find anywhere that sells stamps around here. It's like a ghost town. Plus no one seems to send postcards these days. It's all instant messaging. But I'll find some somewhere. If my mum wants a postcard then I will send her one. She's always there for me when I need her. It's the least I can do.

CHAPTER SEVENTEEN

I could kick myself for falling asleep in the sun for so long on my first day in Thakos. I wanted to go out and do a bit of exploring, not to mention shopping. I've got some peaches in the fridge, which I bought from the street vendor, and some bottled water, but that's about it.

I'd planned on walking down to the beach later to see if Christakis taverna is still there. I can still remember running into the frothy sea and splashing with a little girl called Vicky who was from Newcastle. We promised to be best friends forever, but of course when we got back home I never saw her again. We were both only eight years old at the time and I remember feeling terribly betrayed when she went home three days before we did without saying goodbye.

I went to Newcastle twelve years later for a hen-party weekend and, against all odds, I spotted her in a crowded bar. I was standing there, sipping a cocktail, when a girl came up to the bar and ordered a bottle of white wine. She turned her head in my direction and smiled, and I couldn't believe it. It was her eyes. They were two different colours, one being brown and the other a distinctive green.

'Are you called Vicky?' I enquired, not sure if she would even remember me.

She frowned slightly, searching my face for some sort of clue to our connection, before screaming with delight when she realised who I was.

'Oh my GOD, is that you, Mandy?' she squealed in her Cheryl Cole accent, before grabbing me in a bear hug. She was always the extrovert, even at the age of eight with her cheeky grin and curly brown hair.

She was out with her friend and they joined our hen-party weekend, even staying at the hotel for the night with us. I learned that she hadn't said goodbye to me on holiday because they left at midnight for their flight and we were already in bed.

It was great having a local to show us all around the hot spots. We've had quite a few meet-ups over the years and become good friends, which has been cemented by frequent updates on Facebook. I don't see her as much as I'd like, especially now she is married with two children, but I think our friendship was definitely meant to last longer than those ten days in Rhodes when we were kids.

I'm back on the balcony, reading my book, when I spot Costas collecting glasses from the shaded eating area. He has a slim yet muscular frame, the white T-shirt he is wearing accentuating his arm muscles as he bends and lifts a box of empty bottles. On the way back to the bar he glances up to my first-floor balcony and asks me if I am OK. I suppose I must look like a bit of a weirdo sitting in a shady corner of a balcony wearing a floor-length dress and sunglasses.

'Yes, fine,' I say, smiling. 'Just a bit sunburnt, so I'm staying in the shade today.'

'I have just the thing for you. I will come up in five minutes.'

'What? No, err, it's alright. I'm fine, thanks,' I say, thinking about the slight mess in the apartment.

'It's no problem,' he says, before disappearing around the corner.

I find myself whizzing inside, tidying up my room and wondering how one person can create this much mess as I fling clothes into the wardrobe and kick my shoes under the second single bed. I booked a twin room in the apartments, so I could have more space than a single would offer, and it didn't cost that much more. I then find myself brushing my hair and applying a slick of lip gloss. What the hell am I doing?

A few minutes later, there is a knock on the door and I am staring into a pair of chocolate-brown eyes. He's gorgeous.

'This is for your sunburn,' he says, handing me a bottle of olive oil.

I look puzzled.

'Olive oil?'

'Yes, olive oil. Totally underrated, yet it has many different uses. Rub it into your skin and you will not peel.' He sits on my bed without being asked to and runs his hands along the sheets.

'OK, err, thanks for that. I don't know much about olive oil. I tend to just use the cheap Italian stuff from the supermarket.'

He is suddenly on his feet telling me that I should use nothing but Greek extra virgin olive oil as it is the best in the world.

'We were the first Europeans to use olive oil,' Costas says passionately. 'It was first discovered in Asia Minor, spreading to Iran and Syria before coming to the Mediterranean six thousand years ago. The Greeks had it first before the Romans,' he states proudly. 'It was the source of wealth in the Minoan kingdom of Crete.'

I'm impressed by his product knowledge and I think back to the woman on the department store counter.

'Hmm... interesting,' I say, genuinely.

Costas stands up to leave as he glances at his watch. 'So, as you are avoiding the sun today I will find you a table in the shade downstairs for lunch. I have a break soon, I will join you.'

He doesn't ask if it's OK with me, he just tells me it's going to happen, which I'm not sure I like. Yet, despite myself, fifteen minutes later I am seated at a table, sipping retsina and iced water and facing a huge Greek salad dotted with olives. There is a basket of fresh bread on the table and creamy dips of hummus and tara-masalata. Grape vines are threaded through the beams of a pergola above our head as the sun dapples through the leaves. It's heavenly.

'So,' says Costas in between mouthfuls of creamy feta and crusty bread. 'Why are you on holiday alone?'

I wondered when that was coming.

'Can't a woman be on holiday by herself?' I ask before downing another glass of retsina. It really doesn't taste too bad after a glass or two. Not as good as a decent Sauvignon Blanc, but it's OK.

'A woman,' he says, 'holidays alone if she is getting over a break-up or writing a novel, and I don't see you writing anything.'

'Are you from this century?' I reply. 'Women often holiday alone.'

'No, they don't. They holiday with a partner, a friend or group of friends. Rarely alone.'

I realise he is probably right. Apart from walkers, that is. 'I just needed to relax,' I say, not wanting to reveal anything about my personal life. I barely know him.

Costas smiles at me and leans in towards me to refill my glass, but I put my hand over it. I notice that he is only drinking iced water himself.

'Then you are in the right place. If you can't relax here, then you can't do it anywhere.'

I fill my own glass with water, realising that the retsina has gone to my head, as I imagine Costas sitting on my bed again running his hands over more than the sheets.

I need to get back to my balcony and book. Maybe I will have a siesta inside. I am about to make a move, when Andreas beckons Costas to reception as some new arrivals are getting out of a taxi. He is on his feet at once and doesn't even give me a backward glance as he takes the suitcases from the two blonde, middle-aged women and escorts them to their rooms. I wonder if Costas is just as charming to all of his guests? Maybe he is waiting for the arrival of every plane, so he can charm the ladies. Now that he's gone, I pour myself another drink and decide that I don't mind. It's nice to have a friendly face to chat to either way.

CHAPTER EIGHTEEN

Afternoon drinking has never really been my thing and, after a nap, I awake two hours later to the sound of knocking on my room door. I've been dribbling on my pillow and lying on my arm, which is now heavy and numb. I hope it isn't Costas again.

'Coming,' I shout as breezily as I can, before opening the door and getting the surprise of my life. 'HAYLEY!'

'You're not bloody dead then?' my best friend asks before crushing me in an embrace.

'Ouch, watch my sunburn. Especially my shoulders.' I wince.

'Ooh, that looks sore. Hope you've get plenty of aftersun. If not, I've heard Greek…'

'Yoghurt, I know. Although olive oil is less messy. Anyway, Hayley, I can't believe it! What are you doing here?'

'Well, I needed a break from work. I'm exhausted. And we only bloody got held up by gunmen last week, didn't we?'

'*What?* You mean the bank got robbed? Oh my God, are you OK?'

'Yeah, I'm fine. All the inside staff were OK, actually. It was the guys in the Securicor van that copped it. A couple of balaclava-faced thugs tried to grab the cash as they were making a delivery. They didn't get away with that much, couple of grand I think, as those Securicor guys can hold their own. One of them got badly beaten though, but thankfully he's doing OK now. They gave me some time off to recover. I needed a break anyway.' She sighs. 'It's so stressful lately, with all these ridiculous sales targets we're supposed to achieve. How I'm meant to flog five loans and credit cards a week in an area where everyone's credit rating is zilch I don't know. I'm bloody knackered. I mean we have the kind of customers who ring up to cancel their gas and electricity standing orders but keep their Sky TV. Also… *someone* doesn't reply to their texts, so I thought I'd take a break and check that my friend is OK at the same time.'

I remember guiltily that I still haven't replied to Hayley's messages.

'I'm so sorry, Hayley, I would have got around to texting, you know I would, but I'm only just settling in,' I say apologetically. 'Anyway, I thought you didn't have any holiday left?'

'I had a couple of days left, and the manager gave me some time off to recover from the stress of the robbery. I haven't had a day off sick in four years, so I'd say I'm entitled anyway.' She laughs.

'Hayley, it's so good to see you!' I say, hugging her again gently.

'Come on, let's have a drink.' Hayley smiles. She's wearing a khaki linen jumpsuit and her long brown hair is glossy and thick. As always, she is looking naturally gorgeous. 'I've bought some nice cold Coke to go with this vodka,' she says, waving a bottle at me. 'Oh, and there's decent nightclub five miles away called Strobe, eight euros in a taxi. It's an open-air one in an old amphitheatre or something that gets going about eleven p.m. I got the lowdown from the taxi driver.'

I smile at my dear friend, who has been here all of five minutes and has already managed to discover more about the place than I have in three days. She has also brought orange juice, croissants, crisps, cheese, ham and bread. What more could a girl want?

After a shower and a freshen up, we're both seated on the white plastic furniture on the balcony enjoying chicken-and-salad-stuffed pittas called *gyros*, which are sold downstairs at the street kiosk next door. Hayley has poured us vodka and Cokes (small amounts of vodka as we are pacing ourselves for the evening), and I have pulled a lemon from the overhanging tree and sliced it into our drinks.

Anyone viewing this seemingly idyllic holiday scene would never guess that I am on an emotional roller coaster and putting on a brave face to the outside world. Heartache is such a strange thing. It ebbs and flows like the tide and the pain creeps up on you in the same way. I'm supposed to be here to try to clear my head and attempt to forget about Danny for a little while, but it isn't too long before we are invariably discussing my mess of a marriage.

After her third vodka, Hayley looks at me with a slightly serious expression, before taking hold of my hand. 'I'm here to have a great time with my old friend and to try to cheer you up a bit. But I'm not going to keep this to myself, or what kind of a friend would that make me? I have to tell you something.' She takes a deep breath. 'Danny is seeing someone.'

I'm not quite sure what reaction she was expecting, but I absorb this news quietly as it only confirms what I knew in my heart of hearts anyway. Oh, I knew about the night of his work's party and I wasn't certain that the affair had continued, but I definitely had my suspicions. Danny hadn't exactly beaten a path to my door looking for reconciliation, and I hadn't heard from him for a week before I got the text at the airport.

'Thanks, Hayley, but I think I knew that really. It's someone he works with, isn't it?'

She looks surprised. 'How do you know that? I only found out because I saw them in town on Sunday. Danny tried to dive into a shop, but I'd already spotted him.'

I told her all about him mentioning this Sarah person and then about the text in the coffee shop.

'You'll never guess who this Sarah is,' she says, biting her lip nervously. 'It's Sarah Kelly who was in our year at school.'

I almost spit my drink out. 'Sarah Kelly! No way! Danny is seeing *Sarah Kelly*?'

I can hardly take it in. Sarah Kelly was a nice enough person, but she was a very large girl who used to sweat a lot, especially in the summer months, when she would drag her hefty frame around while constantly mopping her perspiring brow.

'She's not so hefty any more,' says Hayley, flicking her phone onto a picture of a stunning-looking brunette in a bikini. 'Sarah's profile pic on Facebook. Apparently, she's lost five stone since we left school and is now a club leader for Slimming World. As well as working part-time in the offices of Auto Repairs.'

It's weird really, but I don't feel anything much. I'm just surprised to discover that Danny is seeing Sarah Kelly. Maybe he has done me a favour ending a marriage that was simply going through the motions. I don't know what I think, but I do know that I don't want to dwell on the subject. My best friend is here, the weather is warm and the nightlife is waiting. I owe it to myself to try to enjoy a night out.

'Well, thanks for telling me,' I say. 'You really are a true friend. But I don't want to mention it again this evening. We're going to hit the bars before heading down to Strobe. I've got my dancing shoes in my suitcase and tonight they're coming out!'

CHAPTER NINETEEN

A hangover in the heat is hell. I've spent the last hour with my head down the toilet bowl in the blue-and-white-tiled bathroom, while Hayley is bustling around the apartment looking for beach towels. I failed to take my own expert advice about not mixing drinks, as everything from a pina colada to a Slippery Nipple slid down my throat last night.

'Right. That's everything packed in the beach bag. How long are you going to be in there?' Hayley shouts through to the bathroom.

Is she actually being serious? I feel like I am going to die and after several incoherent mumblings from me, Hayley pushes the pine bathroom door open.

'Jeez, the state of you,' she laughs, taking in my mascara- streaked face and last night's pink striped dress, which I slept in hunched around my hips as I hugged the toilet bowl.

Hayley looks amazing. She is wearing denim shorts and canvas wedges, which show off her long, lean legs to perfection. Her dark brown hair is scrunched up in a bun and she is wearing Karen Millen sunglasses and a slick of lip gloss. I don't know how she does it. I don't know how many cocktails she got through last night, not to mention vodka shots, and here she is as fresh as a daisy, while I feel like climbing back under the cool sheets with a bottle of water.

She disappears into the kitchen area, and I can hear a sound of fizzing in water as she returns with a glass of Alka-Seltzer. 'Here, get this down you. I'll give you half an hour. Get a shower. I'll wait on the balcony to make a start on my tan, and then we are going down to the beach,' she orders.

I groan, but Hayley is pushing the drink to my lips and I take a large salty mouthful. My head is pounding, yet somehow I manage to stumble into the shower and, forty minutes later, much to my surprise, I feel half-human again. White linen dress over my bikini, sun hat, water and large sunglasses, and I'm ready to go. At least I can snooze under the shade of a huge parasol.

Andreas was right about the time it takes to get to the beach, as a few minutes later we are paying the sunbed guy for our beds and setting our things down. The little taverna is still there, but it isn't called Christakis any more. It's called the Beach Shack and has surfboards propped up against the bamboo fencing outside.

The sea never changes though. The frothy waves ebbing and flowing over the pebbles along the beach transport me back to my childhood holiday, giggling and splashing in the water with Vicky from Newcastle. I remember losing a flip-flop in the water and crying as the little stones crushed into my feet and my dad came striding into the water to rescue me.

Hayley and I have been there for all of five minutes when a guy strolls over trying to flog us a kite-surfing lesson. 'Morning, ladies,' says the dreadlocked, mahogany-coloured fittie. 'Would you like to try kite-surfing today?'

'No, you're alright, thanks; I'm just here to chill today.' I smile.

He flashes impossibly white teeth. 'Come on, I think you might enjoy it,' he says, eyeing us up and down as we settle onto our beach beds in our skimpy bikinis, a beach parasol completely shading my body. Hayley looks lean and bronzed thanks to a pre-holiday spray tan, whilst I'm giving a good impression of a lobster.

'What I think I'll enjoy is a read of my book and a couple of drinks. I'm here to relax,' I respond, with a forced smile. I hope I don't sound like a snotty cow. I know he's only trying to do his job, but the last thing I want to see right now are flirty blokes.

'Cool.' He smiles again. 'I'll catch you ladies later. Maybe you might fancy it then.'

'Maybe I might fancy *you* later,' Hayley whispers, as she watches his buns-of-steel backside stroll back to the bar. There's two other blokes near the Beach Shack, one working the bar and the other hiring jet skis and surfboards from a bamboo hut with a small reception desk. They are both bronzed and fit and wearing red swimming shorts. I'm half expecting a beach goddess in a red swimsuit to come striding across the sand like a scene from *Baywatch*.

I wish Hayley would find someone nice to settle down with. She is so good-looking she attracts attention wherever she goes, but most of her relationships are short-lived as she gets bored easily. She says she just hasn't met 'the one', which is fine, but (without sounding judgemental) I do worry that she road tests too many guys. She's in her late twenties now and shows no sign of wanting to settle down soon. My mum says Hayley will fall in love one day when she least expects it and I suppose she's right.

I place a large umbrella over me and it isn't long before I am sleeping. I dream about going to the airport to find that it doesn't exist any more and is now a safari park, with tourists being driven around in zebra-patterned jeeps. There are no boats in any of the ports and I am stranded on the island. I think it's the result of that book I've been reading. It isn't long before Danny is in my dream too. He is sailing towards the beach on what appears to be a raft, sporting a beard and shoulder-length hair like Robinson Crusoe. He has come to rescue me; he sweeps me up into his muscular arms declaring his undying love, before we sail off into an orange sunset...

'Do you want anything to eat, or just another drink?' Hayley asks, and I am jolted out of my pleasant dream. 'Do you want a burger or anything?'

I'm not really hungry, but decide to have some fries anyway, as I could probably do with a few carbs.

Hayley swaggers towards the Beach Shack under the watchful eye of buns-of-steel, who quickly engages her in conversation as she orders our food and drink. He's whispering in her ear and she is throwing her head back and laughing, as carefree as a bird. In some ways I envy her. It's one thing being settled into a relationship, but quite another thing when it goes wrong. Being part of a couple has the potential to bring you heartache and there's a lot to be said for not being exposed to that.

'I'm going to have a go later,' says Hayley excitedly, as she returns with our drinks.

I raise an eyebrow.

'Kite-surfing. How hard can it be?'

I point to a bloke who has just smacked into the water with all the grace of a beached whale and is having trouble getting up again.

'Well, yeah, but I'm a bit more graceful than that. It will be a laugh. Why don't you have a go? You're the one who says you should try different things on holiday.'

This is true, of course, but I really don't want to try it today as I'm still feeling a bit hung-over, not to mention having sunburnt skin.

The beach fittie (whose name is Matt and hails from Australia, naturally) brings our food over with a smile that is as bright as the sun, and I consider that he might be alright really. It's just that my opinion of men might not be so great at the moment.

I look at the aquamarine sea and a young couple who are frolicking together. The girl, in a black bikini, is up on the shoulders of her bronzed, broad-shouldered partner, who throws her playfully into the water before scooping her up in his arms and kissing her tenderly. I wonder how their story will go. Will they have their 'happy ever after', or is it just a holiday romance?

I spot some locals with several generations of their extended families relaxing happily side by side, and realise we could learn a lot from the Greek way of living. I've noticed they respect their elderly relatives, who play a vital role in the family, so much.

I open my little tourist pamphlet, which I picked up from reception at the apartments earlier, and note that tomorrow is the start of a five-day religious festival in a neighbouring village called Dremasti. It is a celebration of the Virgin Mary and the streets are cordoned off to traffic, as the road becomes a bustling thoroughfare filled with street dancing and stalls selling their wares.

'Fancy this tomorrow?' I say to Hayley, passing her the little coloured brochure.

But her eyes are more interested in something, or should I say someone, else and I get the distinct feeling that I will be going on my own.

CHAPTER TWENTY

We had a great night at a place called the Banana Bar last night, and when the Antipodean 'rear of the year' just so happened to walk into the bar, dressed in khaki shorts and tight-fitting black vest, that was the last I saw of Hayley. At the time, I was talking to a family from the all-inclusive hotel, who had ventured out for the evening, so I don't think she felt too guilty about leaving me. She hasn't come back today either, so, as predicted, I will be walking into the village of Dremasti on my own.

I slept until noon today and it's late afternoon as I take my coffee onto the balcony and absorb the beauty of the surroundings. The majestic mountains and the azure blue of the sea lift the heart and soul and I briefly wonder what it would feel like to live here, but I don't think I could do it as I would miss my family too much, especially my mum. I can't imagine not being able to call round to see her when I needed a hug and a piece of home-made cake, which she always has in her Cath Kidston cake tin in the kitchen. She loves to tell me about the actors at the Empire Theatre, where she works part time in the box office. She tells me who is a prima donna, who isn't, and who she thinks is 'definitely gay but not out'.

She got the job there several years ago when a friend of mine's dad was the theatre manager. I told him that she needed a little job to get her out of the house, when she started the menopause, and she has never looked back. She loved it from the moment she started, the highlight of her time there being meeting Prince Charles at a Royal Variety Performance. He passed by the kiosk and smiled at her, before commenting that she 'must have been very busy as it's a full house'. She's dined out on that story ever since.

I know it would break her heart if I moved so far away. Sometimes it's a big emotional responsibility being an only child.

I am just walking through reception when Costas passes me. He is carrying a jug of coffee to some residents on the veranda. 'You want some?' he says brightly. 'Or maybe some food?'

'Oh, no, thanks, Costas, I've had a coffee upstairs. I'm off to Dremasti, I'll get something to eat there.'

'Wait here,' he says, before quickly delivering the coffee and reappearing in reception.

'So, you know the buses are only every couple of hours?'

'Yes, I know,' I chirp brightly. 'I'm going to walk.'

A smile spreads across his face. 'You are going to walk?'

'Yes, what's so funny?'

'There is no proper footpath and some crazy drivers. And it will take you one hour to walk.'

'What? But it says ten minutes from Thakos!'

He points to the leaflet again. 'Ten minutes by car. On foot it will take you one hour.'

I really must learn to read leaflets properly. I'm surprised I've even arrived on the right island. The heat is getting up already and I'm not sure I fancy walking for an hour.

'So, you want a ride on my moped? I can drop you off but then I have to come back and work. We can be there in just over ten minutes.'

It seems like a sensible option, and before I know it we are zipping along the dusty road. I don't feel too secure holding on to the metal guard behind me, but feel uncomfortable putting my arms around Costas's waist. I see what he means about the crazy drivers, who just seem to dart out from side streets or overtake erratically. After a few minutes, we are suddenly in heavy traffic heading towards Dremasti. Drivers are hooting their horns impatiently as mopeds, including ours, weave in and out of the queue effortlessly.

'Tourists,' Costas tells me. 'They will have nowhere to park if they go any further. The main village road will be sealed off.'

Five minutes later he deposits me at the beginning of the road to the village, where I can already feel the hubbub of excitement. He tells me to text him later and he will collect me. I think it is sweet of him to be so concerned, but I don't want to rely on anyone. I want to find my own way around on this holiday, as I need to reconnect with myself, having spent so long as the other half of a couple.

I'm dazzled by the colours and sounds of the village as I make my way along the main street. There are dozens of stalls selling gifts; most of them, I notice, are toy stalls brandishing gaudy, overpriced dolls, or remote-controlled cars with flashing lights bouncing at the front of the stall in demonstration mode. There are yapping toy dogs doing back flips, with excited children asking their parents to buy them one. I think you could probably buy most of the stuff for half the price elsewhere but everyone is in festival mood and the parents seem happy to part with their money.

There are ice-cream carts and tall fridges selling ice-cold drinks, and I stroll on past food stalls selling everything from pork souvlaki to pancakes with Nutella. The smell of juicy hog roasts and sides of lamb with herbs, simmering slowly and ready to be sliced into pitta breads, fills the air. My stomach gives a little rumble.

There is already quite a crowd of people, dressed in their best clothes, lingering at the food stalls as spiralling clouds of smoke obscure their faces. Families with young children are mesmerised by street dancers and jugglers, as young men wearing colourful paper hats hand out small nibbles of cheese and meats to advertise their food stalls. There are also fake designer bags and purses for sale and even household stalls selling kitchen equipment, all hoping to cash in on the carnival atmosphere.

I make my way along the road and turn into a market square filled with tables selling jewellery and crafts. My eye falls upon a circular metal necklace with a carved-out scene of a wolf on a hill. It's beautiful and I'm tempted to buy it for myself, but decide to have another wander around first and then perhaps get something to eat. There are seated areas with white plastic tables and chairs and coloured fairy lights threaded through the overhead tree branches. These are the barbecue areas, where pork, chicken and lamb kebabs are simmering over hot coals alongside piles of buns, pitta breads and Greek salad. It costs eight euros to fill your plate, including a soft drink.

I'm back in the main street now, and almost at the end of it, when I come across a long queue of people outside the most stunning white church, its bell pealing loudly into the early evening. The people are queuing to light a candle outside the church before going inside to kiss a gold-framed picture of the Madonna. This is of course the real reason for the festival: the celebration of the Virgin Mary. There is a beggar woman outside the church reaching out to passers-by, but she is soon moved on by the police. A small crowd of people wave their hands in the air in protest and mutter something in Greek, before being spoken to by the police. A woman selling some scarves close by tuts her disapproval and I am not sure whether it is aimed at the police or the protesters.

'Someone's not happy,' I venture.

'The people grow poorer,' the woman says, almost in a whisper. 'Some of them are even sleeping on the beaches. They have lost their businesses and shops in the recession, yet the church is filled with gold and riches. Some people believe the church should open its door to the homeless people. There was a small demonstration outside the church last night but the police quickly moved them on.'

I get the impression she is one of those people who feel the church should do more to help, but is afraid to express that opinion.

'The festival gives traders the chance to make money as people save for months to come here and enjoy themselves, but on the whole the ordinary people are struggling.'

I choose a pretty blue and gold scarf and pay her five euros, for which she is extremely grateful.

After two hours of browsing the stalls and making several purchases (a bottle of ouzo, the scarf and the necklace with the wolf scene), I am seated beneath the branches of an ancient olive tree enjoying my eight-euro barbecue meal with a glass of Sprite.

I get chatting to a young couple from Manchester, who are enjoying their first holiday abroad together and clearly still in the first flush of love. They can barely keep their hands off each other and I resist the urge to tell them that they had better make the most of it, as that urgency of passion doesn't last. Then I wonder when it stopped for Danny and me.

When it's time to leave, I glance at my mobile phone and consider texting Costas, but then decide against it. It's a beautiful, balmy evening and even though dusk is gently falling I feel like walking back to the apartments. I can't believe it would take an hour to walk back as we seemed to get here in no time at all on the moped. The road to Thakos looks well lit and busy enough, so I weave my way through the throng of people to the end of the village road and begin to walk.

After half an hour, as the lights and sounds of the festival fade gently into the distance, I realise that it is actually further than I thought. The traffic has petered out and suddenly I can see only darkness ahead on a stretch of road that is unlit. There is a drone of crickets in the background and I begin to feel a little uneasy, but have no choice but to carry on. I notice the twinkling lights of Thakos village up ahead when suddenly I hear the sound of a moped and breathe a sigh of relief that Costas has come looking for me. But it isn't Costas. In fact, it isn't one but two mopeds ridden by young, dark-haired men wearing jeans and white T-shirts.

'Hey, lady,' one of them shouts, riding alongside me. 'You know a pretty lady like you should not be walking home alone. Anything could happen.'

The other rider laughs and I automatically put my hand on my handbag, and it doesn't go unnoticed.

'So you think I'm going to steal from you? Well that's not very nice. Anyway, who says it's your money I want?'

They are both laughing and circling me on their mopeds now and I start to panic. One of them rides up close and I can smell alcohol on his breath.

'You are a very pretty lady. Do you like me?'

I'm planning my next move, when I suddenly see car headlights coming towards me and then there's hooting and someone waving out of a taxi window.

Hayley!

I have never been happier to see anyone in my whole life as the taxi pulls over and at the same time the moped riders spin their bikes around and zoom down the road in the opposite direction.

'Mandy, are you alright? What the bloody hell are you doing walking home on your own? Get in the taxi.'

I'm sitting in the back seat and I'm shaking. Suddenly I'm back in Liverpool as an eighteen-year-old girl coming out of a nightclub in Seel Street. I'd drunk one too many vodkas and had become separated from my friends on the way to the taxi rank when I stupidly took a wrong turn down a dark alley.

The man came out of nowhere, almost as if he had been lying in wait for someone. He stepped closer and I could smell the alcohol on his breath. My heart almost stopped. I attempted a scream but nothing came out of my mouth. I was praying for help when, miraculously, three women linking arms and singing merrily walked through the alley. I found my voice then and screamed from the shadows. One of the horrified women came to my aid, while the other two gave chase, waving their stilettos and screaming obscenities, as the man disappeared into the darkness like a thief in the night.

I'll never know what might have happened, because he had been disturbed, but the incident shook me up all the same and I had buried it deep in my subconscious. The council, for their part, illuminated the dark alleys shortly afterwards, and *Granada Reports* ran a story about being safe in the city centre when leaving nightclubs.

Tears are rolling down my face now as Hayley crushes me into an embrace with a concerned Matt looking on. I'm happy that she's here, but I suddenly want the arms of my husband around me.

I want Danny. I want to go home.

CHAPTER TWENTY-ONE

It's a fact of life that we always yearn for something familiar during a crisis or at times of stress. Last night I wanted Danny, but after a large vodka and Coke and a good night's sleep I don't feel the urgency to see him any more. Matt went back to his apartment alone and Hayley stayed with me until I fell asleep. She was comforting, as only a best friend can be, as well as honest. She told me in no uncertain terms that I should never have even attempted to walk home alone, and of course she's right. You would think once bitten twice shy for me, but it was ten years ago and I was feeling in holiday mood and beginning to relax.

The patio curtain is waving gently in the breeze and I notice coffee and croissants on the balcony table. The sky is cloudless and as blue as a cornflower.

'I didn't know if you'd fancy eating downstairs, so I asked Costas if we could have room service. He looked a little concerned about you.'

'What did you tell him?'

I sit bolt upright and sip a glass of fresh orange juice that Hayley has placed on my little pine bedside table.

'Relax. I said you have a headache and didn't feel much like talking to people. He thinks it's a hangover.' She smiled.

'I'm sorry about Matt. You didn't have to stay the night with me. It's your holiday too.'

'Nah, don't worry about Matt. I'll catch up with him later. I would never have left you. That's what friends are for.'

She's sitting on the bed next to me now and embraces me in a hug. I'm feeling fine now. Thinking about it, I'm sure those young men on the mopeds would never have actually harmed me. They were in high spirits (literally), but I don't think they would risk the reputation of the village, as the last thing they need would be for tourists to feel unsafe. I decide to put it behind me.

'Anyway,' says Hayley, looking at her watch, 'you've got an hour to get your butt ready. We're going out for a cookery lesson.'

I can hardly believe my ears. Hayley going for a cookery lesson is like a line dancers' convention turning up for 'old school classics' at a local nightclub.

'Just say that again. *You*, sorry, *we* are going for a cookery lesson?'

'Yep. Believe it or not, I've always wanted to know how to cook authentic Greek food. Well, the meat anyway, for a barbecue, and those Greek salads never taste the same when I make them back home.'

'That's because you don't use olives. And cheddar cheese just isn't the same,' I tell her, smiling.

'Well, that's what I mean. I aim to find out how to do it. We can have loads of parties in the summer, when we get home, where I can show my prowess in the kitchen. Now, hurry up and get ready. We're booked in for a two-hour lesson at the Olive Garden Kitchen down the road at twelve o'clock. Twenty-five euros each, including the tuition, and we get to eat it outside for lunch with a glass of retsina.'

It sounds lovely and I'm happy that Hayley is embracing the culture a little. She is normally on a loop of flirting, drinking, sunbathing and sleeping. Also, it wouldn't do any harm for me to brush up on my cooking skills, as I can't live on takeaways from the Bengal Kitchen forever.

The Olive Garden Kitchen restaurant is at the end of the main street, next door to a boarded-up taverna called the Lemon Tree. The metal sign for the Lemon Tree is still there, blowing gently in the breeze, but that is the only sign of life. There is moss growing between the flagstones at the front of the building, where diners would once have eaten and drunk late into the evening. It makes me feel so sad.

We are greeted warmly by a mumsy figure in her fifties who is wearing a white apron and has her dark hair up in a bun. Her skin is a little pale, but other than that she looks every inch the Greek matriarch, so you can imagine our surprise when she opens her mouth.

'Alright, girls, nice to see you,' she beams with a Lancashire accent as thick as a hotpot. She registers our surprised expressions and chuckles. 'I get a lot of that. I'm Joan,' she says extending her hand. 'I'm from Blackburn originally, but don't you worry. I've been cooking Greek food for thirty years now. I married Yannis back in the day and we settled here ten years ago. We lived in Corfu before that.'

I look around the quiet village and can't help asking her, 'Why here?'

'Kids.' She smiles. 'Well, grandkids to be precise. Two, called Spyros and Helena. Our daughter Elyannia works in Rhodes town and settled in Thakos. We wanted to be close to them and so we moved here. It's been great, although we have felt the pinch a little these last couple of years.'

Hence the cookery school, I think. I glance around and count ten other people here for the cookery lesson. They are mainly mature couples, apart from one pair who are in their early twenties and who I recognise at once as being the couple I met at the festival in Dremasti.

'Hi there,' calls the woman, untwining her hand from her lover's and waving to me as recognition dawns. She is wearing shorts and a T-shirt and her dark hair is plaited. Her boyfriend is wearing a T-shirt and a pair of long canvas trousers. I remember that he was wearing long trousers at the festival and briefly wonder whether he doesn't like his legs. When I was seventeen I had a stunning-looking boyfriend who had skinny white legs that hung down like pieces of string. He covered them up in all weathers.

Joan from Blackburn claps her hands together and welcomes us all warmly to her restaurant with a small shot of ouzo, before leading us into a vast chrome kitchen that looks highly polished and spotless. The smell of oregano and garlic engulfs me. She shows all the couples to their workstations before bringing the ingredients to the work surface.

There are soon piles of aubergines and courgettes, waxed lemons and bunches of fresh oregano and potatoes alongside a large metal basin of minced lamb. There are Greek tomatoes the size of tennis balls, slabs of creamy feta and the biggest cucumber I have ever seen (cue raised eyebrow and saucy comment from Hayley!). Huge red onions and bitter green olives complete the Mediterranean mountain of gastronomical delights.

'So, today, everyone, I am going to show you how to make a traditional Greek meal of Greek salad, courgette fritters and, of course, moussaka. There are many slight variations to the moussaka and every Greek woman will tell you that hers is the best. Naturally I am going to tell you that mine is the best, but you can be the judge of that when you eat it later.'

We work hard chopping, slicing, frying and simmering.

'Aye, I'm pretty good at this,' says Hayley proudly, as she flips a pan of translucent onions.

I stop her as she is about to add a tablespoon of cinnamon to the mix.

'Whoa, don't get ahead of yourself, missus. It's one teaspoon of cinnamon, not a tablespoon.'

Hayley roars with laughter. 'Oops! Good job you stopped me there, although what's a tablespoon of cinnamon between friends?'

'Duh… the difference between a moussaka and a carrot cake,' I retort, as we giggle loudly.

I feel we have earned our lunch, which we take outside onto a terrace surrounded by lemon trees and bushes. There is a welcome sea breeze gently wafting across the terrace as we take our seats at a long table covered with a red cotton tablecloth and baskets of bread. My stomach gives a loud rumble as the plates of food give off their delicious aroma and Joan's husband Yannis grins as he brings out several jugs of iced water and places them intermittently on the table. He is a short, wiry man who never stops smiling and singing. He returns with some wine glasses and several bottles of chilled retsina.

The food is utterly delicious. The courgette fritters, which are simply eggs, courgettes, spring onions and feta doused in flour and deep-fried in olive oil, are to die for. Hayley is right about the Greek salad tasting exceptional in Greece. I think it's all about the ingredients, such as the tennis-ball-sized beef tomatoes and the excellent olive oil. I think of Costas's passion for the oil and it makes me smile, but there is no doubt that the star of the show is the moussaka. I find myself oohing and aahing with every mouthful of the tasty dish, savouring every element of it from the creamy béchamel sauce to the tender lamb with a hint of cinnamon. The aubergines are soft and succulent and the unusual egg topping is whipped as light as a feather. It is absolutely stunning.

'Well, I don't know about anyone else's moussaka recipe, but yours is bloody fab,' states Hayley, wiping her mouth with a napkin. Her sentiments are endorsed by everyone around the table, who all have empty plates. They're a nice bunch of people, including a Greek couple who agree that Joan cooks as well as the natives. The Greek wife confides that 'she can't cook to save her life', which is a shameful thing in Greece. 'At least I can now make you moussaka,' she says, smiling at her adoring husband, who probably wouldn't mind if she served him stale bread every day of his life, because she looks like a former world-class super model.

Eventually it's time to make a move and the party disperses with hearty thanks to Joan and Yannis.

'Do you fancy heading down to the beach?' asks Hayley. 'I kind of said I'd meet Matt down there.'

I smile at my friend. 'You go. I fancy a little potter around the shops to walk off all that food. I'm stuffed. And I'm just at a good bit in my book. I'll catch you later.'

My pottering may not take too long as there are only six shops on the main street selling the usual beach towels and souvenirs. One in particular catches my eye and I am surprised that it is much larger on the inside. There is quite a collection of jewellery, including some pretty silver at very reasonable prices. The young lady at the counter looks up from her book and says hello as I enter the shop. I am the only customer.

I buy my mum a pair of silver and turquoise earrings, much to the delight of the shop assistant, who wraps them carefully in some pink patterned tissue paper before taping the end.

I'm not far from the apartments when I spot Costas talking to a shop owner at the front of his shop. As I get closer he says his goodbyes to his friend and falls in step, walking alongside me.

'So, what have you been up to this afternoon?' he asks, smiling.

I tell him about our cookery lesson and he agrees that the Olive Garden Kitchen does indeed have a very good reputation.

'Maybe one evening I will take you there. You won't have to cook it yourself.' He smiles at me again.

My guard goes up immediately. I like Costas and there is no doubt that he is handsome, but I can't even think about romance, holiday or otherwise. I'm a married woman. Well, separated, I know, but even so. I can see I have offended him and so decide to tell him about my situation.

'I'm so sorry to hear that. It must be a difficult time for you,' Costas says gently.

'I can't lie, it's been absolutely awful. I came to Rhodes as a child and have nothing but fond memories, so I thought it might lift my spirits a little if I came here for a holiday.'

'And has it?' asks Costas, as he stops walking and fixes me with those deep brown eyes.

'A little. It's hard not to be distracted by such beautiful surroundings,' I say, managing a weak smile.

When I have finished speaking he looks at me intently. 'I am sorry you feel sad and, forgive me for saying so, but your husband must be a fool.'

We walk the rest of the way in relative silence before arriving back at the Sea View Apartments.

'I have work to do,' he says, as we part. 'Enjoy the rest of your day. But remember, you deserve to be happy.'

He's right, of course, but for now I will settle for having a nice nap.

CHAPTER TWENTY-TWO

I'm awake as the sun is rising the next day and decide to go for an early-morning walk. I had a quiet night with Hayley and Matt at the Beach Shack last night and didn't really drink much, so I'm feeling surprisingly fresh.

I'd forgotten how much there is to miss in the early morning as the world is waking up. I stroll along the road towards the main street as a huge red sun dominates the sky. It's beautiful.

I pass a litter picker, who nods good morning, and watch the shopkeepers sweeping their shop fronts of cigarette ends and other debris. Bar owners are setting out the plastic chairs for the day ahead having hosed down the floors, and a delivery lorry is beeping as it reverses around a corner to the front of a fruit and vegetable shop. I feel happy to see this part of the day unfolding in front of my eyes.

Further down the road, I find an old wooden bench to sit on. It is facing a piece of land filled with olive trees and fragrant oregano plants. There is a fenced-off area with some hens, and an old lady emerges from it carrying a basket of eggs. She is dressed in black and smiles a toothless smile before her slightly hunched back disappears around the corner to the adjacent whitewashed house. An elderly man in a denim shirt and checked cap arrives and begins chopping at some herbs and picking olives, which he puts into a basket. It's all so peaceful.

A young woman emerges from a shop, carrying some milk, and I recognise her from the ceramic shop near the apartments. She says good morning to me, then, to my surprise, she takes a seat beside me on the bench. 'It's going to be very hot today.' She smiles. 'There is going to be a heatwave for a few days.'

'A heatwave?' I say in surprise. 'You mean this isn't one?'

She laughs and tells me that the locals would not consider the recent weather particularly hot. She tells me about the previous July, when temperatures reached a peak of 50°C and the streets literally melted. She introduces herself as Annis and we chat for a few minutes and I discover that she works in the ceramic shop part-time with her grandfather, as well as making jewellery which she sells online and at markets. Before she leaves, she advises me to keep a bottle of water with me at all times.

I buy some water from a street kiosk and decide that I like Annis. I consider she is probably a few years younger than me and I noticed that she wasn't wearing a wedding ring. Maybe it's hard to meet anyone other than tourists in such a small village.

I begin my walk back towards the apartments, enjoying the tranquillity, when Costas scoots past. He stops and does a double take when he realises it's me.

'You are up early,' he says, almost disbelievingly.

'I'm not all about partying and sleeping in till noon, you know.'

'Yes, you are.' He smiles at me.

'Well, OK, most of the time. But there's only a few days left of my holiday so I want to be up early and make the most of them.'

Costas walks his bike slowly alongside me as we head back to the apartments. 'What will you do when you get back home?'

'I really don't know,' I reply truthfully. 'I'll go back to work, of course. I'm looking forward to seeing my friends.'

'What is your work?'

'It's a bit like yours really. I run a bar in a busy bar and restaurant.'

'Not really like mine then. You said busy,' he says raising an eyebrow. 'This season we just about survive, but we do have some bookings from July onward.'

We are almost back at the apartments now. I can't help thinking that Sea View could do with a woman's touch. I don't want to ask Costas about his mother, but he brings the subject up himself.

'My mother died five years ago. She was the life and soul of the place. We were always pretty full then and my father was happy too. One day she went out shopping into Rhodes town and never came back. She was knocked down by a hire car driven by a tourist who was unfamiliar with a bend on a road. Since she's been gone my father is not half the man he once was. His heart is not really in the business. But it is our livelihood. We have to carry on.'

I don't think now is the time for me to say that they can't rely on the sea view as a selling point. The place needs bringing into the twenty-first century and building a pool should be at the top of the list. Now that Costas has talked about his mother, I may be able to offer some advice when the time is right.

Across the road from the apartments there is a huge field that seems to go on forever. It's crying out for something and the longer I stare at it an idea begins to form in my mind.

'Do you have any musicians in Greece?' I ask Costas.

He frowns at me and says no, there are no musicians in Greece, apart from Nana Mouskouri (who?) and villagers who like to play the tambourine and dance around their garden. I realise he is playing with me and feel ashamed of my ignorance. I might as well have asked him if they have electricity (even though it can be a little temperamental).

'There are quite a few decent bands in Greece. There are one or two decent venues in Rhodes town with some fantastic local bands, but the country's biggest acts tend to perform mainly in Athens or the open-air Greek theatre at Epidaurus. Kings of Leon headlined there last year. There is a rock festival in Lindos every June but they're tribute bands like Think Floyd and the Chokers.'

'The Chokers?'

'The Stranglers.'

'That's bad.'

'I know,' he says, and laughs.

I'm staring at the huge field again.

'Oh, and just for the record, my favourite bands are the Kaiser Chiefs and Queen. I grew up listening to them. I don't mind a bit of Michael Bublé either,' he says, looking slightly embarrassed.

'Everyone loves a bit of Bublé,' I say, smiling.

'Yes, it's amazing how I manage to have such knowledge. You can download music from the Internet onto an iPhone or an iPad even in a Greek village,' he teases.

'So... Why do you keep looking at the field?' he asks, looking perplexed.

'When I went to the holy festival at Dremasti the other day, the village was heaving with people.'

'So?'

'So, people like a festival. And you tell me the Greeks like music, so I was thinking why not arrange a music festival?'

'A music festival?'

'Yes, here.'

'Here?'

'Yes, here in Thakos.'

'Here in Thakos?'

'Are you just going to repeat everything I say?'

'Repeat everything you say?'

I whack him on the arm with my water bottle and he laughs.

'OK, crazy lady. I am not sure where this idea has come from but, yes, I suppose you could set up a music venue here. The land is certainly big enough and it might benefit local businesses.' He gives a shrug.

'That's exactly what I was thinking! And I'm not talking tribute bands, I'm talking about the real deal. Just think what it could do for the local community. It might take a few months to organise but I'm sure it could be done. Still, I suppose it would depend on what the local authorities would say. I wonder if they would allow the land to be used for such a thing?'

'There may be a bit of a problem with traffic but they manage it every year in Dremasti. They simply close the road through the village and divert traffic. I'm sure it could be arranged. But the land is no concern of the local authority. The land belongs to my father.'

CHAPTER TWENTY-THREE

An excitement is building inside me as I walk along the village later that day on my way back from a small secluded cove that Andreas told me about. I pay particular attention to all of the restaurants and bars in the village and note that there are actually sixteen of them. Four of them are boarded up (one only the week before I arrived, I was told) and the remainder of them are struggling.

I pass the Olive Garden Kitchen, where Joan from Blackburn is sat beneath the shade of a fig tree enjoying a cup of tea.

'Hello, love.' She smiles at me. 'It's been a scorcher today. I hope you've applied your factor thirty.'

We chat for a few minutes and she tells me that tomorrow night at the Olive Garden there will be a BBQ evening with Greek dancing, if I fancy it. 'No plate smashing these days though,' she says, with a grin. 'Not during a recession – but the Greek dancers are a lot of fun. They have everyone up on their feet.'

I've realised that tourists seem to visit the same places repeatedly, including the Paradise Apartments. (When I spent the day there I overheard a couple telling a lone male traveller that they had been returning to the apartments 'for years and years'.) Maybe it's because these establishments offer the best customer service. They know how to market themselves, from the appearance at the front of the hotel to the service inside. The day I fell asleep in the sun at the Paradise Apartments, I was looked after impeccably by the staff. But, when I returned to Sea View, there was no one on reception as I sloped upstairs with my red, sunburnt skin.

It's hardly surprising, in many ways, that the village is struggling as there is resigned acceptance of the declining situation. But where is the fight? Why aren't they desperately trying to promote themselves? Everything is so understated and I can't work out whether it's pride or resignation, but one thing's for sure – they don't sell themselves. There is a rooftop restaurant five minutes away, with breath-taking sea views, yet on the side of its huge, whitewashed walls the words '*nice view*' have been scrawled in black marker pen. There should be a six-foot-high billboard screaming '*Breathtaking View of the Sea!*'

Later that day, back at Sea View, I think more about all this. I'm a woman on a mission as I take a seat next to Andreas, who is sitting on a plastic chair outside reception having a cigarette.

'So, you are having a nice holiday?' he enquires.

'Well, yes, it's lovely, but it could be even better… Have you thought about building a pool? Not everybody wants to go to the beach.'

Andreas takes a long drag of his cigarette. 'Yes, I have,' he says simply. 'And, yes, maybe now the time is right. I have the planning permission.'

'You do?' I can hardly contain my surprise.

'Yes. I was going to build it at the rear of the property.' I remember that there is a fair bit of land there. 'But then my wife died and my whole world fell apart. I just lost the heart to do anything with the place, but I know I must. I think maybe she would be very angry with me for not getting on with things. She always got on with things.' He sighs.

'Well, you probably needed time. You can't put a time limit on grief,' I say, feeling genuinely sorry for him.

'You are right.' He nods. 'And maybe I need a little advice on how to make the apartments look a little more modern.'

'The apartments are fine,' I say tentatively. 'It's the reception and bar area that need some changing.'

Andreas shifts a little in his seat. 'That was Maria's domain. It does need a woman's touch. It's a pity you have to go home soon.'

I have a sudden yearning to say *No, I don't. I can stay here and help you revamp things*, but I know I need to go home. I have to sort out my life in England.

I take a deep breath and decide to run my idea for a music festival by Andreas. His expression is hard to read. His listens impassively until I have finished speaking and then he slowly gets up from his chair and extinguishes his cigarette into a steel pot filled with sand. I outline my ideas and, after what seems like a lifetime, a huge grin spreads across his face.

'It's an interesting idea. Costas did tell me a little about what you were thinking. Do you really think you could organise it?' He frowns doubtfully.

'If I could, would you be happy for the field to be used?'

He rubs his chin thoughtfully.

'Why not? The land has been empty for so long. I may even make a little money too, huh?'

'And I'm pretty certain it would be good for local restaurants,' I enthuse.

Andreas agrees that it might be worth a shot. I discover that the owners of the closed tavernas and bars live nearby and most of the cooking equipment is still inside the recently abandoned buildings. They could open up at a moment's notice if they thought there was any serious money to be made.

Costas appears then and, after grabbing a bottle of iced tea from a fridge, he comes over to join us.

'So,' he says brightly, 'by my reckoning you have three days left of your holiday and you have not even visited Rhodes old town yet.'

'I was actually thinking about doing that tomorrow. I was trying to figure out the infrequent bus timetable.'

'Well, I have a friend who runs a bar in Rhodes town. They have live music and open mic nights. Maybe we could run a few ideas by him? I was thinking of going tomorrow, if you would like to join me?' Costas looks across at Andreas. 'That is, if my father will give me the day off.'

'Lucky for you tomorrow is quiet. Three guests check out and no more arrive until two days from now. You go and enjoy yourself.' He winks at me.

'You may need a tour guide,' Costas says, his eyes twinkling. 'People have been known to disappear and never be seen again in the maze of the old town.'

'In that case,' I say. 'How can I possibly refuse?' It makes sense to have a local show me around, and meeting up with some musicians sounds great. I suddenly feel quite excited.

CHAPTER TWENTY-FOUR

We decide to take the bus the next morning after a breakfast of Greek yoghurt and honey at the hotel. (As predicted, Hayley has been distracted by Matt, so I'll meet up with her later.) The yoghurt, layered with sweet nectarines and Greek mountain honey, is one of the most simply delicious things I have ever tasted.

When the bus arrives, Costas tells me that we are lucky to get seats and, ten minutes later, as we leave the villages and head on to the main road to Rhodes, I appreciate this. We have made dozens of stops in a fairly short distance as people of varying ages and nationalities have boarded the bus, some of them carrying inflated dolphins and other beach lifesavers, which indiscriminately poke other passengers in the face. We collect holidaymakers making their way to the airport for their return journey, who end up blocking the aisles with their bulging suitcases, as there are no overhead racks on the bus.

As we rattle along the coast road, passing the glorious beaches and the all-inclusive hotels alongside the restaurants of international cuisine, beads of perspiration are forming on the passengers, who are hemmed in like sardines in a tin. The driver brakes suddenly and the people standing near the front collapse into each other like a row of fallen dominoes. This prompts an outburst from a Greek woman and a brief, heated exchange with the bus driver, who is waving his hands in the air and pointing to the offending driver who has caused him to brake so sharply.

I've noticed that Greek people wear their hearts on their sleeves and passionately air their differences in public without any lingering bitterness. I've witnessed shop owners and tradesman shouting and cursing, before going about their business as though nothing has happened.

'Is there no such thing as air conditioning on buses in Greece?' I moan, as a scent of body odour permeates the air in the rising heat.

'Don't be silly,' says Costas, 'we've only just finished inventing the wheel, give us a chance!'

I wipe my brow with a Wet Wipe and take a large slug of water from my bottle, which was ice-cold fifteen minutes ago and is already lukewarm.

'Anyway, we will be at our destination in ten minutes. You can get a cold beer and freshen up.'

I've already realised that there is no point in wearing make-up in this heat, as it literally melts off your face. I don't really need it anyway, as I have now developed a healthy golden glow. I also had my eyebrows and eyelashes tinted before I came away, which is just as well really. Sun lotion on my face and a slick of lip gloss to protect my lips is all I need.

Despite the crush, I'm actually rather enjoying the bus journey. It's nice to be able to look out of the window and just watch the world go by, especially in a foreign country. I notice the houses, shops and people, and realise that, no matter where in the world you are, everyone is just going about their business in the same way. I used to enjoy the bus journey into Liverpool city centre, where you would discover people's life stories if they chose to sit next to you, such is the openness of northern people.

Before long we have alighted at the bus terminus, which is surprisingly small for a large town. Costas buys us each a strawberry Cornetto as we head away from the modern shops towards the old town.

I feel my phone vibrate in my pocket and am stunned to find that I have a text from Danny.

Hi. How are you doing?

What the hell does he want me to say? My heart starts beating as he pops into my thoughts again, just as I was managing to put a little bit of distance between us. Why does he want to know? Have things not worked with him and Sarah Kelly? I don't know whether to reply or not, but he's right back in my head again.

'Is everything OK?' Costas asks, noticing my distracted expression as I fiddle with my phone.

I show him the text from Danny and he thinks for a moment. 'Maybe you need to reply. Or even call him? Ask him why he is asking after you. What does he want?'

It sounds so simple, yet I can't seem to face it yet. I will speak to him when I go home in a few days' time. I decide to put my phone into my square straw bag and try to forget about it.

*

I soon realise that if anything is going to distract me from my broken marriage then it is Rhodes old town.

Suddenly I am transported back to medieval times, as we stand at the end of a long, cobbled street called the Street of the Knights. Costas tells me it is a fifteenth-century street that housed the inns and eateries frequented by the knights who belonged to the Order of St John. It is stunning.

'I think we will take this entrance,' Costas says confidently.

He points out the ancient church and prison cells with the knowledgeable air of a tour guide and I catch one or two English tourists looking at postcards on a stand outside a shop and listening to Costas intently. There are tiny craft shops practically built within the castle walls and the huge twelfth-century castle battlements dominate the skyline.

I never liked history at school, but I might have paid more attention had I not had a teacher who was so boring he could have been employed by the NHS and used as a general anaesthetic. Hayley had a history teacher who was the complete opposite. He used to come into the classroom dressed as a Viking, or whatever, and leap onto the desks. It still didn't capture the kids' imagination, though, because he was basically a prat. I would have loved to have been taught by someone like Costas, full of enthusiasm and passion. He would make a very good teacher.

'So, I am thinking. We will explore some of the streets at this end before we have some lunch. After that we will call at the Olympic Bar to see my friend Adonis and have a chat about some local bands. Then we will explore some more. That is if you have the energy.' Costas smiles at me.

'Aye, I'm pretty fit, me,' I reply, but it's actually a big fat lie. Oh, I used to be. I played netball for a local team and went to dance aerobics at the community centre for a few years. I can't remember when I stopped doing these things, but somehow Danny made me feel like I should spend every bit of spare time with him. He never actually said it out loud, but you could feel the chill in the air every time I went off to do something on my own so, like a fool, I stopped doing stuff.

'Hmm, if you say so. But, be warned, there are actually around two hundred streets in the old quarter that have no name. There is no point looking at a map, there is no grid. People really do get lost here, mainly because most of the streets look the same.'

It's pretty crowded, so I have no choice but to stay closely by Costas's side as we stroll along. The midday heat is increasing now and I'm glad I've brought a straw hat and large sunglasses with me. We are walking along part of the walls of the castle, and before long I have to stop and buy some more ice-cold water from a tiny shop within the castle walls, where you have to duck your head to enter. Further along, we descend via some steps before walking to Simi Square, the home of the Municipal Art Gallery of Rhodes.

The cool marble interior is a welcome respite as we look at some of the fine Greek modern artwork by painters such as Maleas and Vassiliou, whose paintings of unusual style and bold colour are displayed against white walls.

I appreciate all of this but my attention is more captured by the stunning pieces of crafts displayed in the Museum of Decorative Arts, which is one block away within a building that once served as the knights' arsenal. It houses striking pieces from various islands in Greece, particularly Symi. There are intricate, colourful tapestries and carefully crafted wooden vessels, including a smooth walnut fruit bowl that I think would look perfect in my lounge at home. Once outside, we cross the square to view the ruins of the Temple of Venus, thought to date from the third century BC.

Just when I think my brain can't absorb any more of this fascinating history, Costas suggests some lunch and leads me through a small warren of streets until we come upon an open-air market selling all things touristy. We pass some formal restaurants with white linen tablecloths, water features in the middle, and bowing waiters beckoning us inside, but we walk on and soon find ourselves at the end of the market. Costas leads me down a side street that is full of cafés with Greek people having lunch on some not-so-glamorous white plastic tables with paper tablecloths.

'Here we are,' he says, pulling a chair for me to sit down. He has such impeccable manners. 'This is the best food in Rhodes. It's where the locals eat. The tourist restaurants are overpriced and they don't put the same passion into the food,' he announces confidently.

Ten minutes later we are tucking in to the most delicious chicken souvlaki with generous portions of rice, and a fresh Greek salad with a generous slab of feta. We wash it down with large, ice-cold beers and the whole thing costs less than ten euros for both of us.

'Hmm, it's not a bad thing having you as a guide,' I say, wiping my mouth and sitting back on my chair, feeling full, if not slightly uncomfortable. 'I probably would have gone into one of the touristy restaurants and paid double the price.'

'For half the quality and passion,' he says, smiling.

Costas speaks in Greek to the café owner and shakes his hand warmly, before we head off down yet more unfamiliar streets.

Soon we reach the Olympic Bar, which is a basement venue built in the same ancient rock as the rest of the place. I'm surprised to find it is cavernous inside. The owner, Adonis, hugs Costas warmly and kisses my cheek after he is introduced to me. There are a few band members tuning guitars up in a long alcove, getting ready for a jamming session.

Adonis brings cold beers over to a long table and I realise it's a good job that we came on the bus rather than on Costas's moped, as cold beers seem to be the order of the day.

'So,' says Adonis brightly, 'Costas tells me you had an idea for a music festival in Thakos. I can't believe we haven't thought of it before. That field is huge.' He takes a sip of his drink and smiles.

I like Adonis right away. He is friendly and open and has an air of confidence about him. He tells me that the music scene has begun to develop recently and several soundproofed underground bars have popped up around the city.

Costas asks Adonis to recommend some local bands and he rattles several off his tongue. 'Not forgetting these guys,' he says, as a guitarist strikes up a chord on cue.

We are treated to ten minutes of amazing tunes by a band called The Romans. They do two Oasis covers as well as two of their own songs. They are upbeat and brilliant.

'There's loads more bands like this one,' Adonis tells us. 'They'd be only too happy to play a decent outdoor venue. There's never been anything like that round here. They normally have to travel miles. Last year one of the bands travelled all the way to Attica in Athens to support Maroon 5.'

I'm impressed.

'So,' says Adonis, leaning in close enough for me to get a whiff of expensive aftershave. 'Have you done this sort of thing before?'

It's a simple enough question, but when I think about I realise the only thing I have really organised are the acts at the pub.

'Oh, yeah,' I say breezily. 'If it's private land then it's not too much of a problem.' I learned this from Leonard, whose farmer friend had fallen on hard times and leased acres of his land for a concert venue and made a fortune. 'It's more the administrative side – selling tickets, sorting road access, that sort of thing – I may need a little help with. And signing up some good bands, of course. I have someone in the UK who just might be able to sort a couple of big acts to headline, fingers crossed.'

I think of Janet and the card she handed me at the pub the day she visited with her group. I wonder whether she may want to become involved or will laugh in my face. She's done so well for herself and maybe I wasn't the friend I might have been at school. Oh well, I can but try.

'Just call me if you need any help with anything,' Adonis says, with a wink and a touch of my arm. He's a charmer, this one.

We depart with a promise to go along to a music night two days later to listen to some bands. It's the evening before my morning flight so I'm a little unsure, but Costas assures me he will have me home before midnight.

'So now we have sorted that and looked at some of the cultural quarter, I am guessing that now you would like to shop?'

'Well, I'm sure there're at least another hundred streets to explore, so let's go.'

It doesn't seem as daunting as it sounds when I say streets, as they are more like long alleyways, crammed full of shops. Everything from local hand-made lace to modern, intricately designed silver jewellery is on sale. There are rows of shops selling olive oil, soaps, cooking herbs for moussaka and Greek vases and bowls. And bags. Dozens of gorgeous fake designer bags for twenty-five euros and you would be hard-pushed to tell the difference from the originals. I'm in bag heaven as bags of every shape, size and colour hang from shop doorways. I eventually settle on a soft blue 'Michael Kors'.

We weave our way through the throng of people and stop at an ice-cream stand. The vendor has shaped all the ice-cream tubs into animals and I settle on a mint chocolate chip scooped from a butterfly shape, and Costas has a chocolate one from a hedgehog. The nearby children excitedly choose from the array of ice-cream sculptures.

I'm not sure exactly how many streets we have meandered through, but my feet are beginning to ache as the ancient cobbles have awoken feelings in parts of my feet I never knew I had. It is with some relief, then, when Costas suggests we head back towards the bus station. But if I thought it would be a simply a case of waiting for a bus and getting on it I was clearly under a misapprehension. The hundreds of holidaymakers, coupled with the small and infrequent buses mean only one thing... boarding a bus is like fighting your way through a rugby scrum.

I apologise to everyone I make contact with, even the German woman who is poking me in the back with her large camera, and the Greek bloke with the sweaty armpits who is reaching over my head to grab the rail to board the bus. It seems as though I am going to be left on the pavement, when Costas grabs my hand and almost in one fell swoop I am not only on the bus but miraculously seated, while he pays the driver.

'Jeez, I thought the Liverpool bus after a football match was bad, but compared to this it's a train ride in a kiddies' fairground.'

'It's always the same.' Costas shrugs. 'Every year the tourists come but the council do not put any more buses on. The taxis do a roaring trade though.'

'I never thought about a taxi,' I say, rubbing my throbbing feet.

'No need. You have a seat. You are one of the lucky ones.'

I'm exhausted and silent on the way home, and realise that I really do need to get fit. As soon as I get home I am going to join a gym. That is if I can afford it… the thought hits me that I may be the only one paying the bills. Will I even be able to stay in the house? I don't want to think about it, so I plug my iPad in and listen to some music, and it isn't long before Costas is gently shaking me awake as we arrive outside Sea View Apartments.

CHAPTER TWENTY-FIVE

I open the curtains at 6.30 a.m. to see Hayley outside our apartments snogging the face off Aussie Matt before she comes inside to pack for our flight home. The holiday has gone so fast and I'm not sure how I feel about going back to Liverpool. I haven't had any more texts from Danny, which I have mixed feelings about, although I didn't reply to either of his messages.

The sun is already up and the taxi will be arriving in twenty minutes to take us to the airport for our nine o'clock flight.

'Mandy, are we leaving this stuff in the bathroom?' asks Hayley, throwing things into her suitcase.

'Yeah, everything apart from that hair conditioner. It cost a fortune. There's some Sellotape on the dressing table. Just wrap it around the top before you pack it.'

'Aye, what did your last slave die of?'

'Not Sellotaping the conditioner and ruining all my clothes, which resulted in fifty lashes,' I say, whipping her with the beach towel.

'Ow! That hurt. That's the last time I take time off from my horribly stressful job to come out here and join you on holiday,' she says, smiling. Then she sits on the edge of the bed and sighs deeply. 'I really don't want to go home just yet, I've fallen in love with the place,' she says dreamily.

'Is it just the place you've fallen in love with?'

'Yeah, it really is. Matt's great but he's going back to Australia at the end of September. There's no point in falling for a guy who lives on the other side of the world. No, I'm fine, really.'

I'm happy to hear this. I think she was a little stung when her last relationship ended, as she really seemed to like Mike from the bank. I could see it wouldn't last though. He would have been too dull for Hayley in the long run.

'You do know that we might be back here in a few months if we can get the festival idea off the ground?' I say.

Hayley gives me a look that says I really should stop daydreaming. 'Mandy, do you really think you can organise it all in three months? There are tickets to sell and all kinds of legalities to sort out.'

'Well, that's just the thing, there isn't really. A stage can be erected on the field in no time. Most of the local bands are available at short notice. In fact, going by what Adonis was saying, bands would be queuing up for an opportunity like this.'

'Even so, it does seem like a lot to organise,' Hayley says doubtfully.

'It's a good job it's not me organising it, then, isn't it? This is Janet's department. She does this sort of thing for a living, remember.'

'I know. And I'm sure it will be just fine.' Hayley smiles.

I don't think she believes for one minute that the idea will come to fruition, yet I find to my surprise that I don't care what anyone else thinks. I have faith.

CHAPTER TWENTY-SIX

Costas and I had been at the Olympic Bar the previous evening and I was stunned by the talent there. We'd drunk and laughed the night away and even had a little dance together.

Adonis was confident that he could secure the appearance of a popular Greek band and said that a British or international headline would have tickets sold out in no time. I was a bit worried that the people would not have the income to buy them, but he assured me that most of the audience would be university students who had wealthy parents, or diehard fans who followed their music heroes around the globe. He agreed it would be a marvellous thing for the village restaurants and bars. I came away feeling so excited, especially when Adonis informed us that the father of one of the young musicians worked in the council offices in Rhodes town, so could supply any information we needed.

'Things have changed so much in the world. Years ago, you could never consider anything like this without a year of preparation,' said Costas. 'With the Internet, everything is possible so much faster these days. It may be hard to get a big act at short notice, but at least there will be plenty of local bands,' he said enthusiastically.

But I'm sure I can get Janet to supply a big act. I can just feel it.

'This could really happen, couldn't it?' I said excitedly to Costas later that evening, as we made our way home in the back of a taxi. He assured me that indeed it could, and I suddenly believed it too.

As promised I was home at 11 p.m. and went to bed almost immediately. There was a slight pause as we said good night outside my room and Costas leaned in for a kiss on the lips. I leaned my face to the left so the kiss landed on my cheek. Later, I lay awake for ages wondering what a proper, lingering kiss would have felt like.

It's the next morning and I take one last look around the apartment, which is flooded with light, as Hayley trundles our suitcases down the stairs. We make our way to the reception area and are surprised to find Costas already seated at a small table with a tray of fresh coffee and croissants.

'I thought you might appreciate a little breakfast. The airport food is shocking and overpriced.'

I am so touched by his thoughtfulness. We have just over twenty minutes before the taxi arrives as we sip our coffee and eat our delicious warm croissants.

'I will be in touch as soon as I get home,' I promise Costas, who seems a little quiet.

Hayley nips to the toilet and Costas comes to sit beside me. 'Thank you for thinking about the village,' he says gratefully, 'and for your suggestions for the reception area. We will miss you. I hope for everything to be OK for you when you get home.' He hands me a small velvet drawstring pouch and inside there is a smooth tan- coloured pebble. 'This is from Thakos beach. Legend goes that if you take a pebble from the beach you must return.' He leans in and gives me the gentlest of kisses on the cheek.

I suddenly feel quite emotional. 'Thank you,' I say quietly, just as Hayley returns from the toilets, having applied lip gloss and spritzed some perfume, the scent wafting through the reception area. She looks amazing as always.

'Hey, guess what?' she announces, while studying her phone. 'We've been invited to a glitzy party tonight at the opening of Solitaire in Liverpool, VIP tickets and everything. Are you up for that?'

Costas smiles as I roll my eyes.

'Do you remember Gary Cooke, who plays football for Liverpool? I dated him for a while last year. It's his nightclub. I used to think he was the one that got away, so this might be interesting.'

She's incorrigible. Only last night she was all over Aussie Matt and already she's planning her next conquest. I worry about what she will do when her looks fade, before realising that I'm thinking like my mother again.

The navy-blue taxi pulls up outside reception and we say goodbye to Andreas and Costas, as the miserable-looking driver loads our suitcases into the car, obviously expecting a tip.

They embrace us both in a hug and Costas lingers a few seconds longer and for a fleeting moment I wish it could go on even longer.

'I'll email you,' I say to Costas, as I climb into the taxi. 'Remember you've got quite a bit of work to do.'

We wave until we've disappeared around a corner and I suddenly realise that I am heading home. A little knot forms in my stomach. I'm going back to reality and I wonder whether Hayley was right to look at me as if I was daydreaming. Maybe I was. Maybe all this stuff was a way of distracting me from my marital problems. Hayley won't even give this place a second thought once we land in Liverpool, and I'm sure she's already planning her outfit for the party at the nightclub tonight.

We check through the airport pretty quickly and it isn't long before we are seated on the plane. I've got the window seat as I love looking at the clouds. I remember the first time I flew as a child and was amazed that we actually flew above the clouds and looked down on them. I wondered where God was as I was sure that heaven was just above those white fluffy clouds. Hayley can't bear flying and prefers to immerse herself in a magazine and down several vodka and Cokes to calm her nerves.

'So, when are you back at work then?' I ask her breezily.

Hayley pulls a face and plugs her headphones into her iPad. 'I don't want to talk about it,' she says and those are the last words we exchange until we touch down at John Lennon Airport in Liverpool.

CHAPTER TWENTY-SEVEN

We touch down to grey cloud and drizzle. Hello, British summertime! Hayley says we are actually due a heatwave in the next couple of days, which sounds about right, as that is when I am due back at work.

We make our way through to the baggage carousel and Hayley's gold-coloured suitcase alongside my pink patterned one stand out in a sea of black luggage. We are soon outside the airport and trundling our cases to the car park, where Hayley has parked her car. It's several minutes' walk away and I shiver slightly, as my thin, pink cardigan fails to protect me from the chill of the wind and the misery of the faint drizzle, and I grumble all the way to the car park.

'Cheer up,' says Hayley brightly. 'A hot shower when you get home will sort you out, then go through your wardrobe and choose your glad rags for tonight. Or we've got time to pop into town, if you want to buy something new.'

'I don't know if I fancy tonight,' I say truthfully. 'I hardly slept a wink last night with the early flight. I just want to get home, really.'

I think Hayley has forgotten that I'm someone in the middle of a marriage separation. I need to talk to Danny and find out what's what. I'm back to reality with a bang, as I realise how easy it is to put your life on hold when the sun is beating down and you are in holiday mode.

'Well, if you're sure,' she says, breezily. 'But see how you feel later on. You might just need a sleep.'

I love Hayley to bits, but I do sometimes wonder whether she is a bit emotionless when it comes to men. Or maybe it's because she hasn't met the love of her life yet.

I wonder whether Danny *is* the love of my life. I certainly thought he was. We've been together since we were fifteen years old, on and off, so I never imagined myself with anybody else. Hayley doesn't believe that any two people can last a lifetime together. She believes that we evolve and grow so much that couples only stay together because it takes too much effort to make a change.

Twenty-five minutes later, after popping into a shop en route for milk and bread, Hayley has deposited me at my front door. I've only been away a couple of weeks, but I notice that the grass in the front garden needs mowing again. Danny always used to take care of that. I stand staring at the door for several minutes as Hayley speeds off into the distance to prepare herself for her night out. I don't know why I'm hesitating. It's not as though anything will be different on the inside, although I wonder, fleetingly, whether Danny has been round for any reason as he does still have a key.

I unlock the door before I step inside and my foot hits a pile of post. I don't really see the point of neighbours or my parents having a key, as everywhere is securely locked up and there're no goldfish to be fed or plants to water. Plus, we have a Neighbourhood Watch scheme and Dot and Bill never miss anything, so I'm sure any suspicious-looking characters would have soon been interrogated before being given short shrift from Bill.

I remember the time my mum gave a key to a neighbour when we went on holiday. We arrived home several hours earlier than expected and she could still smell the lingering scent of her Chanel N° 5 coming from the bedroom, and Dad swore his whisky had mysteriously vaporised somewhat.

I flick the kettle on before plugging my phone in to charge the battery and am stunned when, several minutes later, seven texts from Danny ping through. They are all pretty much asking me how I am and when I am coming home. The final one says:

Why RU ignoring me?

My stomach does a little flip. Why does he want to know when I'm coming home? He obviously wants to speak to me and I must admit that I want to see him too. I'm home now, and with every passing minute my Greek experience is already beginning to fade into a distant memory.

I sip my tea and ponder my next move, when I hear a car pull up outside. My mouth goes dry as I race to the window, but I'm surprised to find that it's my dad and he's alone.

'Hi, Dad,' I say, breezily. 'I wasn't expecting you. Where's Mum?'

He gives me a hug, but there's an air of tension about him and, for a heart-stopping second, I think something has happened to Mum.

'She's gone into town with her friend Jane. Dress shopping for someone's sixtieth birthday party at work... So how was the holiday?' he asks, accepting a cup of tea and sitting himself down.

'Lovely. Just what I needed really, and with Hayley turning up it was a lot of fun.'

I'm about to scoot off into the kitchen in search of biscuits, but my dad tells me to sit down. 'So how are things between you and Danny?' he asks tentatively.

'You tell me. He's seeing someone else but he's been texting me. I don't know what's going through his mind.'

My dad shifts a little. 'I spoke to Danny last week,' he says, which takes me completely by surprise. 'I bumped into him, actually, at the supermarket in the razor-blade aisle. We went for a coffee in the café and had a bit of a chat. The thing is, I think he regrets what's happened. I'm sure he would like a second chance with you.'

I'm puzzled by all of this. 'Shouldn't he be telling me this, then? Does he know you've come to see me? Has he sent you?' I ask incredulously.

'No, of course not. It just saddens me that you two have been together for so long... don't throw it all away over one mistake.'

'I'm not the one who's thrown it all away, Dad, Danny has. Do you really think I should forgive him just like that? Because, well, excuse me for thinking this but if you have a marriage problem shouldn't you try to work it out, and not go and shag someone you work with? Can you ever imagine doing anything like that to my mum?'

My dad looks down at his shoes and, at first, I think it's because he doesn't know what to say, but then a slow, horrible realisation dawns. *My dad has cheated on my mum.* My lovely, honest, principled father slept with someone else behind my mother's back.

'People make mistakes. We're all human, but if you have a deep enough love you can forgive anything.'

My heart is thumping. I don't want to hear this.

'Are you speaking from personal experience?' I spit, but I already know the answer.

My dad exhales deeply. 'It was over twenty years ago,' he says, without expression, as he stirs his tea. 'There was simply no excuse. I worked with a woman called Marianne in the accounts office and we had a close working relationship that spilled over into our personal lives. I knew there was an attraction between us, but I never should have acted upon it. We got sent on a course to Manchester and stayed at a hotel overnight.'

I want to cover my ears, but at that same time I need to hear this confession from my father. It's like watching a horror movie from behind a cushion but not pushing the off button.

'We all had too many drinks at the bar and the inevitable happened. It was a one-off and I deeply regretted my actions the next morning. Not long after that I went to work for Whitley's Insurance at the Liver Buildings.'

Anger is rising inside me like a bubbling volcano.

'The inevitable happened? The *inevitable*? You say it as though you had no say in it!'

My dad is on his feet now. 'Mandy, I know you're angry, but it was all a long time ago and that's the point of me telling you this. Your mother and I got through it. There isn't a day goes by that I am not truly grateful that she found it in her heart to forgive me. I was young and foolish, but she is the only woman I have ever truly loved.'

My mind is reeling because of what I have just been told. I would never have thought my father capable of something like that, as he is the most loyal, straight-down-the-middle guy you could ever meet, who clearly idolises my mum. He's still a good-looking guy of fifty-five who has a touch of Richard Gere about him. I can imagine he was quite a looker in his younger days.

I sit silently for a while, trying to take it all in.

'I think you should leave now,' I say, after a few minutes.

'I will. It's a lot to take in and I never would have told you had I not believed it might help you in some way. Talk to Danny. I'm sure he will be in touch with you very soon. Don't throw it all away.'

'Close the door on your way out,' I sob, before curling up in a ball on the sofa and bawling my eyes out.

CHAPTER TWENTY-EIGHT

It's only two o'clock in the afternoon and I'm rubbish at afternoon drinking, but I switch my tea to a large glass of duty-free vodka with a splash of Coke. I quickly realise I need to lose my anger over the recent revelation. It was over twenty-five years ago, and I know my parents are happy, so it shouldn't be about me as I'm a grown woman. I'm just shocked that my dad is empathising with Danny. And it's a bit bloody different. My dad's was a stupid one-night stand, whereas Danny has had a full-blown affair.

I don't know what to think. I fire my laptop up and check my emails, to find that I have a message from Costas asking me if I have arrived home safely. He tells me that they have taken some more bookings and that Andreas has decided that work will start on the new swimming pool right away, as he knows some builders who could have it installed in a matter of weeks. He informs me that Adonis has many bands that are keen to take part in the music festival, but they need one or two headline acts before they can begin to advertise or raise any interest from local traders.

I send back a quick reply, as I'm suddenly inspired to actually get this thing off the ground.

I settle down to my ultimate comfort food of cheese on toast and plan to watch the soaps I missed on catch-up TV, when there is a knock at the front door. I think about ignoring it, when suddenly Danny appears at the front window, tapping at it and almost giving me a heart attack.

'Cheese on toast,' he says, noticing my half-eaten slice on the plate on the coffee table as he walks into the living room. 'Bet you couldn't get that in Greece. Not with that Greek cheese.'

'Feta,' I say. 'It's delicious. What do you want, Danny? And what were all those texts when I was on holiday?'

He's standing with his hands in his pockets like a naughty schoolboy who is being admonished by his head teacher.

'I'm sorry, Mandy,' he says quietly. 'I've been a complete prick. I've really missed you these past few weeks.'

'You walked away,' I say, before sitting down to eat the rest of my cheese on toast and washing it down with a large vodka. I start to feel a little light-headed.

'I know I did,' he says, coming to sit next to me on the couch. I notice that he looks tired and has a couple of days' stubble on his chin. 'Things had got a bit jaded between us, hadn't they? But I should have spoken to you instead of looking for excitement somewhere else. I just thought you'd lost interest too. You never seemed to want to come home from work.'

Danny puts his head in his hands and his shoulders give a little shake as I realise to my horror that he is crying. We've been together for so long and I've never seen Danny cry before. Not even when his family cat, Cleo, passed away. I'm not quite sure what to do next, so I go into the kitchen for another glass and pour him some vodka and place it in front of him. He drinks it neat and I pour myself another one. Everything feels soft around the edges. Danny edges his way along the sofa until he is right next to me, and I inhale his aftershave. It's all so familiar and feels completely natural as he hugs me and I bury my face in his neck.

Oh, Danny, I've missed you too, I think. *I've missed you too.*

CHAPTER TWENTY-NINE

I wake two hours later to my phone ringing and vibrating on the coffee table. It's Hayley. She leaves a message on voicemail when I don't answer, asking me whether or not I am going to the party tonight.

It takes me a few seconds to focus before I realise I am half-dressed and Danny is snoozing gently on the sofa. The bottle of duty-free vodka is almost empty and my head is slowly beginning to throb. *Oh God, what have I done?* Danny just walks through the door after almost two months and I end up having sex with him. I'm angry at myself, although a part of me obviously wanted to, and I suppose he is still my husband after all.

Maybe my father is right. We have far too much history to just throw it away, and I suppose I should be pleased that at least we are talking again (although if I'm honest I don't remember much talking). It felt good to have Danny's arms around me again and when he kissed me, although there weren't exactly fireworks going off, it felt safe and comfortable as I sank into his familiar embrace. I hadn't realised how much I missed having a man's arms wrapped around me like a protective cocoon. I'm not really a touchy-feely person on a daily basis, but I guess I was feeling pretty unloved.

Danny stirs slightly, before pulling me down onto the couch and kissing me again. It's not a passionate kiss, just a kiss on the forehead. He gets up and goes into the kitchen to brew some fresh coffee before returning and handing me a black and white striped mug. He then grabs his coat saying that he needs to go out, but will return later.

'Where are you going?' I ask in surprise.

He comes and sits down next to me again. 'Mandy, I haven't been living here for weeks,' he says gently. 'I've got to go and collect all my clothes and stuff. And I think it's only fair that I tell someone I've been seeing face to face that I'm back with you.'

I know that he's been seeing someone and for a brief moment I feel almost sorry for Sarah Kelly. Danny should never have got involved with anyone else when he was still married, as somebody was bound to get hurt. But, on the other hand, she knew he was married, the slut. Suddenly I'm angry again.

'Whoa, hang on there! Who said we are back together? Isn't that the sort of thing you normally have a conversation about?' I say sharply.

I suppose I do want Danny back in my life, but I am totally affronted by his lack of effort. He can't just rock up and pick up where we left off. What a bloody cheek. He is going to have to work a bit harder than that.

He looks puzzled. 'But I thought—'

'You thought that a bottle of vodka and drunken afternoon sex was going to get you back into the marital bed permanently? Do you have such little respect for me?'

He doesn't appear to know what to say to this.

'Well, err, what now then?' he says, doing his lost-schoolboy look again. I suddenly want to shake him and it strikes me in that moment that maybe Danny just wants to be back with what is familiar and easy. Maybe Sarah Kelly was high maintenance so he's returned to his comfy slippers. Well, I'm not bloody having that.

'I don't know,' I reply. 'Surprise me.'

He nods and slopes out of the door and I wonder what the hell I am doing. My mother always said that if a man cheats you should not forgive too readily or he will walk all over you. Little did I know that she was talking from personal experience, and I wonder how long it was before she truly forgave my dad?

The phone's ringing again and it's Hayley. I answer and tell her that I won't be going tonight and that Danny has returned.

'And?' she replies. 'He's been gone for bloody months. One more night won't make any difference.'

I take Hayley's point, but my mind is made up. I don't feel like going clubbing and realise that deep down I am more interested in sorting my life out.

I nip upstairs and stand under a steaming hot shower. Everything is exactly as it was in our terracotta-tiled bathroom with its chrome fixtures and fittings. We invested in a giant shower cubicle built for two, and I glimpse our dressing gowns hanging side by side on the back of the door. I suddenly wonder if Danny had a dressing gown at Sarah's place, or did he wander around naked? I luxuriate in my jasmine shower gel and wonder if this is how it's going to be. Will I always be wondering about what he did with Sarah, where he went, what they did in bed? Will I drive myself crazy? Maybe you can never fully forgive an affair, as part of the trust will be gone forever.

I grab a soft white towel from the heated rail and wrap it around my body. It's strange that only ten hours ago I was in a Greek apartment, wrestling the plastic shower curtain that was sticking to my legs as a drizzle of water attempted to escape the white plastic nozzle.

I'm out of the shower and dressed, when Danny returns two hours later carrying his holdall and a bunch of red roses.

'I've booked us a table at Luigi's on Bold Street tonight for nine o'clock. I know how you used to love it there,' he says, with a grin as wide as the mouth of the Mersey.

A feeling of nostalgia engulfs me and I consider that if there is any place to rekindle the romance then Luigi's is the place. We've still got a long way to go, but I think this is a good start. Maybe it's not the end of my marriage after all?

CHAPTER THIRTY

It's ten o'clock in the morning and Danny and I are lying in bed, having a cuddle but nothing more, despite Danny's attempts at stroking the inside of my thigh. I think about the vodka-fuelled sex of yesterday, but don't want him to think I'm a pushover. And a thought keeps circling round in my head: *Is this what I really want?* If I close my eyes I can visualise the sun-drenched beach at Thakos, where I left my worries behind.

Danny and I did have the most amazing night at Luigi's though. We were delighted to find that Luigi was hosting front of house, as he has semi-retired from the restaurant, leaving most of the work to his son. He crushed us in a warm embrace when we arrived and asked about my parents. 'Why you not come and see us any more?' he asked, turning his mouth down at the corners and feigning sadness.

I realise it's probably been about eighteen months since we last visited as there haven't been any milestone birthdays to celebrate. There was a time when we would go as regularly as every fortnight, just to celebrate the arrival of the weekend. It makes me realise the extent of the rut we had got into.

It was almost as though we were on one of those celebratory evenings as we sipped Chianti and ate the most delicious meal of seafood linguine for me and garlic-chicken pizza for Danny. Whenever we eat in a restaurant he always thinks that my meal looks better than his and sits there with the expression of a starving dog until I give him a taste. It drove me mad when we first met, as he was constantly sticking his fork in my meals and helping himself without asking, until I accidentally stabbed him in the hand as I stopped him from eating my chilli chicken fillet. Funnily enough Danny hasn't helped himself to my food ever since and still refers to the 'stabbing' as an attack rather than an accident.

Towards the end of the meal last night he fell silent and reached for my hand. 'I thought I'd lost you forever,' Danny whispered, as we shared a large portion of tiramisu. 'I've been such a fool. We've been together so long I just can't imagine having a future with anyone else.'

I wasn't sure what to say to this as I dug into my creamy tiramisu. After all it was Danny who changed everything. Besides, the distant future isn't something I think about, if I'm honest, as I can't imagine myself growing old. These days I don't think about the future or the past, as I prefer to live in the present. I'm not entirely sure we even have a future together any more, but I feel as though I owe it to our marriage to give things another try.

Danny's taken the week off work, but I don't know what he's going to do after that. I really hope that we can spend this time trying to get to know each other again, although I admit to still feeling a little guarded with my emotions. Maybe I needed a little longer in the Greek sunshine to ponder our future.

Sarah Kelly still works in the same office as Danny so he has decided to look for another job, although I'm realistic enough to know that it's not going to be as easy as it sounds. He's worked at Auto-Repair for twelve years and is on a decent salary now. He's also built up quite a customer base. I asked him if he had ever considered setting up his own business, but he thinks it's a bit too risky in the current economic climate.

I mull over the conversation with my dad again, who left his job after his brief dalliance with Miriam or whatever her name was. I'm not sure if I'll be able to trust Danny when he returns to his old job. Perhaps I'm just going to have to see how things work out. I've always believed that 'what will be will be' in life. But that's the hypothetical view. In the past, I've advised girlfriends that there's nothing you can do about it if someone is unfaithful; they do it of their own free will regardless of anything you might say or do.

I swore I'd never forgive an infidelity, but then when it happens to you it's a whole different scenario. It's all such a mess. I still feel like I could bloody kill Danny at times, but for now I've got to give our marriage a second chance. I don't think I could forgive myself if I walked away from our relationship without at least trying one more time.

'Oi, your turn to get up and make the coffee,' I say, poking Danny in the ribs. 'And I think there are some sausages in the freezer, if you fancy making us a sausage butty.'

I don't really like frozen sausages. In fact, I hate frozen anything really, but there are times when junk food just hits the spot. A friend of mine used to freeze cheese, milk and anything else she found in the supermarket that had gone past its sell-by date and was being sold off cheaply. I tried to argue that she was effectively freezing dodgy food, and she finally agreed when she froze, defrosted and ate manky fish, which she had bought from the fresh fish counter for under a quid, and was then off work for nearly a week with food poisoning.

'Nope,' says Danny, snuggling further down into the duvet. 'There's no ketchup in the cupboard and you can't have a sausage butty without it. There isn't much in the cupboards at all as you haven't done any food shopping for weeks…' he says, walloping me over the head with a pillow. I retaliate and we are having a full-blown pillow fight with the feather-filled pillows, when the doorbell rings.

Danny pulls on a T-shirt and a pair of grey joggers, before going downstairs to answer the door. I hear muffled voices and a few seconds later Danny is leaping up the stairs two at a time to tell me it's my mother.

'I think I'll go and grab a shower,' he says, keen to make himself scarce.

'Mum!' I say, squeezing her in an embrace and also feeling slightly embarrassed that Danny has opened the front door. Her expression is hard to read.

She takes her blue cotton gloves off and places them on the kitchen table. She always wears gloves, my mum, which give an air of eternal elegance. Black leather gloves in the winter and various shades and fabrics throughout the rest of the year.

'I was a bit surprised to see Danny opening the door,' she sniffs. 'You've only just got back from holiday.'

'I know, Mum,' I say gently, thinking of how she must have felt all those years ago when my dad strayed. 'But I want to make my marriage work. We've spent too many years together to just give up.'

'Well, that may be true,' she says thoughtfully, 'but you can't stay together out of sentiment. You're still young, so think very carefully about how you want to spend the rest of your life.'

I'm not going to tell her that Dad visited me and told me all about his infidelity, as she has never once discussed it in all these years.

'I love him, Mum,' I say simply.

'Well, I know you do. Or you think you do. You haven't got much to compare it to really, have you? Just remember a leopard can't change its spots, is all I'm saying,' she says, in a tone that tells me the conversation is over.

I'm a bit thrown by this remark, as my dad swore that his indiscretion was a single moment of madness. Was he telling me the truth? Surely he proved that a leopard can indeed change its spots?

'Well, if that proves to be the case, Mum, then I will leave our marriage behind. There will be no more chances, I promise you, but I think everyone should be forgiven one mistake,' I say honestly.

Her expression never changes. This is the one opportunity she would have to tell me all about Dad, but she doesn't. I know she just wants to protect me from the truth and doesn't want my dad's mistake to taint my opinion of him, and I love her for that. But I'm an adult, a friend as well as a daughter, and I would like nothing more than to embrace my mum in a hug and talk about it, but I realise it's never going to happen. Sometimes it's better to let sleeping dogs lie.

'So,' I say brightly. 'Do you want a cup of tea? There's even some fruitcake. Not home-made, though, I'm afraid. I didn't inherit your baking skills. It's shop bought.'

Much to my surprise, she declines the offer. 'No, it's alright,' she says, picking her gloves up from the table. 'I'm in work in an hour. I just wanted to drop in to see if you are OK, but I can see that you are.' She raises her eyes to the ceiling as Danny closes the bathroom door.

She forces a smile as she makes her way towards the front door. 'Just remember what I said, Mandy. You deserve to be happy. Make the right choices. Oh, and tell that errant husband of yours the grass needs cutting.'

CHAPTER THIRTY-ONE

Ten days later, things start to settle back into a normal routine, just as the blood-red roses are wilting in the vase and dropping petals onto the windowsill. Danny has started leaving wet towels on the floor in the bedroom and bathroom again, and is not jumping up quite as frequently to make a brew. Small things, I tell myself.

We certainly can't afford to eat at Luigi's as frequently as we have done these past couple of weeks, which has consisted of two lunch dates, ditto dinner, and a four-pound weight gain according to the scales. The recent second-honeymoon period could not be expected to last forever, I suppose, but at the moment I'm feeling happy enough. That is, until Danny brings up the subject of returning to work.

It's Saturday evening and Danny is sprawled on the couch with a bottle of Asian beer in his hand. We've just had an Indian banquet for two from the Bengal Kitchen, as the owners have added a couple of new dishes to the menu. I've drunk nearly a bottle of Prosecco, which was half-price at the supermarket and tastes divine.

'You do know I'm back at work on Monday,' Danny says casually, as he flicks channels and tries to stop at yet another re-run of *Top Gear* on Dave before I snatch the controls from his hand.

'So you're going then,' I say, sipping the last few apple- flavoured fizzy drops of the bottle and wishing I had another one in the kitchen. We had a fully stocked wine rack once upon a time, but as both of us seemed unable to resist drinking wine on a daily basis, it was either buy it at the weekend or join Alcoholics Anonymous.

'Well, of course I'm going,' he says, without a hint of regret in his voice, which pisses the hell out of me.

Danny notes my expression before quickly adding, 'We've got a mortgage to pay and I can't just walk into another job, much as I'd like to. I'm not looking forward to it, believe me. I'll go back but I'll start looking elsewhere. I've told you that. I know that's what you want,' he says, without his eyes leaving the television screen.

I can feel the irritation rising inside me like a bad case of heartburn.

'You'll look for another job because it's what *I* bloody want? How stupid of me to think that *you* might actually want to make a fresh start and not have to face the tart that you had a fling with every day,' I rant.

It's something I've tried to avoid thinking about, if I'm honest. I really don't know how I'll feel knowing that Danny and Sarah will be seeing each other in work each day. I'll probably pick away at our marriage until it falls apart.

I'm seriously considering walking over to the Bengal Kitchen for another bottle of wine, when I remember that there's some port under the kitchen counter, which my mum brought over at Christmas. We were supposed to have it with a cheeseboard after Christmas lunch, but we were all so stuffed on Christmas pudding and Bailey's cheesecake that the cheeseboard was shelved along with the port. I like a port and lemon now and then, even though Danny says it's an old woman's drink.

It's funny how certain drinks become unfashionable or evoke memories of childhood. Babycham, advocaat and sherry all remind me of childhood Christmas parties with my extended family, sipping drinks in the kitchen, and munching on cheese-and-pineapple on sticks that were stabbed into a foil-covered cabbage. My mum loves a 1970s vibe at parties and her buffets always include vol-au-vents, cocktail sausages on sticks and Black Forest gateau. I remember devouring half a sherry trifle with Hayley, telling her that it would get us really drunk, but, much to our disappointment, it did nothing but make us feel extremely sick.

I pour myself a tumbler of port and lemon, glad that I have a bottle of lemonade in the fridge, even though it is a little flat. There're some sliced lemons in a jar in the fridge and I plop one into my aubergine-coloured drink before returning to the lounge, where an action film is about to start.

'You wanna watch this?' Danny asks, placing the control down on to the coffee table, telling me that the decision has already been made.

'Whatever,' I say, taking a large glug of my drink, which isn't the most pleasant taste, if I'm honest, but I feel like getting pissed. 'I think I might go upstairs, actually. I still haven't watched that girlie DVD I got in the Secret Santa last Christmas.'

While I'm upstairs, I also look in the long drawer under the double wardrobe. It's where I stash all my unwanted Christmas presents, which can be thoughtfully recycled for other people throughout the year. There's a chunky vanilla-and-lime candle

(I don't like candles); a magnolia bath set (magnolia gives me a rash); a romantic comedy DVD (I prefer real-life drama to yet another romance disaster); and an assortment of other trinkets, including a pair of silver earrings and a silk scarf in various shades of green.

It occurs to me that people selected these gifts without actually thinking about who they were buying for, as I don't wear scarves or have pierced ears. It disappoints me slightly that gifts are bought so generically, although it does save me time and money when I can re-gift them, I suppose.

To my dismay I notice a missed call from Costas earlier in the evening, and wonder if it was important as we agreed to correspond by email. In his last message, he told me that the popular Greek band The Hunted had expressed interest in performing at 'Greekfest', as it's now being called. For a second, I wish I was back in Rhodes with the sultry heat and evenings spent in the beach bar, but I suppose we all feel that way when we return from holiday. There's a steady drizzle of rain splattering against the window outside, reminding me that I am firmly back in the North of England.

I discover a mini vodka cocktail set, which I decide to crack open, and twenty minutes later I am snuggled in bed with blue-berry- flavoured vodka as a nightcap and a packet of cheese and onion crisps which I found in a cupboard. I can hear sounds from downstairs spiralling upwards as Danny snores like a sleeping lion.

He's always the same after beer and food and I can barely recall a time he has actually watched a film to the end before sleep takes over. I usually end up going downstairs to wake him in the early hours of the morning, to find the television blaring and a beer bottle balanced precariously in his hand. He did it with a glass of red wine once, which ended up all over the wooden floor.

I open my bedside cabinet drawer to get a tissue, when I notice the little card that Janet gave to me at the pub several weeks ago. I turn the card over in my hand and think about dialling the number.

Costas has told me that the village won't be able to raise any national interest in ticket sales unless there is a big act to headline the musical festival so, emboldened by alcohol, I find myself dialling the number, which goes straight to voicemail.

> *'Hi. This is Janet Macey's phone. I'm sorry I am unable to take your call at the moment but please leave your contact details and I'll get back to you as soon as I can.'*

I hesitate for a few seconds before breezily (and a bit drunkenly) introducing myself and briefly outlining the idea for the music festival and asking if she can help.

The name Janet Macey rings a faint bell somewhere in the back of my brain. I didn't expect that she would still be called Janet Dobson, but Macey just seems familiar somehow. I consider going downstairs to wake Danny, but as I'm already cosy and settled I switch my bedside lamp off and snuggle into the duvet with the freshly washed cover that smells of lily and jasmine, and I'm soon sleeping and gently snoring in unison with my husband in the room below.

CHAPTER THIRTY-TWO

Hayley and I have both finished work and we're on our way into Liverpool city centre when a blue Vauxhall Corsa is edging precariously close to us, veering erratically from the centre to the edge of the adjacent lane. A glance sideways reveals that the vehicle is being driven by a man who looks about a hundred years old and has a distinctly unhealthy-looking pallor.

'Jeez, is he alright?' I say, glancing at him but also trying to keep my eyes on the road ahead. There's a low sun in the sky that's making vision difficult, especially as I have forgotten my sunglasses.

'Is he even alive?' quips Hayley.

I'm beginning to feel like I'm on the dodgems as I skilfully swerve my car away from the blue Corsa. Vehicles are tooting behind us and I'm beginning to worry about how this is going to end up.

A minute later we approach traffic lights, and the metallic-blue car glides quietly through a red light like a dragonfly on a pond, before stopping in the middle of a junction. It's as if it's all happening in silent slow motion before the calmness is shattered by the continuous shrill of the car horn as the old man's head hits the steering wheel.

It's a good thing it's just before the rush hour, as goodness knows what kind of chaos could have ensued then.

I dash to the scene to try my first-aid skills, but can tell at once that the poor man has gone. It's the second time I've seen a dead body, the first one being in the pub, when a portly man dropped dead of a heart attack at the bar after ordering a pint of Wagtail bitter. All I could think of for days afterwards was the fact that he never even got to drink his pint.

After the police and ambulance arrive at the scene of the stalled car in the road, and we have given witness statements, Hayley and I go to a restaurant in town to steady our nerves, and for a late- afternoon meal.

We're in Marrakesh, a Moroccan haven down a side street away from the crowds of Church Street and Liverpool One shopping mall. We're sitting on dark wooden benches covered with stripy-orange padded seats and cerise-coloured cylindrical cushions with gold tassels. Bejewelled brass-and-coloured-glass lanterns are suspended from the ceiling, and a gentle scent of burning cinnamon sticks is wafting gently through the air.

My stomach gives a little growl as I realise that I haven't eaten since breakfast. I eventually settle on lemon-and-herb chicken tagine with couscous and Hayley opts for apricot-stuffed lamb.

'Anyway,' says Hayley, as she attracts the attention of a waiter to take our order. 'What's going on with you and Danny? I never imagined you'd get back with him so easily.'

'I don't honestly know, truth be told. I'm just seeing how things go. I can't throw away all those years without a fight.'

'Well, don't be a pushover, that's all I'm saying. Make him work for it, you deserve it. And if it doesn't work out, you can always go back to your Greek island!'

I know Hayley's right. Being back with Danny just doesn't feel the same. I thought I loved him and that I'd be lost without him, but I'm starting to realise that maybe I've changed as well as Danny. I don't like chicken Kiev or Mel Gibson films any more but Danny still has a penchant for both.

We order large Cokes with our food and settle in for a chat when my phone rings. I take it outside as a waiter arrives with a carafe of iced water and sliced lemon.

'Mandy, darling,' drawls the unmistakeable tones of Janet Dobson-now-Macey. 'I'm just returning your call. You said something about a Greek music festival. How intriguing. I must admit I didn't quite catch your entire message so I thought you might like to meet up and have a chat.'

It's hardly surprising she didn't catch my message, as I now recall the amount of alcohol I'd consumed before making the call and rambling on about goodness knows what.

Five minutes later I'm back inside, just as two lime-and-orange-striped glazed terracotta tagines are arriving at our table. Hayley is flipping her phone closed, having taken the opportunity to have a quick chat with Gary Cooke, Liverpool FC football star and current nightclub owner. She's been dating him after hooking up with him at the party on our return from Greece.

We simultaneously lift the lids from our tagines and inhale the fragrant scent of the dishes. My mouth is watering.

'Sorry about that,' I say, in between mouthfuls of fragrant couscous, 'you'll never guess who that was.'

'So tell me if I'll never guess,' Hayley replies, shovelling tender pieces of lamb into her mouth like she hasn't eaten in a month.

'Janet Dobson. And what's more she wants to meet with me for a chat.'

'You're not still thinking about that music festival idea, are you?' Hayley laughs.

'You may mock, my friend, but Janet Dobson is very big in the music industry, so why not?' I say, before chewing an utterly delicious piece of lemon-and-herb chicken.

'I just don't want you to be disappointed, that's all. Everything seems possible on holiday, but it's not the real world, though, is it?' she says gently.

'Well, I think anything is possible, if you believe in it passionately – and obviously Janet thinks it's a good idea.'

'Is she your *new* best friend then?' teases Hayley.

'She might be after next Thursday.' I grin. 'I'm going down to London to meet her. Don't get jealous now.'

'As if I would. Nothing could ever come between us,' says Hayley, laughing.

'You're right. You know too many of my secrets.'

'Best friends forever,' says Hayley, chinking her glass against mine.

I know I'll always be friends with Hayley – she's like a sister to me. In the light of recent events, though, I might be forgiven for wondering, *Is there really any such thing as forever?*

CHAPTER THIRTY-THREE

The train journey whizzes by, as I am treated to the life story of a thin-faced, middle-aged woman, with short dark hair, who is seated in the opposite seat. She is going to London to hear the reading of her recently deceased brother's will. I am informed that her other sibling has already been into the brother's flat and 'helped himself' to his forty-two-inch plasma flat screen television, before declaring that the other sibling was always 'a robbing bastard'. She tells me how the deceased brother was the only member of the family who had gone to university, and how he had then carved out a successful career as a writer living in London.

I'd forgotten about the magical effect of London, which feels exhilarating and refreshing the second I step out of the station. Even the station itself, with its cacophony of sounds and cubes of small shops, reminds me of the airport at Liverpool, which has expanded over the years. It now features Blow 'n Go hair salon incorporating the services of 'lash in a flash', so every appearance-conscious lady can arrive at their holiday destination looking like a million dollars.

I love my hometown of Liverpool, but there's something special about London. It seems to wear its badge as capital city of England

and flaunt it proudly, whipping you around the face and demanding that you love it.

I check the address Janet gave me before taking a seat in the front cab of a long black snake of continually moving taxis. The driver recognises my accent and tells me that he has an aunt who lives in Bootle, which is a mile away from where I live. He then tells me a tale of how on a visit to said aunt, he saw a woman walking down the street in her pyjamas. He slowed his car down alongside the pavement before asking if she was alright and, 'Is there anything I can do?' He was informed that she was perfectly alright and that he was 'a fuckin' kerb crawler'.

The cab driver chuckles at the memory. 'I'd never seen anyone out in the street in their pyjamas before; I thought there had been an 'ouse fire or summink. The following year I went back and blow me they were out in their pyjamas AND wearing heads full of rollers. I ain't never seen the like of it before until I went to Liverpool,' he says with a throaty chuckle.

It's less than a five-minute drive before the amiable cabbie drops me outside the address of a flat in Bayswater. It's a striking white-stuccoed building and I happen to know that even the smallest apartments in this area cost well over a million quid.

For some reason, I feel a little nervous before I press the intercom for Flat 3 to announce my arrival. I'm unsure as to why I feel like this, as things seemed perfectly cordial at the pub back home and Janet did give me her business card after all. And she's agreed to see me *and* she paid my train fare, so I can't really understand my reservations. All the same, I take a deep breath as I press the button before hearing the familiar tones of Janet.

'Dahling, hi! I'll buzz you up.'

The door slowly opens and I'm inside a hallway that looks nicer than my front lounge. There're modern-art prints on the white walls and potted plants in corners, standing on a highly polished floor.

I climb the stairs to Flat 3 to find Janet stood in the doorway of her apartment, smiling. I can see at once that the place is sensational. There's a never-ending hallway lined with photographs in blonde wooden frames that match the floor. Most of them are of a smiling Janet with a number of well-known celebrities. I had no idea she was this well connected, and I gasp at the gallery where she is pictured with every celebrity in the category from A to Z. There's a larger framed photograph that takes pride of place in the centre of all the rest, where she is standing with Nelson Mandela. I'm staggered.

'Charity auction at the Ivy,' Janet informs me. 'Made a substantial amount that year for a malaria appeal in West Africa. Not forgetting introducing one of our band members to his future wife. People raised eyebrows over the age difference at the time.' She smiles. 'But they're still together, co-hosting a prime-time breakfast programme. So, Mandy,' she trills. 'Would you like some tea? Or maybe some champagne? I've got some Bollinger in the fridge. Or perhaps some food? I can get us a table at Nobu for lunch.' She flashes a smile so white that I swear it bounced off the white walls and cast a blue shadow over the fireplace.

This place is a white palace. Yet there appear to be ever-so-slightly different tones. The hall has an almost grey hue to the white, while the enormous lounge, with huge bay windows that flood the room with light, seems to have an ice-blue tinge. I mention this.

'Oh, I can't tell you what a palaver it was to get the hall right. We tried ten shades of white before we got the right one. The lounge only took three attempts. There are so many shades you could write a book about it,' Janet says, grinning.

'I bet it wouldn't sell as well as the one with the various shades of grey,' I say, smirking.

She ignores me.

Jesus Christ. Ten shades of white? Well, you can't really call it white if there're other colours in it, can you? Is this what it comes to when you have more money than sense? I wonder. *Does she send for fabric samples to peruse before she buys her knickers? Does she even buy her own knickers? Maybe she has them made to measure. Perhaps she has an arse-measuring maid.* I'm laughing to myself at the thought, when Janet asks me what's so amusing.

'I don't know – just you, me, and everything really. Here I am in your apartment yet I hadn't set eyes on you for fourteen years before you came into the pub. It just all feels a bit weird. I'm really pleased that you've done so well for yourself though.' To my surprise I find that I really mean it. 'I knew you would. You always worked really hard at school,' I say, sitting down, as Janet gestures to a sofa.

Janet sits down beside me on a huge gold-and-cream striped-fabric sofa. 'Well, that's true,' she says quietly. 'But I decided to concentrate on my studies because I just couldn't bear the thought of living on a council estate. And I wasn't exactly the most popular girl in the school.'

I feel a sudden stab of guilt. I expect she had a heart of gold really and would have done anything to be accepted by us popular lot, but we never welcomed her into the gang.

'We were just kids.' I sigh. 'And look at you now. Look at this,' I say, waving my arm around the enormous room that is straight out of a beautiful homes magazine. There are ornate antique coffee tables dotted around the room, holding huge glass vases filled with fresh lilies and magnolia. Expensive-looking modern art hangs majestically from the 'off white' walls and silver chandeliers shimmer from the ceiling. This is contrasted by a huge black rug and a baby grand piano in the corner of the room. It manages to look both opulent and homely.

Over fresh coffee and tapas in a smart deli down the road (I told her I don't do afternoon drinking) I learn that Janet has been married for six years to a property developer called Simon.

'He's currently in Montenegro looking at some holiday apartments. Most of the property has been purchased from in and around London, but he's breaking into the foreign market now,' Janet tells me, as she sips her Blue Mountain coffee. 'I could have gone with him, but I'm organising a new reality TV show for The Crypt.'

I thought I was hearing things.

'The Crypt? You're the agent for The Crypt?' I say in disbelief.

'Among others,' she says, with no hint of smugness.

The name Janet Macey, which has been bugging me in the back of my brain, suddenly comes to the forefront as reality dawns.

'Oh my God! You used to be one of the Night Owl girls, didn't you? That's where I recognise your name from!'

The 'Night Owls' had a column in a tabloid as well as columns in just about every celebrity magazine known to man, several years ago. They were constantly photographed with celebs and opened doors to all kinds of paparazzi. Think Perez Hilton but British.

'I was.' She smiles. 'I was very young at the time, and I think they wanted me more for my journalism skills. I'd just completed a university course when I ran into Amy Adler, another of the "girls", who was actually thirty-five years old. She was a top model and could usually access all areas of nightclubs, but needed someone to take photographs and do the write-ups. That's where I came in. Her two stunning sisters joined us after I managed to secure a column in a celeb magazine, and the Night Owls were born. It opened all kinds of doors for me, but I eventually settled on being a music agent and the rest, as they say, is history.'

I sip my coffee in disbelief. Janet Macey, agent to the stars, and I went to school with her. Who'd have thought it? I never recognised her in those magazine photos six years ago, because her hair was a dark shade of plum and she was nearly always wearing sunglasses. I would never have made the connection, not in a million years.

'Anyway,' she says, ordering another coffee for herself and a pot of tea for me, 'that's enough about me, what about you? I didn't realise you had gone from hospitality to organising concerts. And in Greece of all places. How did that come about?'

I tell her about the village of Thakos and how it is struggling to survive. 'It's just so heartbreaking,' I say. 'I loved it there as a kid and was saddened by the demise of the tourist trade. Then I noticed all this land just sitting there and doing nothing. There are no immediate plans to build anything there as there's not much money about. It turns out that the land is owned by an apartment owner who has never thought about doing anything with it.'

'Hmm, it does make sense to try to utilise it in some way, I suppose, but do you really think people would be interested?' Janet asks uncertainly.

'Well, yes, I'm certain of that,' I say enthusiastically. 'There are hardly any music festivals in Greece, other than in Athens. The annual Rockwave festival at Terra Vibe in Malakasa attracts huge crowds, but there's nothing local. Most of the village festivals seem to have a religious theme, celebrating the Virgin Mary usually. That's what gave me the idea of a festival. People travel from all the other islands to Athens to the open-air concerts, and the Rockwave festival is always a sell-out. It features local bands as well as international headline acts over four days. A friend has contacts in Rhodes to organise the local bands, but we need a big headline. That's when I thought of you.'

Janet smiles a slow smile and looks at me. I'm not sure what she's thinking, yet a part of me is waiting for her to burst out laughing and ridicule my fanciful idea. But she doesn't.

'I can help,' she says simply. 'It's true that most of the musical activity goes on in Athens. I know that for a fact. I was managing The Flowers when they headlined a concert there several years ago. It's an interesting idea to make things a bit more local, bring music to the masses. But could the village people afford to attend?'

'Well, I was hoping for a bigger act than the Village People,' I reply, grinning. 'Are they on one of those comeback reunion tours?'

She throws her head back and laughs. 'You always were the joker, Mandy. Nothing ever changes with you, does it?'

'Well, I haven't been laughing too much lately,' I confide, as I tell her about Danny and his recent affair. She looks shocked.

'I must say I'm surprised you've forgiven him. The old Mandy would never have taken him back,' she says, raising her eyebrows in surprise.

I think she may be right. Somewhere along the line I've softened. I can't make up my mind if that's a good thing or a bad thing.

'Perhaps,' I say, not really wanting to think about the person I have become lately.

'Anyway,' says Janet, standing up after paying the bill, 'I think you have a very interesting idea here. Would you like to stay over tonight? Simon's not back for another day or two. We could go out to dinner tonight and discuss it some more.'

A little tingle of excitement is building inside me. Who would turn down the chance of a night in London with a good chance of celebrity-spotting in a swanky restaurant?

'I think I'd enjoy that,' I say. And to my surprise I really mean it.

CHAPTER THIRTY-FOUR

We're sitting in a smart Italian restaurant called Diciannove in the city, sharing a large antipasti platter and sipping chilled Prosecco.

The place is beautiful with its chestnut-leather banquettes and highly polished wooden floor. It's a far cry from Luigi's on Bold Street back home. There are chunky wooden tables with stylish pendant lighting suspended from the ceiling and not a checked tablecloth or fake flower in sight. It's all about the food for me though, so I shall reserve judgement on that until I get to the main course, to see if it can match Luigi's in Liverpool, which is legendary.

Danny was a bit quiet when I spoke to him earlier, telling him that I would be staying overnight. I did ask him to book the day off work and come and join me, though, but he told me it was far too short notice.

I take another sip of the extra-dry Prosecco, which smells of honey and has an apple-scented fizz that bursts on the tongue. It's refreshing and delicious and I feel myself beginning to relax.

I still can't quite take it in. Here I am sitting in a stunning restaurant in the centre of London with Janet Dobson-now-Macey. A well-known TV chef has just walked into the restaurant and been shown to a discreet corner booth with a young, giggling brunette in a short dress who clearly isn't his wife.

'So,' says Janet, fishing some Dior glasses from her bag to peruse the wine list. 'Let's not forget why you are here. When is this proposed music festival going to take place?'

'Later in the year,' I say brightly, which almost causes Janet to choke on her salami.

'*This* year? You can't be serious. Most of my boy bands are booked up and touring for at least the next twelve months. I could probably get someone a little less high profile, but I don't think they would be a crowd puller,' she tells me, looking a bit disappointed for me.

I'm suddenly crestfallen and wonder what the hell I was thinking. Did I really expect a world-class band to just happen to have a free window for a week in September? I feel like a complete fool.

'Look,' says Janet gently, noting my disappointed expression. 'I'll have a think. Actually, if I'm not mistaken I think New Horizons have a gig in Istanbul around about that time. Leave it with me. They could possibly fly over for a day, but they're on a tight schedule, these guys.' She spears an olive with a cocktail stick from a bowl of mixed olives and is quiet for a moment as she chews.

I swallow slowly. New Horizons is currently the biggest boy band in the world. 'You manage New Horizons?' I say weakly, hardly able to take it in.

'Oh, yes. Lovely bunch of lads they are. Well, when I say lads, some of them are in their mid-twenties now so the next teeny-bopper boy band is right behind them. It's a short shelf life for these acts. Some do go on to last for the duration, but they are few and far between. Take That had the songwriting talent of Gary Barlow to sustain them.'

The mention of Gary Barlow makes me recall seeing his lookalike at the Leeds and Liverpool Canal about fifteen years ago. *Where does the time go?* I wonder whether he and his fishing partner are still together, and whether they were actually a gay couple at all or were just trying to let me and a flirty Hayley down gently.

'I'll be onto it first thing in the morning. I must admit the whole idea has me intrigued.' Janet smiles before ordering another bottle of Prosecco as, to my surprise, we have already finished the first one. 'I can really see the potential with this. You're right, there aren't too many venues outside of the big cities in Greece. It could really put a small village on the map. I love the smaller venues anyway, and when it's private land there aren't as many complications so it's pretty low risk.'

Janet picks up her phone and begins to flick through her contacts, before turning the screen to me.

'Any preferences?' she asks, as I scan the list of superstar bands.

My mouth is gaping open. 'Whoever you think,' I stammer. 'It's all a bit surreal to me.'

I think of the chubby-cheeked Janet of fifteen years ago and not for the first time I feel a little guilty. It strikes me that Janet knew what she wanted even as a teenager. She wanted to be part of the most popular group in school. From a young age, she had a desire to mingle with the beautiful people, so maybe in some way we inspired her. Suddenly I don't feel so bad any more.

CHAPTER THIRTY-FIVE

We're back at Janet's luxury apartment, and I'm using her laptop to check my emails, when I notice a message from Costas. He tells me that his father knows someone who is able to organise the essentials for the event, such as toilets, medical stations and so on, and closing the road off is not a problem as it's a very quiet village with a suitable diversion close by. Local bands are of sufficient interest to the students, but a couple of bigger acts are going to be essential to attract a wider audience. He needs to know as soon as possible if we can secure some well-known names before tickets can go on sale.

I fire an email straight back explaining that I'm currently with Janet and mention New Horizons as well as The Miracles, who are also massive. He tells me that even though business is done over the Internet, the Greeks very much like to see who they are dealing with and wonders, once the act is confirmed, whether I may be able to come over for a couple of days. Maybe even bring my friend Janet with me. I smile at the thought of her being my friend. We lead completely different lives now, but who knows, maybe we could be friends?

Janet asks why I'm smiling as she brings us coffees onto the huge outdoor terrace, which is just as stylish as the interior with its dark wood table and chairs and huge ferns in silver pots.

'I've just had an email from Costas,' I tell her. 'He says I should go over there and meet some of the organisers. They like to do business face to face apparently. He's also pushing for some decent headline acts or it may be a bit of a damp squib. Oh, and he says I should bring you,' I say, laughing.

Janet is very quiet for a few seconds before saying, 'OK, great. When do we leave?'

I'm too stunned to speak. 'But you do know it's the most basic of Greek villages,' I remind her. 'Even the phone signal's a bit dodgy. Would you really want to go? I suppose there is a large hotel just outside the village though, if you prefer that?'

She sighs as she comes and sits next to me. 'Mandy, frankly I think it would be like a breath of fresh air. Simon's still away and, in all honesty, even when he returns it won't be long before he's off again somewhere else,' she says with a faraway look in her eyes. I wonder if there's a glimmer of trouble in paradise. 'I can do business from anywhere in the world and my diary doesn't have anything I can't cancel for the next four days. It'll be good to get a bit of sun. So, first thing in the morning I'll confirm with New Horizons and The Miracles. I may also be able to get Apocalypse. I know their drummer is from Greece so that might be a welcome gig. Once confirmed we can get a flight to Rhodes from Heathrow. They're pretty much daily flights, I think.'

'With a budget airline,' I remind her.

'Mandy, will you stop,' she says firmly. 'I may have lots of money but I'm not a snob. Besides, it will be Aegean Airlines, which are perfectly fine, but of course if you really want to upgrade the flights I'd be happy to do that.'

'I don't! Of course not! It's just that you are enjoying the finer things in life now, so I didn't know whether you did budget airlines, that's all.'

'Well, whatever is available is fine by me. Just remember I went to the same school as you and I lived in the same area. We have the same background.'

This isn't strictly true. Wherever you live there are always two sides of the tracks and Janet lived on the better side, with a detached house and a two-car driveway, as opposed to our tiny terraced home, which was immaculately kept, but a terrace all the same. Janet's mother owned her own boutique in Crosby and her father was a head teacher, whereas my mum dipped in and out of part-time jobs and my dad worked at an insurance office. Janet may have gone to the same school, but that was because it was the only Catholic school in the area.

'You don't seem to realise I envy your life, in a way,' she says quietly, as she sips her Ethiopian filter coffee, which is from a vast collection I noticed in the kitchen earlier.

'You envy me?' I say incredulously. 'What on earth for?'

'Well… normality, I suppose. Things like going to your parents' house for Sunday lunch, still being in touch with Hayley… all that stuff. I hardly ever see my parents,' she says, without emotion. 'And like you I don't have any siblings, so it has made my family situation very small.'

'Did you fall out with your parents?' I ask carefully, wondering if I am being too intrusive.

'Not really,' she says, matter-of-factly. 'It's simply that we aren't very close. They were very remote when I was a child. My father smiled and charmed everybody from the children to the parents at his school, but pretty much ignored me.'

I'm taken aback.

'Oh, yes,' Janet continues, 'I've had ex-pupils stop me in the street to tell me how wonderful he was, encouraging them in their future career and so on, when he didn't give a damn about what I was up to.' She says this casually and without a hint of bitterness.

'What about your mum?' I venture.

'Oh, she was completely off her head. Drank herself stupid most days and had affairs with the blokes that came into her shop when they were buying underwear for their wives. I remember being there when I was about ten and she was offering to model some stockings for some bloke and flirting away. I was mortified. She thought I didn't know what was going on, but I did. She was such a good-looking woman I suppose she just wanted a bit of passion, as Dad was such a cold fish. I don't think I was ever on their radar really. But you know what, they are who they are. As an adult, I just pity them. My dad obviously feels guilty because he has tried to build bridges with me recently, but I'm afraid too much water has gone underneath. We do still exchange cards and gifts at Christmas though.' She smiles.

My heart melts and I feel the urge to just wrap her in a huge hug, which I instinctively do but I can feel her body tense up as she clearly isn't used to such open displays of affection. I think of my parents' kitchen back home, filled with baking smells and full of warmth and security.

I wonder about her husband Simon. Is he distant or affectionate towards Janet? Often people subconsciously seek out partners who are similar to their family, even if they don't realise it at the time.

'Won't you just be leaving as Simon is due to arrive home?' I ask.

'Not a problem,' says Janet, standing up and smiling. 'We're quite often like ships that pass in the night, but we've got a week in Rome coming up in a couple of weeks, just the two of us. And we talk on the phone every evening.'

I know for a fact that she didn't speak to him last night.

'So,' says Janet, placing the coffee cups onto an expensive-looking slate tray to take indoors. 'Shall I book those flights then?'

CHAPTER THIRTY-SIX

I've contacted Lyndsey at the Pig and Whistle, who is more than happy to cover my shift for a couple of days, as she's been trying unsuccessfully to save for her sister's hen do in Ibiza.

Danny is not so happy about my 'gallivanting', until I tell him that it's only going to be for a couple of days and remind him that he went AWOL for weeks. He mutters something about hating being on his own, and fails to see the irony of this statement.

I'm staggered by Heathrow Airport, which I've never been to before. It's like a small city! Liverpool Airport could fit into one small corner of this cosmopolitan wonderland and, not for the first time, I am totally blown away by London.

I was slightly worried that I had only brought clothes for an overnight stay in London, but Janet came to my rescue. We are roughly the same size and, when she opened the doors to her walk-in wardrobe, I found myself in designer-label heaven. I threw a couple of Boden summer dresses into my case, along with a pair of gold Gucci sandals, some long linen shorts, and a few vests that would probably cost more than my shopping budget for the entire year. Oh, and Janet even threw in a pair of genuine Armani sunglasses. My previous ones were fake ones that I purchased in a Greek market for a few euros.

We're at the airport and Janet has disappeared for a few minutes to make a phone call.

'Well that's New Horizons on board,' Janet says, as she returns to our table at the airport bar and takes a sip of her lager.

'I can't believe it! New Horizons have actually agreed to do the gig?' I say, agog.

'Well, I'm their manager, so they don't have a lot of choice. They've been on a whistle-stop world tour recently and a couple of the younger members are completely exhausted. I think Sam is almost on the edge and I don't want him quitting. There's a few more UK concert dates before they have a little break, then it's Istanbul. After that, a few days chilling in Greece will probably do them good.'

Apocalypse and The Miracles were all happy to be on board too and I can't wait to tell Costas and Adonis.

For some reason, I suddenly feel a little selfish jetting off with Janet at a moment's notice, when I'm meant to be getting my marriage back on track. Brian at the pub has been really accommodating about the whole thing, too.

I send Danny a text:

Be back before U know it. I'll ring U when I arrive xx
Love U x.

He doesn't reply, but he's probably underneath an engine or something. He takes his work very seriously and hardly ever looks at his phone during working hours.

The flight goes smoothly and soon we have collected our suitcases and are wheeling them to the taxi rank outside, where the searing heat on my bare shoulders reminds me to apply sun cream.

One short, slightly less bumpy ride than last time, and we are deposited close to Sea View Apartments. I smile to myself as I recall my reaction the first time I arrived. The same little boy who was there on my last visit is kicking a ball around and lifts his arm and waves at me as recognition dawns.

The taxi driver is astonished when Janet gives him a twenty euro tip, which is twice as much as the taxi fare, and quickly asks if she would like to book him for the return transfer.

I turn to Janet, expecting to see her horrified expression at being in the middle of nowhere, but to my surprise she is smiling.

'Ah, fresh air,' she says taking a deep breath and exhaling slowly. 'You forget just how dirty London is, much as I love the place. You can really feel the pureness in the air here.'

I feel relieved. We are just lifting the handles on our bags to pull them up the slope, when Costas appears and, to my great surprise, my heart gives a little flutter.

'Why did you not call me?' he says, embracing me briefly. Costas attempts to do the same to Janet, after I introduce her, but she swiftly intercepts him with a handshake. 'I would have collected you from the airport,' he says.

'It's no problem,' I say brightly. 'It's only a short journey and I don't want Andreas having a go at me from keeping you away from your chores.'

'This is true.' He laughs before taking our cases in his strong hands and practically running up the slope with them. I am reminded, yet again, how unfit I am, as I am puffing slightly when we walk into reception. Janet is as cool as a cucumber and clearly in good shape.

'You never told me he was so good looking,' says Janet, when Costas is out of earshot taking our cases up to our room

'Hey, behave, you're a married woman,' I say, feeling slightly uncomfortable.

'So are you,' she reminds me. 'But don't say you hadn't noticed.'

Andreas welcomes us warmly into the bar, which has been painted a shade of pale blue. The checking-in desk has been de-cluttered and the fake flowers have been replaced by a vase of fresh wild flowers. The party-revellers photo board has been replaced by a cork message board, displaying tourist information and a Holiday Watchdog certificate of excellence. I'm impressed.

I spot Annis from the ceramic shop at the new-look bar with a young man and she comes over to say hello. I introduce her to Janet, before the young couple depart for a night at a restaurant and then on to a nightclub, Annis tells me excitedly. There is a glow about her, which tells me this is a blossoming new romance.

Over a large gin and tonic for Janet and a vodka and Coke for me (well, it is just after five o'clock), Andreas tells us how the village is buzzing quietly with news of the music festival.

'The business people feel they could make some real money,' he tells us. 'They have seen the religious festivals in neighbouring villages and how everybody benefits from them. They want the same. I still can't believe you have arranged for such well known bands to perform at our village,' says Andreas, turning to Janet.

'I think they were only too happy to oblige. It's hard to connect with fans in huge arenas. A lot of artists prefer a more intimate gig, given the chance, but their popularity means that isn't really possible. In that respect they become victims of their own success,' says Janet, as she sips her gin.

We are invited to a barbecue tonight to meet the local events organiser, who is a friend of Andreas and helps with the religious festivals. Adonis is coming along too, with a few of the local bands. Andreas tells us they are desperate to hear from the horse's mouth whether these world-class bands really are coming to Thakos.

I suppose it must all seem a little surreal really. Who would have thought that a Greek village struggling in a financial crisis would be hosting a music festival with the biggest boy band in the world headlining it? There are food outlets queuing up to sell their wares from all around the island, apparently, but the local village traders are to take priority according to council laws. Even Nikos's taverna, which closed several weeks ago, is planning to open its doors in the hope of making up for a disastrous year so far. Nikos had been running his restaurant at a loss for some time, hoping the recession would pass before finally admitting defeat. These days he runs a small snack van close to the beach.

The barbecue takes place at the Olive Garden Kitchen and Yannis and Joan have pulled out all the stops, with tantalising dips and Greek meze, and a huge moussaka taking centre stage. There are chunky cream candles in glass storm vases illuminating the crazy-paving path that leads to the dining area. The whole place looks incredible.

Adonis arrives shortly after us with The Romans, who I met in the Olympic Bar in Rhodes town. He makes a beeline for Janet and wastes no time in flirting with her and telling her how beautiful she looks. He is dressed in smart, olive-coloured chinos and a white linen shirt with the top button open. He is wearing tan-coloured suede loafers on his feet and smells of expensive aftershave. His curly black hair is tousled around his coffee-coloured neck. We have a Greek god in our midst.

'So,' Adonis says, grabbing a glass of champagne from a passing tray and handing it to Janet. 'I cannot believe that you are manager to such international bands. You are so young, which means you must be very talented,' he fawns, fixing her with his huge brown eyes.

Janet is unimpressed. She's seen it all before in London and far less obviously, I would imagine.

'It's not the most difficult job in the world and I was lucky enough to be in the right place at the right time.' She shrugs. 'It's a job like any other and it's not all glitz and glamour. Some of the band members can be right little divas, not to mention the fans, who range from the mildly obsessive to the downright psychotic.'

'I bet you've got some tales to tell,' Adonis schmoozes and I can tell by Janet's face that he has stepped just a little too close and is now invading her personal space. She is saved by the arrival of Andreas and his events-organiser friend.

Over dinner and several ouzos, everyone is in relaxed mood. It has been decided that the music festival will take place in the last week in September, which gives us just under three months. The price of the tickets will be fixed at fifty euros and the event will run for four days. The main tourist season will almost be at an end then and the university students, of which several thousand are expected to attend, do not return to their studies until the beginning of October.

'My brother had a food stand at the Dremasti holy festival last month,' a man called Tinos tells me. 'He made enough money over the week to help keep his family going through the winter months.'

Tinos goes on to say that most of the Greek villages rely on tourism, although many people are virtually self-sufficient with their own vegetable patches and chickens and goats in their gardens.

'I've told Danny I'll be home in two days, but there's a flight tomorrow evening to Liverpool that I might catch,' I tell Janet, as I pick at a delicious filo pastry fig tart.

'Well, the nature of this evening was business, that's true, but I thought you might like to spend a couple of days in the sun?'

'I would really, but I just feel a bit guilty jetting off again when my marriage is still a little fragile.'

'Maybe that's all the more reason to give it a little space, although it's entirely up to you, of course,' Janet says gently.

I've decided it's Janet's domain from here on in and, despite her suggestion that I take a later flight, my mind's made up. She can take a flight to London at her own leisure, but I feel the need to go home. My marriage is just beginning to get back on track and I need to invest time in it. A huge part of me wants to stay, even though I know I'll be returning here soon enough.

There's something about this little Greek village that's wrapped itself round my heart…

CHAPTER THIRTY-SEVEN

I've booked an aisle seat on the plane but after several interruptions from a fifty-something blonde bombshell with a weak bladder I suggest we change places. It's going to be late when I get home so I want to try to sleep for a couple of hours.

'Oh, thanks, doll. I'm ever so sorry to be a pain in the backside; this over-active bladder thing has only happened since the menopause. It's all downhill after fifty,' she cackles.

I tell her it's no problem, remembering the problems my mum went through, then pull my cap down over my eyes and settle in for a snooze. I begin to dream. I'm up on the stage with New Horizons, belting out a tune, when I feel a hefty nudge in the ribs.

'Sorry, doll, but you were singing and making funny noises. There's a couple with a sleeping baby in the row behind, who didn't seem to appreciate your vocals.' She winks.

Oh my God. What is it with me? Why can't I just bloody sleep without singing or wailing? I think it must be when I'm overtired. I turn around and apologise to the couple with the baby and notice that the husband is smiling but the pale-faced wife isn't. It must be hard having a new baby, I reason. She's probably exhausted and I wonder, not for the first time, what the appeal is in taking children abroad on holiday.

There's an hour and a half of the flight left, so I decide to stay awake and engage the woman next to me in conversation.

'Did you have a nice holiday?' I ask cheerfully.

'Oh, yeah, love, it was great, thanks. We've got an apartment in Rhodes near the beach, so I bob back and forth. My husband lives there all the time now. It was his dream to live there when he retired.' She smiles.

'Wasn't it your dream too?' I find myself asking, and hoping I don't sound like a nosy cow.

'To be honest, yes, it was at first. We'd spent many years holidaying in Rhodes and I was quite happy to retire in the sun. But that was before we had any grandchildren. Honey came along three years ago and I completely fell in love with her. Some days I would be just sitting on the balcony reading a book, and I would suddenly yearn to go home and give her a cuddle. So I'd book the next available flight and come back to Liverpool. We discussed moving back home, but Ken was having none of it. He's worked all his life as a builder and he's basically bloody knackered.' She laughs, then orders a gin and tonic from the drinks trolley. 'He always wanted to retire to a place in the sun, and I must admit his health's improved no end since we went out there. So, I flit back and forth and sometimes my daughter and granddaughter come out to us. It has to be before the summer months, when the temperatures reach their peak, though, as Honey's a porcelain-skinned redhead. Cute as a button she is,' she says proudly, fishing a picture out of her purse to show me a sweet toddler in a white cotton dress, with a mass of copper-coloured curls. 'It's an arrangement that suits us all. Our Joanne always laughs about the fact that we chose one of the hottest places to retire to – with three hundred days of sunshine a year – and she goes and gives birth to a ginger kid!' She guffaws, before stopping the drinks trolley on its journey back down the aisle to order another gin and tonic.

It makes me think that there are all types of marriages, and if yours works for you then I suppose that's all that matters. My neighbours Dot and Bill have been married for forty years and have never spent a night apart. Even now they still hold hands. They will probably be the type of couple that die within weeks of each other.

The next hour flies by as the woman, whose name is Irene, regales me with all kinds of humorous tales from the garden centre where she works. 'Some of those pensioners are as mad as a box of frogs,' she laughs. 'We even had a wedding there last year. A couple who had met in the garden centre café and shared a piece of carrot cake, after they'd discovered it was the last slice and had almost had a punch up, were married in the courtyard under a rose-covered archway.'

As we disembark she fishes a voucher out of her handbag and hands it to me. It's a Family and Friends 20% discount card for purchases in the Canal View Garden Centre.

'Only Monday to Friday though. Bring your mum along. The lemon drizzle cake in the café is to die for.'

There are so many lovely people in the world, I think to myself as my taxi speeds along Speke Boulevard towards home. I'm a bit concerned that the driver is going well over the speed limit, but at least I'll be home sooner than expected.

I think about Irene's marital arrangement and – having just returned from Rhodes – I reckon it sounds just about perfect. I wonder whether that kind of thing could only work with older couples though.

I arrive home just after ten thirty, when I realise I only have euros in my purse. The driver keeps his engine running as I nip inside to get some emergency cash, which I always keep in a tin in the hall cupboard.

The lamp in the lounge is gently illuminating the front garden, which I notice needs a little bit of pruning and weeding around the borders, a lone thistle almost reaching the window ledge. Maybe I ought to do a little more gardening apart from tending the small vegetable patch in the rear garden. My parents have a pretty garden at home, with a bowling-green lawn and bursts of rainbow-coloured plants and shrubs. My dad built a beautiful bridge over his garden pond, which always reminded me of Monet's garden at Giverny. Maybe it's something I will be more interested in when I'm older.

As I put the key in the front door and enter the hallway, I inhale the spices of the Bengal Kitchen and my stomach gives a little rumble. Typical Danny, I smile to myself, can't be bothered cooking for himself. I take in the sight of the littered takeaway trays on the coffee table in the lounge, but there is no sign of my husband. I also notice a half-pint glass containing dregs of beer, which is strange as he usually just drinks it straight from the can.

I open the door to the hall cupboard, where I keep my cash tin, when I hear voices coming from upstairs. I can't understand why he's got the telly on upstairs when he's forgotten to switch off the TV in the lounge. Perhaps he's had one too many beers. As I make the descent up the cream-carpeted staircase to announce my arrival, I freeze halfway up in horror. The voices are replaced by giggling and far more intimate sounds as I realise with a pounding heart that Danny is in our bedroom. And he's not alone.

CHAPTER THIRTY-EIGHT

A strange composure envelops me as I descend the stairs and go outside to pay the taxi driver. I'm surprised Danny hasn't heard the car outside the house, but then I suppose he is rather preoccupied.

I go back inside and walk calmly upstairs. I push the bedroom door open and I'm greeted by the sight of Danny's bare backside. The young woman is the first to spot me; she looks like a rabbit caught in the glare of headlights. She's shaking Danny's shoulders and trying to push him off her, but he ignores her, obviously thinking it's some kind of foreplay. I stand in the doorway, taking in the whole performance, before he finally registers that there is somebody watching him and turns around to meet my gaze.

'Jesus Christ!'

I say nothing.

The woman, who actually looks no more than about nineteen or twenty years of age, is off the bed and scrambling for her clothes with a terrified look in her eyes.

'He told me he was separated,' she says, shooting Danny a disgusted look. 'I'm so sorry.'

'Just get out,' I say quietly, and she does as she's asked, gathering her bag and flying down the stairs and out of the front door, probably grateful that I didn't skull-drag her down the stairs. I'm not angry with her. How was she supposed to know that he's a cheating bastard who is very much married, with a wife who has only gone away for a couple of days.

Danny is as white as a sheet.

'I thought you weren't coming back until tomorrow,' he says, as if it's my fault for coming home early.

'Downstairs,' I say firmly.

Danny looks a bit uncertain. He's probably thinking about the recently sharpened knives in the knife block in the kitchen.

I feel numb as I turn on my heel and descend the stairs. I go into the kitchen and quietly put the kettle on for coffee before placing two mugs on a tray and carrying it into the lounge. There are no late-night floods of tears, just a quiet feeling of stomach-churning resignation that my marriage can't be saved.

Danny appears in the doorway of the lounge and can't meet my gaze. 'I don't know what to say,' he says, coming to sit on the chair opposite me. 'I didn't plan it. I just went out for a few drinks with the lads and ended up completely wasted.'

Just like the last time, he doesn't appear to be that drunk.

'Anyway, I know it's no excuse, but I just hate being on my own,' he says, staring at the floor pathetically.

'What, even for a few days? I managed without you for weeks without jumping into bed with someone else,' I say as I sip my strong coffee.

I can't bear to look at his face.

'That's because you're a good person,' he says quietly. 'The thing is, Mandy, you can do so much better than me. I've proved I'm a shit for the second time now. You deserve so much better.'

'This is only the second time you've cheated then?' I enquire. 'Or are they the only times I know about? Can I even believe a word that comes out of your mouth?'

We talk until the sun comes up and the dawn of a new day signifies the end of our marriage. Maybe my mother was right, all those years ago, when she expressed surprise at me getting married so young. I've come to realise over the years that my mum is a very wise lady. But you never take advice when you're young, do you? You always think you know better.

The funny thing is I'm grateful, in a way, that I walked in on this situation, otherwise I think Danny and I would have limped along far longer than was necessary, slowly destroying each other.

It's almost six in the morning when Danny walks into the kitchen and flicks the kettle on for more coffee, before I go for a shower. I am aching all over with tiredness and need to sleep. I'm due in at work at two o'clock this afternoon and feel I should make the effort. Brian has been very understanding so far but I don't want to push it.

As I stand in the shower the tears come. They roll freely down my face like a stream racing down a mountain. They are not tears of pain, I realise, but tears of immense sadness for the end of this chapter of my life.

I dry my hair and slip into the cool sheets of the bed in the spare room. I think of all the time I've invested in the marriage and can't face the thought of having to do it all again with somebody new. Maybe I won't. Perhaps I'm destined to be on my own from now on. I don't mind my own company. In fact, I quite like it.

CHAPTER THIRTY-NINE

I return to work at the Pig and Whistle and quickly inform everybody of the end of my marriage, and request that they say no more about it, which they respectfully acknowledge.

At breaktime I'm checking my phone for messages, when I discover a missed call from Janet. I text her, telling her about me and Danny, and within two minutes my phone is ringing.

'Oh my goodness, are you alright?' she asks, sounding genuinely concerned.

'Yeah, I think so,' I say honestly. 'I literally found him in bed with someone else.'

I hear a gasp at the other end of the line.

'Perhaps it was meant to be – me coming home early like that – or I might never have discovered what he was up to. I always said I would never forgive him a second time. I'm not quite sure why I forgave him the first time really. Something to do with not failing, I think.'

'Not to mention hellfire and damnation from the Catholic Church,' she reminds me.

She has a point. It was instilled in us from a very early age that divorce was a no-go area. I found out in later years, however, that it very much depended on the reason for divorce as to whether you burned in hell or not. And it seems that adultery is scriptural grounds for divorce, so I am saved from the burning pit of the abyss.

'What now, then?' Janet asks, her voice full of concern.

'I'm not sure, to be honest. We'll probably have to sell the house. Neither of us can afford to run it on our own and I'm not sure I'd want to live there anyway. Danny can share a room in a mate's flat in town, so he's sorted. There are actually four bedrooms above the pub. Brian has one, but the other three are vacant. They'll need airing but are reasonably decorated, as Brian refurbished them a couple of years ago when he toyed with the idea of bed and breakfast. It never came off, but the rooms are OK and I can have one for a peppercorn rent, if I want one.'

'Hmm... that might not be such a bad idea. Give you a chance to save.'

'I was thinking the same. It's not ideal, but hopefully it won't be forever and I'll never be late for work,' I say, realising that I've even managed a smile.

'And you can come down to London whenever you want, you know, for a change of scenery. I really mean that.'

To my surprise, I think that may be rather a nice idea. I've grown up a lot since my schooldays and have come to realise that Janet is a pretty good sort. And I think I'm pretty alright too.

'I was going to phone you later anyway,' she says. 'I had a really lovely time in Thakos. In fact, I haven't long arrived home. The people there are just so lovely. They don't have very much in those villages, but they are all so grateful for what they do have. It makes you think...' She tails off. 'Anyway, all systems set for September.

There's a real buzz from the musicians. You missed a brilliant impromptu show after you left. I think I'm going to stay during the festival week myself. I might even be able to persuade Simon to come with me,' she says brightly.

We finish our conversation and I quickly nip to the toilet before returning to the bar area, which is heaving with people. A coach trip en route to Southport has just rocked up, as the satnav has taken the group from Burnley in completely the wrong direction. They have called in here feeling ravenous, and asking if we do pensioners' specials. We don't – I'm expecting a mutiny.

'We don't do any specials, ladies and gents, because as you will discover from the menu the food is very reasonably priced. It's freshly made, which may involve a small wait, but we will gladly provide unlimited refills of tea and coffee while you wait for your order.'

There are mutters and nods of agreement as Lyndsey shows the forty diners to two large window tables, before diving into the kitchen and telling the chefs to gird their loins for an onslaught of fish and chips. Mutiny averted, I think.

An hour and a half later, the pensioners have been fed and watered and are complimenting us on their wonderful lunch.

'It's a blessing in disguise our driver getting us lost,' says one blue-rinsed old dear, smiling as she departs. 'That was the best lunch I've had in a long time, and as long as we've got time for a game of bingo and a walk along the promenade I'm happy.'

Brian sets them on their way with clear directions to their destination and they all wave until they are out of sight and heading for the motorway.

'It's good to have you back at the helm,' Brian says, as he pats my arm with his Cumberland sausage fingers. 'We've missed you.'

He waddles off to the microbrewery, as Lyndsey and I clear the pensioners' tables and tidy the bar area.

And I agree. It's good to be me again.

CHAPTER FORTY

Hayley is reading the pages of a well-known tabloid and shaking her head in disbelief.

'Honestly, the state of her. As if Gary would go anywhere near a little tart like that!' she says, poking the photograph in the newspaper with such force that she puts her finger through it.

Rhianna from Runcorn has sold her kiss-and-tell story to the well-known tabloid, claiming she spent the evening with him at his luxury apartment on the Liverpool waterfront.

'Stupid cow hasn't even done her research properly or she'd know that we live together now. Where was I supposed to have been when all this was taking place?' Hayley rants. 'And why do the bloody newspapers believe it?'

For a split second, I wonder whether this liaison could have taken place somewhere else and the girl is embellishing the truth, but quickly remind myself that Gary and Hayley adore each other and are usually inseparable.

'Hazard of the job, I suppose,' I say, crossing the room and wrapping my friend in a hug. 'There are loads of these little slappers looking for their fifteen minutes of fame. They know the accused never take them to court as it just adds fuel to the fire in the eyes of the public. And who pays all the court costs? Not the person playing games, that's for sure.'

'You're right.' She smiles. 'Gary said the same thing. We're never apart in the evenings, so I know it's a load of balls, but I don't want people to think I'd be accepting of that situation, that's all. I'd never put up with that shit and he knows it. I'm not a prostitute.'

She's right about this. She's a smart cookie, Hayley, as well as being impossibly gorgeous. She could have anyone she wants and I think Gary Cooke is well aware of this.

'So, forget about it,' I say, screwing up the offending news article and tossing it in the bin. 'Tomorrow's fish-and-chip paper. Talking of fish and chips, shall we go and get some lunch?'

'OK. Not fish and chips, though. It's Sunday, which can only mean one thing.'

'Carvery at Duke's,' we say in unison.

'Mmm, yeah, roast beef and Yorkshire pudding,' I say.

'Roast chicken for me every time.'

'Maybe lamb with mint sauce and crispy roast potatoes.' I'm beginning to salivate.

'I've never been able to eat roast lamb since we were kids,' says Hayley, reminding me of something I had pushed firmly to the back of my mind.

We'd gone on a day trip to north Wales with Gillian Taylor in our street, and me, Gill and Hayley had a wonderful time on the beach at Llandudno. We strolled along the pier eating ice cream, and rode on the helter-skelter and the swing boats. Our day was ruined on the journey home when Gillian's dad pulled up at the roadside near some rolling hills, where sheep and lambs were lazily grazing. He got out of the car and jumped a low barbed-wire fence and proceeded to wrestle a startled, bleating lamb, before putting it in the boot and closing the lid.

He jumped back into the driver's seat of the Ford Mondeo as though nothing had happened, with me and Hayley sitting there with our mouths hanging open in shock. Gillian never uttered a single word as she immersed herself in her teen magazine. Her dad was a butcher, and he proceeded to take the lamb home, slaughter it, bone and wrap the joints, before selling them down at the pub for a tidy profit.

My mother got wind of the whole thing from one of our neighbours at the hairdressers and forbade me from ever hanging around with the family again, declaring them 'barbarians'. She ran into Gillian's father a few days later in the street and told him exactly what she thought of him.

'So don't you eat meat, then?' he'd asked, in reply to her protestations.

'Yes, I do,' she'd answered calmly. 'But I like to buy it from a butcher's shop. I wear leather shoes, too, but I don't go and scalp a cow in a field!' This rendered him speechless, although I think that was probably due more to the expletives my mother had used, as she was generally considered very ladylike, with her penchant for gloves and occasional hats.

'Oh, yes! Gillian's dad and the lamb! I'd forgotten all about that. Your mum gave him a right mouthful, didn't she? I remember my mum telling me that she'd heard he'd had a roasting from "the duchess".'

'The duchess?' I say in surprise. 'Is that what people called my mum?'

'Yeah, but in the nicest possible way. She gets on with everyone, doesn't she, your mum? But she has such style. I think she stood out in the street really; never one for idle gossip, but quite happy to give practical, honest advice.'

I suddenly feel quite proud of my mum. She was never one to compromise her style or her beliefs, no matter where she lived.

'So, what about Gary then?' I ask.

'What about him?'

'Is there any point in asking him if there's even a grain of truth in the story? I'm sorry, Hayley, but I have to ask.'

'No, honestly, there isn't. I'm with him most of the time and even when I'm not, I trust him. There's no point having a relationship otherwise is there?'

I think about this. I trusted Danny implicitly and he let me down. He tried to make out like it was my fault for working so many hours at the pub, but the fact is he never spoke to me. Never tried to put things right. There was no communication between us, he simply went off and did as he pleased.

'No, you're right, of course. Without trust, there's no point to a relationship. I'm sure it's a load of rubbish too. Just someone after their name in the papers. Anyway, come on, get a shift on. Duke's gets packed out on a Sunday and I'm starving.'

I pick my bag up when a text pings through. It's from Costas. He tells me how much he enjoyed meeting Janet and how she had made quite an impression on the people of Thakos. He says he hopes all is well with me. I'm not sure how to tell him about Danny so I just reply to say that I'm looking forward to the next trip to Thakos.

Costas tells me that he is looking forward to seeing me again and has thought about me often since my visit to Greece.

If I'm honest, I've been thinking about him too. He's the total opposite of Danny – and perhaps that's exactly what I need. But do I really want to risk my heart being broken for a second time?

CHAPTER FORTY-ONE

Duke's is a popular restaurant at the top of Duke Street, which has a reputation for great food and fabulous carveries in particular. It's packed to the rafters every Sunday with diners that range from loved- up couples, who have only just got out of bed at midday, to large family gatherings celebrating special occasions, or just the fact that it's the weekend and catching up with each other.

It's an old Victorian gin palace and the restoration has left the stunning historical features of the building intact, which makes it a glorious place to dine. There's an enormous bar with a mirrored backdrop, where every type of spirit is displayed. The high ceiling seems to go on forever, with a rose-patterned skylight at the pinnacle. The carved wooden seats are dark brown with green leather upholstery and have a feeling of grandeur about them. The highly polished floor is original and uneven, and the whole place has such a sense of history that it's hard not to imagine raucous nights of sailors and prostitutes downing flagons of ale and singing sea shanties.

The place is bursting at the seams but we manage to slide into a corner table just as a middle-aged couple are leaving.

'I'm starving!' says Hayley as the waitress appears and gives us our ticket, which means we can go up to the carvery as soon as we are ready. She quickly takes our drinks orders and is back in a flash with two cold pints of amber-coloured cider. I wonder where Hayley puts her food, as she appears to grow leaner and fitter by the day. I briefly considered, at one time, whether or not she was bulimic, as I had never seen anybody eat so much food without gaining an ounce. I discounted this idea when I once spent almost every minute with her on holiday and never remember her puking in the bathroom or spending excessive amounts of time in there.

I only have to look at a roast potato and it takes up residence on my hips, along with its friends: burger, cream cake and curry (OK, lots of curries). I walk miles and work hard to keep the pounds at bay, but the fact is I'm a shapely woman who can quickly become chunky, if I don't watch it. Hayley has a lean, boyish figure and is constantly telling me she would love my boobs, while I would kill for her long, tanned legs. We're never satisfied, are we?

I can see Hayley listening in to the conversation of the couple at the next table. She's a real people watcher, Hayley, even more so than me.

'She's just said her new boss has got a chin like the corner of Curry Street,' she whispers to me. 'I wonder how big the corner of Curry Street is? And where do all these weird sayings come from?'

'You mean like saying someone's the bee's knees?'

'Or the cat's whiskers.'

'The dog's bollocks.'

'Ugh, the dog's bollocks. Sounds gross!'

'But that's the ultimate compliment. When something is the dog's bollocks it's the very best.'

'I know – weird, isn't it?'

I'm salivating as we queue for the carvery. The aroma of the huge golden turkey is competing with the scent of the succulent beef, and I don't know what to choose. There is also the biggest side of ham I have ever seen. Giant, puffed up Yorkshire puddings like golden cushions beckon for me to pile them on my plate.

'What will it be then?' asks the young chef, smiling, with sharp knives poised over the great hunks of gleaming roasts.

I dither. 'Ooh... the beef, I think... I just fancy roast beef and Yorkshire pudding. That ham looks good though... so does the turkey... I've got too much choice here,' I say, grinning.

'Bit of everything?' he suggests as he begins slicing into the huge side of ham.

Well, I didn't want to appear greedy and say that myself, but as he's suggested the idea I decide to go with it. I manage to pile some broccoli, cauliflower, carrots and roast potatoes on top of my meat feast, with a huge Yorkshire pudding on the summit of the food mountain.

We squeeze our way back to our table and begin the assault on our food, oohing and aahing with every mouthful. I've eaten just about every type of cuisine in various international restaurants at home and abroad, but I reckon a good old roast dinner is very hard to beat.

'How are you?' asks Hayley, as we sit back stuffed to the gills and yet still perusing the dessert menu. 'I mean how are you *really* feeling now that it's over with Danny? Do you think it's completely finished?' she asks, taking a sip of her cider.

I sigh deeply. I've done nothing but ponder this myself. I know I'd be a fool to return to a relationship with trust issues, but I do still miss him. A lot. Despite what he did. We had been together a long time after all. On balance, I think I'm doing alright though. I'm busy at work and I have some great friends there, who are always ready for a chat and a laugh. They really do cheer me up no end. And, of course, Hayley always has and always will be there for me whenever I need her.

If only we could have a crystal ball to look into the future. How many bad decisions would be averted in our lives? I would never have spent so long with somebody just to break up with them; it seems such a precious waste of time. We never had any children together, which brings me sadness and relief in equal measure. I could never imagine having children with anybody other than Danny, but I guess that's because he's all I've ever known. Yet again my mother's words of wisdom pop into my head: 'You can't stay together out of sentiment.' And, of course, she is absolutely right. A relationship deserves a hundred per cent trust and commitment on both sides. I would never have cheated on Danny.

'I'm fine,' I say to Hayley, and I really mean it. I realise it's time to look ahead and move on. I reach over and place my hand over her tanned fingers with the beautifully manicured red nails. 'I've got great people around me. Don't you worry about me. There is something I need your advice on though,' I say, adopting a serious expression.

'Yeah, anything, what is it?'

'Sticky toffee pudding or berry pavlova?' I smile.

CHAPTER FORTY-TWO

Hayley has unbelievably managed to polish off a huge slice of hot chocolate-fudge cake with ice cream, while I struggled with my berry pavlova, even though it was the lighter option.

It's turned out to be a glorious sunny afternoon, so we decide to walk down to the Pier Head to burn off some calories, but not before I've nipped to the toilet. Hayley recognises someone from the bank and, as they strike up a conversation, tells me she'll meet me outside.

I'm just washing my hands and applying some pink lip gloss when I notice somebody through the mirror staring at me.

Maybe she's admiring my long blonde hair or shade of lip gloss, I think, before turning around as she quickly averts her eyes. There's a glimmer of recognition, but I can't place it.

She glances at me again before taking a deep breath and speaking to me. 'It's Mandy, isn't it?' she says hesitantly.

'Yeah,' I say, before searching her face for a clue.

'I'm Sarah,' she almost whispers. 'Sarah Kelly.'

She looks nothing like the Sarah Kelly I remember from school. She is tall, dark and, well… gorgeous.

'Sarah?' I finally manage to say, before remembering that this is the woman who had an affair with my husband. Why the hell would she want to speak to me?

'Look,' she says, quickly noting the darkening expression on my face. 'I could have legged it out of here, but the fact is I wanted to speak to you. I wanted to say sorry.'

'Sorry. What for?' I realise I want to hear this.

Sarah looks momentarily stunned.

'So, go on, what are you sorry for?' I repeat, keeping my tone even.

'Well, for seeing Danny,' she says uncertainly. 'But it was after you broke up, or at least I thought it was.'

Suddenly her face turns pink and to my great surprise she begins to cry. Huge, heaving sobs. I wasn't expecting that. *Where's Hayley when I need her?*

'What are you crying about?' I ask, in an attempt to disguise my soft side, which is actually beginning to feel sorry for her.

'Oh, I'm sorry,' Sarah says, going into the toilet cubicle and grabbing some tissue to dab at her eyes. 'I just feel such a fool. I worked with Danny and we got along really well, as mates only, obviously, but he always paid me loads of compliments about the way I looked.' She stops for a moment. 'I'm sorry if this is hard for you to hear… Anyway, he told me you were separated, so we started going out together, just for a drink after work at first.'

I recall the nights he came home later than usual, saying he'd gone on a roadside recovery.

'Go on,' I say.

'Well, we started seeing each other properly after a few weeks and then he moved into my flat. It all happened so quickly. Obviously I thought you were apart by then. I swear I would have never gone anywhere near him had I known you were still together. But

I bloody fell for him, didn't I? Next thing he's back with you, but his attention was wandering somewhere else, towards a new, young receptionist at work called Kate.'

'With waist-length dark hair, by any chance?' I ask, as I recall the young woman fleeing down the stairs at home.

'Yes.' She sniffs, dabbing at her eyes before a fresh bout of tears erupt. 'He cuts me dead in work now. I just feel so used.'

'And what… Am I supposed to feel sorry for you?' I snort.

Sarah meets my gaze. 'No, of course not. I don't expect that at all. I just wanted you to know that I never would have looked sideways at him had I known you were still together – still married. I'm not that kind of girl.'

I know this to be true. She was always a nice girl at school. Not quite one of the A-team crowd, but a mid-division sort who was well liked by all.

'Look,' I say gently. 'It sounds as if he's hurt us both. I do believe you when you say you thought he was single. But forget about him. I was with him for nearly fifteen years and I'm moving on. He obviously wants to lead the single life again, so let him. You can do better.'

I don't take any pleasure in seeing her distress. I suppose it took some guts to approach me in the first place. To my surprise, I don't feel anything, really, other than a massive realisation that I am definitely doing the right thing in moving on. I join Hayley outside, who is now chatting to a group of flirtatious lads who are having a cigarette. I link arms with her as we set off towards the Pier Head to enjoy the rest of the day.

CHAPTER FORTY-THREE

The searing heat is massaging my aching bones as I sink down into the warm sea. I'm lying on my back and floating along, thinking how I might just like to stay here forever. There's the distant sound of a horn coming from a ship that is travelling across the Mediterranean towards Corfu. I think of the paths of the ancient mariners, as they visited the Greek Islands to deliver silks and spices from far-flung lands. The ship's horn is fading into the distance as the water beneath me suddenly feels surprisingly cool. My foot jerks into something solid, and I wake to find myself in a stone-cold bath and the alarm clock on my mobile phone is bleeping furiously. *Shit!* My shivering body steps out of the bath and into the warmth of my towelling robe, which is draped over the heated towel rail.

There's a couple coming to look at the house today. We put it on the market several weeks ago and there hasn't been much interest until just recently. I suppose it's because the weather has improved again after a surprisingly wet spell in July.

It's hard to explain how I feel about showing potential buyers around our home. *Our* home. The words stick in my throat. The home that we spent eight years lovingly creating will soon be ripped apart and replaced by something to the taste of the new owners. They won't care how we deliberated over the kitchen until we almost fell out over it, or how we spent hours traipsing around the shops looking for the perfect-sized sofa that wouldn't swamp the fairly modest-sized lounge. There will be no thought given to the hours spent cultivating the small vegetable patch at the end of the garden, which has given us a steady supply of beetroot, carrots and onions over the years. We were never very successful at growing potatoes, but as they are so cheap to buy from the local farm shop it didn't really matter.

As I towel myself dry, I can feel tears threatening to spill over and I give myself a brisk talking to.

I knew the time would come to give up the house. The room at the Pig and Whistle is all ready for me, but I've been staying here as long as I can. Danny is paying half the mortgage until the house is sold, and is currently enjoying a bachelor lifestyle at his friend Adam's flat. It's not in the best area of the city, but the cheap-and-cheerful rent gives them disposable income to enjoy the entertainment of the city, namely the bars and nightclubs. We are both putting in extra hours at work, although Danny's overtime is to fund his new-found lifestyle, whereas mine is to take my mind off the failure of my marriage.

With hindsight, I'm not sure we should ever have married at all. I loved Danny in the beginning, there is no doubt about that, but we were just kids. I remember my wedding day being the best day ever but, looking back, I realise that this was largely due to the excitement of the huge gathering of family and friends, not to mention the gifts of money and a table full of presents. I don't recall any stomach-churning emotion as we exchanged our vows, but more an acceptance that this was the expected thing to do.

There was no passion back in the bridal suite on our wedding night either, as Danny paid several visits to the bathroom, vomiting the entire contents of a litre bottle of Bacardi.

I'm dressed and downstairs when the doorbell rings to announce the arrival of the prospective buyers. I welcome the suited estate agent and the excited newly married couple into the house and offer them a cup of tea, which they all politely decline.

'No, thanks,' says the bubbly young woman with the cropped platinum hair. 'We thought we'd have a look around and then go and have a drink at the pub down the road. I think it's called the Pig and Whistle.'

I hope they're not time wasters.

The estate agent says he will take an incoming call outside and tells us he'll 'leave us to it'

'They do a nice Sunday lunch at that pub,' I say, smiling.

'Ooh, even better,' says the handsome husband with the goatee beard. I notice they have their hands firmly held for the duration of the house visit and reckon they can't have been married for very long.

'So, is this your first home?' I ask, as we make our way around each room, to which they give very positive comments.

'Yes, we've been looking for a few months now. We've been renting, but we want something outside of the city. This is the first time anything like this has come on the market. It looks like a lovely place to bring up kids,' she says, exchanging a loving glance with her husband.

I think of the similar dreams I shared with Danny and hope their story has a happier ending.

They seem particularly impressed with the garden, which has a fair-sized lawn and a flagged patio area. The young wife enthuses over the vegetable patch, telling me that she loves growing things and currently has window boxes full of herbs in their city flat.

I really like them and after half an hour of looking around, I'm convinced they are genuine about wanting to buy the house.

'Have you had much interest?' asks the husband.

I tell a little white lie and say that there have been several interested parties, with one of them coming for a second viewing next week. They look at each other.

'If we were to make you an offer today, would you take it off the market? We love it,' they say, exchanging more affectionate glances. 'It's exactly what we've been looking for.'

'Oh right, brilliant,' I reply, almost too stunned to speak.

They go off and have another wander around the garden, before coming back inside to make me an offer. In the current market, Danny and I agreed that we'd go five grand below the asking price, but to my surprise the couple offer only two grand below. I snatch their hands off without giving away too much excitement. There won't be much profit once we've paid off the mortgage, but there will be a few thousand pounds to make a fresh start, and that's all I want now.

We go inside and open a bottle of Prosecco that's been sitting there waiting for an appropriate celebration, and toast their future.

'Oh, it's just so lovely,' the wife, whose name is Jane, keeps saying. 'And I love the décor. That stone fireplace works so well with those cream walls. We'll hardly change a thing. I'm having fabric sofas though.' She smiles. 'I find leather so cold, especially on a winter's morning.'

'I agree. Leather's more practical if you have kids though,' I suggest. 'Wipe clean.'

'Oh, I hadn't thought of that,' she says, laughing. 'But we're not planning on having any just yet.'

I really like these two and think that they will fit into the small community very well. I tell them about my job at the Pig and Whistle and inform them of the quiz night on a Tuesday and the forthcoming barbecue in two weeks, which may give them a chance to meet some of the locals. They seem really excited at the prospect.

'I'll ring the estate agent first thing in the morning and they will be in touch with you. I'm not in a chain so the sale could go through pretty quickly,' I tell them.

Jane gives me a big hug and her husband Aidan shakes my hand warmly. I have a feeling these two could become good friends. Maybe if me and Danny'd had more couples to socialise with our marriage might not have become so stagnant.

They wave out of the window of their white Mini until they disappear around the corner, and I go back inside. I am just pouring the remains of the Prosecco into a champagne glass when my phone beeps a text message. It's from Janet, who is in Liverpool next weekend at the Echo Arena with one of her new bands. Her husband Simon is coming along, too, and she wonders if I'd like to meet up. They will probably stay in one of the stylish new hotels on the waterfront at the Albert Dock. I fire back a message saying that would be great. I'll ask Hayley and Gary along too. It's only after I suggest the idea I realise that I won't be part of a couple, and the realisation startles me. I suppose it's something I will just have to get used to.

CHAPTER FORTY-FOUR

I knock on the black-painted door of the city-centre venue and wait a few minutes for a response. There's no signage outside the bar or even a door number. It's just an inconspicuous door on an unremarkable street. Unless you know about it.

A few minutes later a doorman appears and, when I tell him I am with Gary Cooke's party, allows me to enter. Janet is probably more well-known nationally, but a Liverpool player in his home town has real celebrity status.

I follow the barman up a narrow staircase before entering a large, softly lit room, the strains of jazz music in the background.

Janet spots me first and she raises her hand and beckons me over. 'I've ordered you a cocktail!' She grins, pointing to a blood-red drink in a tall glass. 'I know you like vodka so it has a vodka base. It's called a Caribbean Calypso.'

'Ooh, thanks,' I say, taking a quick sip before greeting the others.

Janet's husband, Simon, is on his feet with his hand outstretched as Janet introduces us. He's wearing a smart shirt with a cardigan over it, giving him a clean-cut, preppy look.

'I must say I love this place. It's like a secret speakeasy with the red-velvet curtains and the jazz music. And the style of the barmen... I love it!' enthuses Janet.

The barmen in question wouldn't look out of place in a spaghetti western, with their red waistcoats over white shirts and their designer beards and moustaches.

The conversation is flowing, when two slightly self-conscious young men approach Gary and ask him if he would mind having a photo with them. I think to myself that it must be a right drag being recognised every time you go out, but Gary doesn't seem to mind and obliges the young men with a smile. They thank him fervently before no doubt putting the photo on Facebook, for all their friends to admire.

I was worried about not being part of a couple when I came here tonight but thankfully it's been OK. I'm on my second cocktail, when the conversation invariably turns to the Greek concert preparations.

'So, how's everything going with the festival?' I ask Janet, while Simon laughs at Hayley, who is telling a funny story.

'Pretty much perfect. The Greek acts are all on board, as are the international bands. Andreas and his friend have sorted all the legalities, and the food stalls and toilet facilities have all been arranged. I spoke to Adonis, who tells me there's a real buzz about the village and the musicians from his bar can't wait to perform.'

'Sometimes it's hard to believe that it's really going ahead,' I say as I pick a piece of pineapple from my cocktail. 'To think I had the idea for it by just staring at that field.'

'With Costas, as I recall. Sounds quite romantic, staring out across the empty field together,' teases Janet.

'It wasn't, actually. I'd just been for a bit of a walk and I bumped into him.'

'If you say so.' She smiles. 'Well, anyway, empty land has to be used for something. And as they say in the movie *Field of Dreams:* "If you build it, they will come."'

I hope she's right.

The evening passes in a relaxed manner as we dine on steak and chips. Us girls have an ice-cream cocktail called 'a floating mermaid' for dessert, while the boys opt for another bottle of beer.

It's going to be a busy day tomorrow, because I'm unpacking more boxes at the Pig and Whistle, where I'm now staying. This evening has been lovely, though, and the mention of Costas has suddenly made me feel less lonely.

CHAPTER FORTY-FIVE

Things are not too bad staying at the pub. The bedroom is huge, with a modern en suite and it overlooks the car park, with miles of rolling hills and farmland beyond. Summer has been quite a blast here, with lots of barbecues and fundraising days, as the weather, after a wet start, has turned out to be glorious. I'm slowly coming to terms with the single life, which I intend to enjoy for a while, despite the attempts of some keen male customers to persuade me otherwise.

The house sale went through in the quickest time possible and Jane and Aidan have, as I predicted, settled in well and are already regular visitors to the pub. Jane has even started a book group, which has been very well received by the local community. I joined them reading their first novel, although I struggled with the dark themes in the story. It felt strange going into our old house at first, as nothing much has changed apart from some new sofas and some very tasteful soft furnishings.

And now it's almost the end of September and I can hardly believe that I'm packing my suitcase in readiness for the Thakos music festival. Costas has informed me that there's great anticipation for miles around and it's all over social media now too! The Facebook page that has been set up by Janet is showing that thousands of people are hoping to attend the event. I'm so looking forward to being back at Sea View Apartments, where I am informed by Costas that a swimming pool has just been installed.

Simon and Janet will be staying at Sea View Apartments for a few days, too, arriving before the UK bands headline. It turns out Simon is a really lovely guy. He and Janet have been up here a couple more times since the Liverpool Arena visit. He's a self-made millionaire with no airs and graces about him whatsoever, and he clearly adores Janet. I've watched her withdraw her hand from his once or twice, as she's uncomfortable with public displays of affection. But Simon told me over a few glasses of wine one evening that Janet is becoming more accustomed to his affectionate nature; it's simply that she has never experienced anything like it before. I feel so happy for Janet that she has such an understanding and considerate husband.

I've had to pretty much take all of my annual holidays over this last three months, but I suppose it's a one-off this year and I can't think of a nicer place to enjoy a holiday than a sun-drenched Greek island. I've just been trying on some of my summer clothes and find to my dismay that a few of my dresses have become a bit tight again. I remember all the lunch dates with Hayley, which have included roast dinners and copious amounts of alcohol, so it's not surprising really.

I've always loved my food. As I child I was always hanging around the kitchen, inhaling the fragrant aromas of food in eager anticipation. I would peer through the oven door, watching the cakes rise, desperate to sink my teeth into the light-as-a-feather cakes my mother would bake. Luckily, I have a very small waist, which gives me an hourglass figure, but I do have to rein myself in now and again.

There's a gentle tap on my door and I'm surprised to find that it's Brian. His room is at the other end of a long landing, close to the second wooden staircase that leads to the bar area. Our paths rarely cross.

'I'm off out shortly, so I may not see you before you leave. I just wanted to give you this. I found it in the pocket of a summer jacket from last year's holiday to Spain.' He hands me fifty euros. 'Don't think I'll be going abroad again in a hurry, it's far too hot for me,' he says, chuckling.

I give him a hug and can just about get my arms around his huge frame. I couldn't ask for a better boss, who, over the years, has become a true friend.

'Thanks for the money, Brian - and for everything.'

'No problem. Have a safe journey, love,' he says, as he waddles back to his room.

I suddenly get a wave of anticipation. In just over a week Thakos village will be holding a music festival to rival anything in Athens, or anywhere else for that matter. There are top acts headlining this event and I had the inspiration for the whole thing. I can hardly believe it. *Me! Who'd have thought?* I watched a programme on TV once about a man who just set about doing anything he wanted and never saw any obstacles. He reckoned people spend too long just thinking about things rather than just going for it.

I hear the tooting of a car horn in the car park, which tells me my taxi has arrived to take me to the airport. And I haven't even finished packing! I open the sash window and gesture I'll be five minutes, to which the driver gives an expressionless nod and turns off the running engine.

I throw the last bits and pieces in the case and take a quick trip to the loo. I stuff the fifty euros from Brian into my bag and I'm ready to go.

Downstairs I say my goodbyes to the staff amid comments of 'you lucky cow' and Lyndsey saying she wished she was back in Ibiza again.

'Well, this will be the last holiday I'll be having in a while,' I say, 'so I intend to make the most of it. See you all soon.'

As the taxi joins the motorway for the airport I can barely contain my excitement…

CHAPTER FORTY-SIX

The Sea View Apartments look stunning. Costas had recently told me that the addition of a pool and a poolside snack bar has seen bookings steadily rise and they are now fully booked right through until the beginning of October. The buzz of the music festival has no doubt had an impact on bookings too.

Andreas welcomes my arrival with a huge grin. 'Mandy!' he says with genuine warmth. 'You are here! Why did you not ring from the airport? I could have collected you.'

'Well, I have to keep the local taxi drivers in business, don't I?'

Andreas ponders this for a second before breaking into a laugh. 'You are very kind,' he says. 'Always thinking of other people.' He beckons me into the dining room, which looks stylish and cool with its ice-blue painted walls and white voile curtains waving gently in the slight breeze. Over lunch of an omelette and Greek salad, he tells me about the excitement in the village.

'Nikos is planning to open his restaurant for the festival, although there has been some problem with the electricity. People are also setting up barbecue areas and food stalls. In fact, they are planning to sell anything and everything.' Andreas grins. 'There is great anticipation. It's not every day international bands come and play at our little village.' He beams proudly. 'You should go along later and see how they are getting along. I will introduce you to some people.'

I suddenly feel really proud. I think that Janet Dobson was meant to walk into the Pig and Whistle several months ago. Of all the bars in all the north-west she happened to walk into mine – and I'm so glad she did. It was meant to be. For the music festival and for our new friendship.

Even Hayley thinks she's really cool, despite her initial reticence when she recalled our schooldays together and Janet's penchant for Alice bands and all things wholesome. We all grow up, though. Some people say that we never really change, but I disagree. I think our basic character traits remain the same, but we grow and change with every experience in our life. I think of my own journey, as I feel a little of my old confidence returning.

There's a crashing sound outside, followed by a loud expletive. It sounds like Costas has dropped a crate of beer bottles. A dog is barking wildly.

I stroll outside into the sunshine and Costas raises an eyebrow and smiles. 'Sorry about the language,' he says.

'It's a good job those bottles were empty,' says Andreas, appearing with a brush and shovel. 'I don't want you pouring my profits down the drain.' He winks at me. 'We will hose it down later.'

'So how are you?' asks Costas, as we sit down for a coffee when he has a break.

'I'm OK, thanks.'

'Why are you alone again? Where is your husband?'

I decide to be honest about the recent developments in my marriage. 'We split up,' I say simply.

Costas is quiet for a moment before he speaks. 'Are you alright?' he asks, a concerned look on his face.

'You know what? I think I am. If I'm honest, I think things were over between us a long time ago, I just didn't want to face up to it. Anyway, there're lots of thing to distract me here.' I smile as I drain my coffee.

'Distractions can be a good thing,' replies Costas, holding my gaze. My heart gives a little flutter.

There's a palpable excitement over the next few days as the village prepares for the festival. Traffic-diversion signs are ready to be displayed, in preparation for when the main street will be pedestrianised. Lorries have been delivering food and beer to local restaurants, which are hoping to profit from the event, and technicians are due to arrive tomorrow to do a final sound check. Local children excitedly chase every new vehicle that arrives on the vast field, some of them even lucky enough to receive sweets and coins from the drivers.

I notice Annis, who is busy setting up a stall, from which she hopes to sell some beautiful carefully selected ceramics, as well some simple bracelets made with coloured thread and leather.

She waves and calls me over when she spots me. 'Mandy, how are you?' She beams. 'Can you believe this is actually happening? It's so exciting!'

Two young women, who I haven't seen before, are whispering to each other when one of them pushes the other one towards me. 'Are you Mandy?' the raven-haired teen asks.

'Yes, I am. Hi.' I smile.

'It is true, isn't it? New Horizons really are coming here, to this village,' she asks uncertainly.

'They certainly are,' I say, beaming.

A look of sheer excitement spreads across her face as she thanks me and runs back to her friend, squealing.

I chat to Annis for a few minutes, with a promise to meet up for a drink later, and I carry on walking around the site absorbing the atmosphere. I'm not sure how many Greek pots and trinkets will be sold to a hoard of invading students at a festival, but I admire Annis's optimism. Maybe some kind-hearted sons will buy something nice for their mums.

The huge stage has been erected and several of the local bands have already held some practice sessions, attracting the attention of the local teenagers who are enjoying the remainder of the school holidays, lazing about on the grass with their clandestine bottles of cheap beer.

I pass Yannis and Joan from the Olive Garden Kitchen, staking out a place for a food stall. It doesn't appear to be going well. Yannis and Nikos, a stout, balding man, are throwing their hands up in the air and throwing expletives at each other. Joan, grateful for the distraction, I think, steers me away from the warring men to a couple of white plastic chairs near a refreshment van. She buys two bottles of iced lemon tea and gives one to me.

'What are they arguing about?' I ask.

'Territory,' replies Joan, raising her eyes to the sky. 'Nikos is unable to get his restaurant fully up and running due to a problem with the electricity, so he's having a food van instead. Right in the place where Yannis was going to set up. It's a pity they never discussed it before. Anyway, love, they'll sort it out.'

Sure enough, several minutes later the shouting has stopped and the pair are hugging and patting each other on the back.

'So, love, is everything sorted with the music then?' asks Joan.

'Yep, I think so,' I say confidently. 'Janet has taken over organising the programme.'

'Oh, that's good. I'm really looking forward to it myself, so is my daughter Elyannia and her family. Who have you got presenting it?'

'Presenting it?'

'Yeah, you know, the compère. Who'll be introducing the acts and pulling it all together?'

I'm staring at her as if she's just been talking to me in Swahili. I hadn't even thought about it. The compère! I think about all the quiz nights and karaoke evenings that I have hosted at the Pig and Whistle. It can't be much different than that. Can it?

'The compère,' I say, sounding more confident than I feel. 'That would be me then.'

I can't believe I hadn't thought about who would be presenting it! And I'm surprised nobody else mentioned it either. Not even Janet. Jesus! What was I thinking? Did I expect the acts to just rock up without any introduction?

I'm strolling along the beach back to the Sea View, thinking about watching YouTube videos of people hosting Glastonbury, when my phone rings. It's Janet ringing from London. And what she has to say makes me drop my phone in shock.

CHAPTER FORTY-SEVEN

'Say that again *slowly* please, Janet, just so I know that I am not hearing things.'

'Oh, Mandy, I'm so sorry. I can hardly believe it myself. As you know, New Horizons have been doing a concert in Istanbul and now they're stranded there. There's an air-traffic controllers' strike.'

'But can't they get on a private plane?' I say, desperation rising in my voice.

'It wouldn't make any difference if they did, I'm afraid. Without air-traffic clearance all flights are grounded. There are no incoming or departing flights for the next forty-eight hours.'

Oh my God, it can't be true.

I can feel the colour draining from my face and a throbbing pain in my temples. I haven't listened to the news today so I had no idea of any airport strike action.

'But surely this might be resolved?' I almost plead to Janet as though she was personally responsible.

'Mandy, I really don't know. No one does. All they are saying is that all flights are grounded for the next two days. It's obviously being done to have maximum impact in the holiday season,' she says, sighing.

I don't want to hear this. I don't want to bloody hear it. *It can't be true!* Everything is ready here. Tomorrow the festival is kicking off with the local musicians followed by the 1990s' band Stairs, who have recently re-formed and are now touring. They've all recently arrived, expecting to be the warm-up acts for the main event.

This can't be bloody happening. Why now?

For a single split second, I wonder whether Janet is secretly smiling at my soon-to-be spectacular flop, waiting years for her revenge, but quickly admonish myself. Nobody could predict anything like this. It's just bad luck. Huge, freaking bad luck.

I'm speechless for a moment, just trying to take it all in. Surely the strike won't take several days to resolve. It simply *can't*. We've sold thousands of tickets.

My head is suddenly pounding as I race my way back to my apartment to switch on the television. Sure enough, Sky News is showing dozens of holidaymakers stranded at Istanbul Airport in Turkey.

I need a drink. I leave my apartment and go shakily downstairs to the bar, where I order a large vodka and Coke and knock it back in one go.

'You look as if you've seen a ghost,' says a concerned Costas, as he pours me another drink.

'Oh, err… I just feel a bit stressed… that's all. Maybe the scale of the event is… just beginning to hit me,' I say, fumbling for words.

I don't want to say anything to Costas just yet, although he will find out soon enough. He never has the television on during the day, but it will be on later this evening as there is a big European football match being screened. I figure there is no point in worrying anybody unnecessarily. Maybe the problem will be resolved sooner than expected.

I can't think straight and I find myself heading down to the sea, just trying to clear my head. I walk to the far end of the beach, where there is an old Greek man hiring out speedboats near a little jetty.

Several minutes later, after being given a map and strict instructions that the petrol will run out after two hours, I set off across the glistening Mediterranean Sea as I try to gather my thoughts. The wind is blowing in my hair and, if I close my eyes for a moment, I can pretend that I am vanishing off into the distance to an unknown destination.

I wish I could just bloody disappear. I feel personally responsible for this predicament, although I realise that is such an irrational thought. I think about the villagers. What will they say when the news reaches their ears? Half of the teenage population for miles around have thought of nothing else other than seeing their heroes New Horizons. Their hearts are going to be broken. I can't bear it.

I'm following the map along some small bays when realise that I have come rather a long way out. A glance behind shows the speedboat guy like a dot in the distance. I pull over to a small cove and step out onto a secluded strip of sand. I unwrap a sandwich that I bought earlier from the Beach Shack when out of nowhere a wasp appears. Then another. Within minutes there is a swarm of them attacking my ham-and-cheese sandwich. Where the bloody hell have they come from? I toss the sandwich into the sea and they disappear in search of the bread, which is now bobbing on foamy waves and attracting the attention of seabirds.

This just isn't my day. My water bottle is of little interest to predators, so at least I can keep hydrated. I take a long swig of water that is quickly becoming lukewarm.

I sometimes wonder whether there is any point at all in making plans in life. Oh, I know we have to have short-term plans, or else nothing would ever get done, but there are just so many things that can change everything in an instant. There was a couple at the Pig and Whistle who had been planning their retirement to France for many years. They lived for the day when the husband's lump-sum pension would come through so that they could head off for their new life. In some ways I think they put their life in England on hold, or at least stopped enjoying it as much, in anticipation of the French retirement. When they finally made the journey, they were involved in a collision with a lorry on a French road and the husband was killed outright. The wife returned to England to live with their daughters in the Midlands. There's a moral somewhere in that story. Perhaps it's that we should live each day to the full? The thought is enough to make me stand up and go skinny-dipping, rather than moping around.

I climb back into the speedboat and fire up the engine. My journey takes me past secluded coves and little wooden jetties. After a while, I hear a slight *phutt phutt* from the engine and realise with horror that I may be running out of fuel. I glance at my watch and I'm startled to see that I have been out for two hours and twenty minutes.

I can't be running out of fuel!

I can't even see the shoreline any more as I have curved round the rocks. I am surrounded by nothing but ocean.

No!

There's no way I'm going to make it back to the shore and I'm starting to panic, when I notice something in the distance high on some rocks. As I draw closer I see that it's a bloke doing some sea fishing. I round a corner near yet another secluded cove and my eyes are drawn up the rocks to the most stunning whitewashed villa.

My boat does another little *phutt phutt* before dying at the bottom of the rocks near the fisherman. He stands up at once and shouts down: 'Alright?'

'Err... no, not really. Think I've run out of fuel.'

To my surprise, a smile spreads across his face. 'Well, you're not the first and I don't suppose you'll be the last,' he says, as he skilfully makes his way down the rocks. 'I take it you didn't use the map.' He grins.

I suddenly feel like a fool. What was I thinking? I could have been stranded out here.

'I've got some boat fuel in my garage at the villa,' says the helpful stranger, pointing up to his stunning home. As he comes closer and removes his sunglasses I am stunned to find that I am staring into the mesmerising blue eyes of superstar Roddy Wilson!

CHAPTER FORTY-EIGHT

We scale the steps to Roddy Wilson's villa and he offers me a glass of fresh lemonade, and we take our drinks outside on an elevated patio area that commands stunning views over the Mediterranean. A housekeeper appears several minutes later with a plate of olives, Greek bread and hummus. I feel as though I am on the set of a Bond movie.

'So,' says Roddy, 'what brings you around here on your own?'

Here we go. A woman is supposed to have a rugged man at the wheel of a speedboat, fighting off sharks or any other perils that may come their way. I tell him this and he laughs.

'Nah, I just meant right out here. Most people have a whiz around the sea but are keen to keep sight of the shoreline. Bit of an adventurer, are you?'

I ponder this. There was a time when I would definitely have just taken off with wild abandon, but today I took a speedboat simply because I wanted to disappear from the village. I realise I will have to go back soon though. I tell Roddy about the problem with the festival and he listens with interest.

'That's a tough one. Especially with so many tickets already sold. I haven't watched any news today. I only arrived here this morning. I was just trying to catch some fish for a barbecue tonight.'

'Before you were so rudely interrupted,' I say.

'Don't worry about it. There was nothing biting anyway. I'll try again later. Anyway, what's this about a concert? I usually get over to Thakos at some point, although I was planning to just chill here for a few days. I'm burnt out.' He grins.

Roddy doesn't look burnt out. He looks fit, tanned and irresistible.

I proudly tell him all about the festival and how my friend was organising New Horizons as the headline act. His ears prick up when I mention Janet's name.

'I've met Janet a few times, back when she was one of the Night Owl girls,' he says, with a twinkle in his eyes. 'Nice lady.'

Janet never mentioned meeting him. Once again, I'm staggered by her connections.

Roddy sips his lemonade and is silent for a few moments, just staring out at the open sea.

It all seems a little surreal. A few hours ago, I was eagerly awaiting the arrival of one of the UK's biggest bands and quietly congratulating myself, now I'm being shown hospitality at the villa of Roddy Wilson and dreading going back.

'I might be able to help you out,' he says finally. 'I'm supposed to be taking it easy, but a village concert sounds like fun.'

I'm wondering if I've had too much sun. Maybe I've fallen asleep in the heat again and am actually hallucinating?

'*You?*' I say, barely able to get the word out of my mouth.

'Why not? If the others turn out to be a "no show"... I'll do a few tunes, if you like.'

I can't speak. I'm suddenly overcome with emotion and, to my surprise, I burst into tears. I wonder, not for the first time, what the hell I've been doing? Why could I not just have enjoyed a holiday like anybody else? I was getting over a marriage break-up, for goodness' sake. Why did I have to poke my nose into the affairs of the villagers? I suppose I've always been this way. When I'm stressed I always throw myself straight into something else to occupy my thoughts.

Roddy disappears inside and returns with a box of tissues and places them in front of me. He asks me to write my mobile number down on a piece of paper and tells me he will ring me tomorrow.

'Best not forget the fuel,' he says, jumping to his feet and heading towards a large storeroom. 'I don't do bed and breakfast,' he tells me, winking.

That's a shame.

Despite arriving back at the jetty to be greeted by the annoyed expression of the boat man, who is tapping his watch, I dare to hope that just maybe things may not turn out to be such a disaster after all.

CHAPTER FORTY-NINE

I arrive back at Sea View Apartments as Costas is putting little bowls of nuts and crisps onto the bar, ready for an expected influx of tourists and locals coming to watch tonight's football match between Manchester United and Real Madrid. Andreas invested in a fifty-inch television screen as part of his refurbishment, and Sea View has been a popular venue on match nights in recent weeks.

'Hi, would you like something to eat?' asks Costas with a cheery smile. 'There is some beef stifado in the kitchen.'

I'm not hungry. I actually feel physically sick, although I did manage a few olives and a piece of bread at Roddy's villa. *Roddy's villa!* It seems crazy now I think about it and I wonder whether I am in the middle of a strange dream.

'Err... no, I'm alright, thanks. I've got a bit of a headache actually. I think I'll have an early night and head up to my room.'

'At six thirty?'

I feign a yawn. 'Yes, I know, but I've been awake since very early this morning, I didn't have a very good night's sleep.'

'Your bed is not comfortable?' Costas frowns.

'The bed's fine, Costas. I'm just exhausted. It's the heat, I think. I'll see you in the morning,' I say, plastering a smile on my face. 'Good night.'

'You are exhausted, yet you sleep alone?' says Costas, with a playful grin. 'Maybe I will join you for a nightcap in your room later. It might help you to relax.'

Any other time I would be flattered and vaguely interested in this proposition, but today I'm stressed to hell, so I bid him a hasty good night.

Costas places some beer mats on the bar and nods good night with a slightly puzzled expression on his face.

I'm dialling Hayley's number and forcing myself to think positively. I mustn't panic. This could simply be nothing more than a temporary hitch.

'Hi, Hayley. You OK?'

'Hi, babe. Yeah, I'm fine. What's up?'

I tell her about the airport strike and she flicks the television on to Sky News. 'Oh no, what's this all about?'

'It's about one bloody big disaster, that's what. I mean can you even believe it? Just my luck.'

We've had this conversation many times about my bad luck. Hayley always puts things in perspective for me by telling me people are subject to far more unfortunate experiences than I have been privy to, and I have to agree. I am unlucky though.

Once, on a first date with a new boyfriend, we had to be evacuated onto the street when the restaurant kitchens caught fire. Then there were the fires on holiday. And, I kid you not, I actually picked out the numbers for the five numbers and the bonus ball on the National Lottery once, but couldn't place my money in time. The list goes on and on...

And now this.

'Listen, Mandy, everything will turn out alright, I can feel it. The main acts aren't due to appear for a day or two anyway, are they?'

'I suppose not. And someone else has offered to perform if the flights are still grounded.'

'Really? Who's that then?'

'Roddy Wilson.'

There is silence at the other end of the line.

'Sorry… for a minute there I thought you said Roddy Wilson.' Hayley laughs.

I tell her all about meeting him and having a drink at his villa and her responses are peppered with expletives and gasps of, 'Oh, wow!'

'I know, I can hardly get my head around it myself. Most of the crowd would be delighted with Roddy. But I just keep thinking of all those young girls who are desperate to see New Horizons. I'd feel terrible.'

'Listen,' Hayley says, finally calming down and becoming the voice of reason. 'It's not your fault if there's an airport strike, is it? People would understand, I'm sure they would. Roddy Wilson, eh, who'd have thought?'

We chat for several more minutes and she tells me about the events of her day, which have included lunch at Malmaison on the Albert Dock and a tarot-card reading, where she was told she will live in America and marry a city banker.

'I don't believe the fortune-telling most of the time. It's just a bit of fun,' says Hayley, laughing. 'I accept the good bits, though, like being told I'm going to live to a ripe old age and never have to worry about money. She's way off the mark with the American thing though. I'm more than happy right here in Liverpool with my Gary.'

We finish our call with promises to meet again soon, as she's flying over with Gary for the second part of the festival.

I'm suddenly overcome with exhaustion after my adventurous jaunt on the high seas and, even though it is now only just past seven thirty, I am soon snoozing gently on the top of my bed, the balcony curtains wafting gently in the warm summer breeze.

It's shortly after ten o'clock when there is a loud tap on my bedroom door. I adjust the straps on my top, wipe the dribble from my chin and stumble to the door in the now near-darkness. It's Costas. I have a distinct feeling of déjà vu.

'I take it you have seen the news?' he says, waving his phone at me and striding into my apartment uninvited.

Oh balls.

'Yes.' I sigh. 'I just didn't see the point in saying anything just yet.'

'We've sold ten thousand tickets!' Costas tells me, as if I need reminding.

'Well, I know that, but what can anybody do about a bloody air- traffic controllers' strike? It's hardly something you could see coming. There's no point in worrying about it. The problem could resolve itself in no time, and it's not as if there aren't plenty of other acts on the bill,' I say, trying to convince myself.

'But people are paying to see the big UK acts. They can see the local bands in Rhodes town any day of the week,' says Costas, wearing a rather deflated expression.

I'm starting to feel annoyed. It's not my fault this problem has decided to present itself during festival week. I ask Costas to leave, as my head is thumping and all I want right now is a good eight hours' sleep. The festival kicks off tomorrow afternoon, with several of the local bands from Rhodes, which I'm sure will get everyone in the right mood. And, who knows? Maybe this time tomorrow everything will be back on track for flights to resume normal service.

I decide to try to get some sleep or I'll be fit for nothing tomorrow. Somehow, though, I think it's going to be a restless night.

CHAPTER FIFTY

I toss and turn, alternating between sweating and shivering, as my flailing limbs have twisted my thin cotton sheet into a rope. I think I might be coming down with something. Flu, maybe even pneumonia, in which case I will have to be admitted to hospital for bed rest. Everyone will sympathise…

> It's early evening and, as I look out of my window, there are hordes of villagers. Some of them are screaming my name and brandishing barbecue tools. They are the Greeks of yesteryear, wielding their pitchforks in preparation for the Greek resistance to protect the villages. They are shouting my name and, before long, they are banging on the windows. I can't breathe. The banging sound is getting closer.
>
> 'What do you want with me?' I cry. 'Please, have mercy!'

The knocking sound is followed by a rattling of keys as my apartment door is flung open, and then Andreas is standing over me.

'Are you OK?' Andreas asks, as his face slowly comes into focus.

I grab the sheet, wrap it around my body and race to the balcony. 'Where are the people?'

'The people?' Andreas repeats blankly.

'Yes, there were dozens of them shouting my name and banging on the windows...' The words trail off as I realise it is yet another one of my funny dreams.

'Banging on your windows on the first floor? Who were they? A Spider-Man convention?' Andreas laughs.

I look at him and smile. Then I laugh and so does he. I chuckle again until I am soon howling a mildly hysterical belly laugh, with tears streaming down my face. Andreas has stopped laughing now and once again looks concerned. This makes me laugh even more.

'Are you ill?' Andreas finally asks, which is enough to set me off again after a short intake of breath.

I eventually regain some composure and reassure Andreas that no, I am not ill, I'm simply having nightmares. I tell him all about the possible 'no show' of the UK bands and he sits impassively and just listens.

'Some things are simply out of our hands,' he says, shrugging. 'The people will enjoy the concert anyway. They will make the best of it.'

'I'm not sure,' I tell him. 'This is supposed to be the concert of a lifetime for the village. So many people are looking forward to it. Costas tells me it's the highlight of their year... their decade!'

Once again, I think of all the young fans who must have talked of little else these past few months. How can I go ahead with hosting the festival? I can't face them, I simply can't.

'You mustn't make yourself ill over this,' says Andreas wisely. 'Today is the opening day of the festival. Many Greek bands will perform and Stairs have already arrived along with The Miracles.

They will keep everybody happy. There are still twenty-four hours until the other acts are due to arrive.

Andreas has such a calming manner that I momentarily relax. He's right. How can anyone possibly know how long this strike will last anyway? Emergency talks can resolve everything in an instant.

'Get yourself ready,' he says. 'The first acts are starting the concert in less than two hours. Adonis will be arriving soon to meet Costas. I hope to see you downstairs at the bar shortly.'

I'm about to grab a quick shower when my phone rings.

'Hi there, you alright?' asks Roddy Wilson in a chirpy tone. 'I've just been watching the news. It doesn't look like flights are going anywhere, any time soon.'

'I know.' I sigh. 'Some local bands are kicking off the concert tonight as well as Stairs, who are hugely popular again. It's a waiting game really, but I have a feeling you might just have to save the day. It's just the young girls I feel sorry for.'

'Oh, cheers!' says Roddy, laughing.

'Sorry... it's just the New Horizons fans.'

'I'm teasing. I'll try and get over to Thakos tomorrow morning, see what's what.'

I feel a sense of relief. A few hundred teeny-boppers might be disappointed if New Horizons fail to show up, but everyone loves a bit of Roddy. He knows how to work the crowds. It will be OK, I tell myself. With Roddy on board, I realise that I may have unwittingly pulled off the greatest concert ever!

CHAPTER FIFTY-ONE

I'm about to head down to the bar to meet Adonis and Costas, when my phone rings. It's my mum.

'Hi, Mum, are you OK?'

She takes a little while to answer before telling me that yes, she is OK and to remind her again when I was planning on coming home.

'Sunday, as soon as the festival has finished,' I tell her.

'Well, good luck with it all, love. I hope it goes off well. I know how much effort you have put into all of this.'

I think about this and decide that most of the effort has not been of my doing. The Greek people themselves and, of course, Janet have done most of the groundwork. I merely planted the seed.

'We must go out for lunch when you're home,' Mum says, before she rings off, 'and have a proper catch up. You can tell me all about the concert.'

I remember the voucher for Canal View Garden Centre and decide to take her there when I get home.

'It's a date. See you soon, Mum.'

'Bye, Mandy. Love you.'

I put the phone down feeling slightly uneasy. My mum is from the generation that doesn't spout 'love you' casually at the end of every sentence. I hope there's nothing wrong.

I'm jolted out of my thoughts when my phone rings yet again. This time it's Janet.

'Mandy, how's things there? I can't believe the flights are still grounded. It seems one thing money doesn't have control over is people's principles. But, don't worry. I'm working on a solution.'

'A solution? I'm intrigued.'

'Well, I don't want to say too much, in case it's not possible, but I'll be in touch.'

'Janet, I—'

The phone signal breaks up and then she's gone. I try to return her call but it goes to voicemail. A solution? I wonder what on earth that's all about. How can there be a solution? There are no flights getting out from Istanbul.

I try to push all thoughts of New Horizons out of my head as I get myself ready. There are plenty of excited musicians ready to perform, so the show can and must go on. I am finally ready to party in my black cotton jumpsuit, set off with my wolf-scene metal necklace that I bought in Dremasti.

Costas is sat on a bar stool deep in conversation with his face close to a stunning-looking woman sat next to him. A broad smile spreads across his face as he notices my arrival and stands up to greet me.

'Mandy, here you are.' He beams. 'I would like you to meet Athena. I have been telling her all about you.'

A caramel-skinned brunette, with soft, blonde highlights steps forward and shakes my hand.

She chats politely for a few minutes, but I hardly hear a word. A strange sensation has enveloped me. I'm not sure what it is exactly.

All I know is that the glossy surroundings of the bar party have suddenly taken on a dull matt veneer.

'Right, see you later,' says Athena, as she drops a kiss on Costas's cheek. 'My date's here.' She smiles, nodding towards a tall, dark, bearded bloke who has just walked in.

Costas notices my puzzled expression, before explaining that Athena is his cousin. I feel relief wash over me and my shoulders relax a little.

After a quick drink at the bar with Adonis, we all head out across the road as the first acts are tuning up. Andreas introduces me to a man called Stavros, who is wearing a cream suit and puffing on a large Cuban cigar. I quickly get the impression that he is very well respected in the village, as every single passer-by waves and says hello to him. He asks me some questions about myself and I feel like I'm being interviewed by the Godfather. We chat easily for a few more minutes before he kisses me on the back of the hand and takes his leave.

There's a steady stream of people filtering through the main street and lazing outside the local restaurants, soaking up the atmosphere, much to the delight of the restaurant owners. And there's a buzz about the place that Costas says he has never experienced before.

'My father tells me it's like the old days,' he says to me, as we cross the road with a throng of people.

'Holidaymakers would arrive here in droves and sip ouzo in the cafés, before heading down to the crowded beach,' continues Costas. 'The roads were full of tourists in hire cars, who would call in for lunch on their way to Rhodes town. Many of them would fall in love with the village and stay for a week or more.'

I can understand why.

We arrive at the festival and the air is alive with the sound of music, thanks to local DJ, Mika, who I enlisted to showcase his set for the warm-up acts. The crowd are in ebullient mood as they shimmy their hips and sing along to the pulsating rhythm. It's incredible. If it's like this with warm-up, I'm imagining what it will be like when New Horizons arrive. They *will* arrive. I must have faith.

I glance across the road to the main street and see the waiters zipping in and out of the cafés like worker bees, placing food and drinks onto heaving tables, and I can't help but feel a wave of immense satisfaction, no matter what happens.

A little later, I climb onto the stage for the first time to introduce The Romans, who kick off the concert with a cover of 'Twist and Shout' by the Beatles. I can't believe I did it! It felt nothing like hosting a quiz night at the pub, as I faced a sea of excited, expectant fans singing and waving their arms in the air. Annis and another DJ from a local bar have agreed to help with the presenting later on.

As I watch The Romans belting out their songs and rousing the crowd, I suddenly feel a little emotional. It's actually happening. And it's just too wonderful for words.

CHAPTER FIFTY-TWO

There's frenzy down at the beach the following afternoon as a speed-boat arrives and parks at the little jetty. Even with a baseball cap pulled down over his eyes, and a pair of designer sunglasses, there is no mistaking the appearance and demeanour of the enigmatic Roddy. The old Greek man on the jetty nods and exchanges a few words with Roddy, before he heads along the beach towards Sea View Apartments. That's when a group of sunbathing young women recognise him. A curvy redhead in a multicoloured bikini is on her feet in seconds, screaming and waving.

'Roddy, oh my God, girls, it's Roddy Wilson!' she is screeching to her stunned friends, who race along the scorching sand, tripping over in their haste to put their flip-flops on. Roddy is presented with various parts of the redhead's anatomy to autograph, much to his amusement.

I'm watching with laughter from my balcony and manage to catch his attention as he approaches the apartments. I usher him through reception before opening a back door and letting him into a private area.

Roddy is meeting up with Adonis and Costas, who are enjoying a cold drink inside a private gated area inside the grounds. Many years ago, Andreas commissioned a 'secret' garden for his own family and guests, which is a small area dotted with lemon trees and several wrought-iron tables and chairs. There is a stone circle pattern paved into the middle of the courtyard, giving it a focal point. In the evening, the trees are strung with candles inside storm vases, creating a magical, romantic feel.

Three hours later, as darkness begins to fall, Roddy bursts onto the stage, much to the surprise and delight of the unsuspecting crowd. He launches into the opening of bars of 'Love of My Life', and soon has the crowd in the palm of his hand. Even Joan from the Olive Garden Kitchen is strutting her stuff.

I introduced him onto the stage too. *Me!* Somehow, I told the crowd my name too. And, much to my delight, they whooped and cheered! They even began to chant '*Mandy! Mandy!*' It's insane!

I feel as if I'm in the middle of a dream. A good dream this time, I hasten to add. The crowd are going wild as Roddy thrusts his microphone towards them following the line in the song that says, 'Now scream'. The crowd duly obliges. Three songs later he gives me a slightly sweaty squeeze as he exits the stage. The shouts from the crowd are deafening.

'Ladies and gents! How about that! Give it up one more time for Roddy Wilson!' I hear myself say. More applause.

I'm loving this! My confidence is growing and for a brief moment I don't even think about the stranded UK artists.

But it's day three tomorrow. There are exactly thirty hours before the other UK acts are due to perform. I haven't been able to contact Janet. And I'm wondering whether Roddy Wilson will be around to entertain the crowd for just a while longer…

CHAPTER FIFTY-THREE

I had a restless night and it's late morning now as Costas is banging on my bedroom door. Again.

He practically drags me down to reception and along the village to the main road, where there is a frenzy of beeping horns and screaming people. The coach crawls along the road and the crowds are parting to make way for it. Gary Styles waves to a young woman in the crowd, who promptly faints.

The sleek machine finally purrs its way to a standstill, where a bevy of security keeps the crowds at bay. How on earth has Janet managed to pull this off? The bands are hurriedly and expertly ushered inside a large hotel just outside the village.

'You drove?' I say in astonishment to Janet over drinks in the Hilton hotel bar an hour later. 'You actually drove here?'

'Well, I could have flown straight here from the UK but as the band's manager I thought I would fly to Bodrum and travel part of the way with them on a tour bus. It was only Istanbul that was affected by the strike and Simon was keen to do it as he thought it might be a lot of fun. And do you know what? It actually was. We passed through some stunning landscapes, as well as having a good laugh, so it gave us quite an experience. It reminded me of when I was in the Night Owls and we drove across France, stalking the boy band Black in the hope of an interview.' She laughs. 'We called at some beautiful Greek islands on the ferry, too. I will never forget the sight of the harbour at Symi, with its colourful sugar-cube houses on the hillsides, spiralling towards the sky.'

Most of the crowds are on the field listening to a rousing set by the Mandolins followed by The Miracles. I have briefly left my hosting skills to a friend of Adonis, who is a bar owner and part-time DJ, who is alternating with Mika. Outside the hotel, a ten-minute walk away from the festival, a group of diehard New Horizons fans have taken up residence in the grounds of the hotel, being intermittently shooed by security.

We are joined by the band, who are showered and changed and causing a sensation in the foyer, where Sam from New Horizons is making eyes at the stunning-looking receptionist.

I'm still in a state of shock. 'I can't believe it!' I keep saying over and over.

'Neither can I really,' Janet says, draining her glass and ordering another from a passing waitress. 'I'm just so happy everything turned out alright in the end.'

Janet's husband, Simon, is smiling at Janet in admiration.

When we are all seated in the restaurant, the band members of Apocalypse join us and regale us with stories of their road trip. I have hair envy of lead singer Mick's blond, flowing tresses. He keeps moving his chair closer to mine and fixing me with his steel-blue eyes, unnerving me ever so slightly. You can tell he's been accustomed to a steady supply of groupies.

'That journey was a blast,' says Mick, in between mouthfuls of lamb and green bean stew. He wipes his plate clean with a hunk of bread. 'We haven't been on a long trip in a while. But the show must go on, eh, gorgeous,' he says, winking at me. I can feel the eyes of Costas boring into him.

'Indeed it must,' says Janet. 'But, for now, I think we should all get some rest, it's been an exhausting journey. You're up first tomorrow.' She speaks directly to Mick from Apocalypse.

'You're kidding, babe. The day is young,' he says, before beckoning a passing waitress and ordering another beer. 'I think we'll have a wander over to the concert field, see what's what.' He grins. 'The concert has been going for a good few hours. It will probably be a bunch of drunken revellers by now,' says Janet.

'Sounds good to me,' says Mick with a lecherous wink.

New Horizons decide they will be happy to 'hang out' around the hotel, much to the delight of the receptionist, who has been joined by some equally attractive female staff.

Janet looks exhausted, and I am overwhelmed with admiration for her that she actually made this happen. It took sixteen hours of driving, although they all did their fair share. She had to dissuade Mick from picking up two gorgeous-looking girls at the harbour in Kos and letting them on the tour bus. She did tell me that she had enjoyed the adventure though.

I'm suddenly overwhelmed with gratitude and reach over and give Janet a lingering hug, which I notice she doesn't recoil from.

'Well, we're going to our room now,' she says turning to a yawning Simon, who is on his feet in an instant.

'Good night, Mandy. See you in the morning.'

Janet kisses me on the cheek as Simon smiles and I am happy to see that she has come a long way, in more ways than one.

CHAPTER FIFTY-FOUR

Apocalypse are rocking the crowd into a frenzy, while Roddy is causing a stir near one of the bars, chatting to a bevy of beautiful blondes.

'This is just unbelievable,' says Costas, as he snakes a hand around my waist. It's so lovely being here with him stood next to me and, in some ways, I still can't quite believe it. All I know is that it just feels so natural being with Costas now, even though I haven't really known him for that long.

He's not much of a drinker but he has sunk quite a few pints tonight, which may explain his amorous advance towards me. His fingers are gliding gently up and down my back, arousing feelings I am enjoying, when a passing reveller trips and spills his beer over Costas, causing us to spring apart.

The music is intoxicating and by the time I introduce New Horizons on to the stage, things have reached fever pitch. Costas is stage-side, swaying along to the music with a drunken grin on his face, and I wonder whether he will even remember his affectionate gesture towards me in the morning.

Gary Styles has targeted a striking brunette in the audience and is singing a line from their most recent bestseller, to which she shakes her head and screams in response.

I've never seen anything like it in my life. I've been to a few concerts at the Echo Arena in Liverpool, but they never had an atmosphere like this. The place is literally bouncing. I spot Simon and Janet squeezing their way through the crowds to join us near the stage.

'Are you having a good time?' asks Janet, who looks fresh and relaxed in a stone-coloured linen maxi dress with a statement necklace.

'I'm having the time of my life, it's just fantastic,' I say, suddenly feeling choked with emotion. 'The crowds seem to be having an amazing time. And I can't believe how much I'm enjoying hosting the show! It's the best feeling ever. Actually, I hear Daniel O'Brien is leaving *The Next Superstar* show. I might apply for his job. Can you get me Simon Cowell's phone number?' I joke.

It's hard to believe that a few short months ago, this was nothing more than a dream. It seems dreams really can come true.

'I can never thank you enough for what you've done and neither can the people of the village,' says Costas, as he takes a drunken stumble towards Janet before crushing her in an embrace that she quickly releases herself from.

'It's been an absolute pleasure. The big events don't have the heart that this one has had. I can feel the appreciation all around. I don't think I'll ever forget this.' She grins. 'But let's not forget Mandy,' she says, turning to me. 'This would never have happened if it wasn't for you. This was your idea.'

'Well, ideas are one thing, turning them into a reality is something else,' I say modestly, while secretly feeling very proud of myself.

Simon is singing along to a cover version of 'One Way or Another', while Janet throws him an adoring glance.

The party continues in the field long after the final acts have finished, and we are sitting on blankets in the soft moonlight while Costas gently snores.

'He is not one for too much alcohol,' notes Andreas as he comes along to say good night. 'I think he may have a bad head in the morning.'

'I'm dreading going home,' I say, pulling a cardigan over my arms as the temperature cools a little in the early hours of the morning.

'Me too,' says Hayley, swigging from a bottle of pink rosé and looking as gorgeous as ever.

Gary is lying down beside her and stroking her arms lovingly. They are as loved up as ever and I think Hayley may have finally found the one she wants to spend the rest of her life with.

'We'll just have to count down the days until next year, won't we?' says Hayley brightly.

'Next year?'

'Well, yeah. This has been bloody brilliant. Surely it's going to be an annual event?'

An annual event? I'd never even considered it! It makes sense though. Most festivals, if a success, become annual events that everyone really looks forward to.

'Hayley,' I say, crushing my friend in a tight embrace with a tingle of excitement. 'You are the dog's doodahs!'

CHAPTER FIFTY-FIVE

I've been home for two days and I'm still buzzing with the excitement of the festival, which has been hailed a huge success by everyone concerned. Some of the restaurant owners spilled tears of gratitude when they counted up their week's takings, declaring that it was more than they had made in the last six months.

It's Saturday afternoon and I'm off to collect my mum to have lunch at Canal View Garden Centre, which is a twenty-minute drive away. I like garden centres. They've come a long way since the days of just lawnmowers and bedding plants. These days they have some beautiful gifts and outdoor dining solutions, and invariably a café selling delicious home-cooked food. I admire a huge barbecue, which I think I might suggest to Brian for the pub's beer garden.

We're seated near the window admiring a lemon tree in a glazed blue terracotta planter and I think of the lemon trees in Thakos.

I'm surprising my mum with an afternoon tea that I pre-booked, and there is an array of goodies in front of us. There are little sponge cakes cooked in mini terracotta plant pots, ceramic wellies filled with elderflower cordial, and a selection of mouth-watering sandwiches and cakes, including the heavenly lemon drizzle cake. They are all laid out on a miniature wooden picnic table. It's charming, but I didn't quite get the response from my mum that I expected.

'Are you alright, Mum?' I ask, in between mouthfuls of an utterly delicious slice of lemon drizzle cake.

She nibbles distractedly on a smoked ham sandwich before placing it down on her plate and taking a sip of tea.

'Now, I don't want you to worry, but the thing is I've found a lump,' she says quietly.

My blood runs cold.

'A lump?'

'Yes, in my breast. I wasn't too worried at first, you know, with not having any family history of it. Your grandmother and great grandmother both lived to be in their late eighties. Anyway, I found it in the shower and went to the doctor's last week. They sent me for tests.'

The dreamy lemon drizzle cake that had melted on my tongue seconds earlier turns sour in my mouth.

'So what have they said?' I ask, hearing my own heart beating loudly through my chest.

'Well, it's a slow-growing cancer, apparently. I'm going to have it removed. A lumpectomy, I think it's called, then several sessions of radiotherapy. The outlook is good,' she tells me with a forced smile.

I'm trying to process what my mum has just told me. She seems to think it's going to be a simple procedure, or maybe she's just trying to shield me from the truth. I know low-grade cancers generally have a better prognosis, but the fact is we just don't know. Everybody reacts differently.

My mum musters a smile and takes a bite of a cherry Bakewell, which she concedes is better than hers.

'Don't be worrying. I'll be fine. Now then, tell me all about that Greek concert,' she says, grinning.

I can't string a sentence together. *My beloved mum might die.*

I manage to hold it together for the duration of our tea with positive platitudes, but when I get home I cry like a baby and wish I had someone to hold me.

What am I going to do? *My mum has cancer.*

CHAPTER FIFTY-SIX

It's been a horrible few weeks. I was already on a holiday downer when I returned to Liverpool, but returning to the news of my mum's cancer was devastating. She seems to be doing alright now though. The lumpectomy has been performed and the cancer hadn't got into any lymph nodes. She's had two sessions of radiotherapy so far, without any real ill effects, and I've been spending as much time with her as possible. I must admit to missing the sunshine in Greece, though, as well as all the wonderful friends I've made.

Leonard Walker's in hospital, too. He's recovering from a stroke that everyone seemed to think would finish him off, including his son Greg, who travelled over from Australia to find a smiling Leonard sitting up in bed and thankfully over the worst.

I've prayed a lot these last few weeks, having lapsed a bit of late. When I was younger I was always talking to Jesus and asking him for things. Mainly big boobs when I was a twelve-year-old with a chest as flat as an ironing board. They say good things come to those who wait and I was duly rewarded with an ample thirty-six-inch bosom when I was fourteen years old, which drew envy from the girls and admiration from the boys.

Greg Walker is a handsome forty-something with a touch of Pierce Brosnan about him. He's caused quite a stir in the pub, where he occasionally comes in and sits on the bar stool that is usually occupied by Leonard. He finds it quite amusing that, since his arrival, he has been asked to join the book club, has been invited to dinner by Dorothy Burns, the spinster of the parish, and has become the object of desire for at least a dozen other women who have started to frequent the pub. He's good for business, I tell him, and he laughs and says he's happy to help. I also tell Greg how his father helped me when my marriage was in trouble, and he raises his glass to him.

'That's typical of Dad. He's a good old stick. I wanted him to come out and join us in Australia, but he was having none of it. Too set in his ways. Anyway, he adores that house, which he and Mum shared together. He'll never leave it.'

Greg's wife has stayed in Australia to look after their ten-year-old twin boys and Greg is flying back in a few days, now that he knows Leonard is on the mend.

'You'll break some hearts when you leave,' I say, raising an eyebrow as Dorothy Burns enters the pub and makes a beeline for him.

'It's a cross I have to bear,' he jokes.

I like Greg and can see a lot of Leonard in him.

'When will you be over here again, do you think?' I ask, as I pull a pint of bitter for a regular who has placed his pint pot on the bar for a refill.

'Christmas time. It was my original plan to visit with Dawn and the boys anyway. I'm sure they'd love to meet you. Why don't you come and have dinner over Christmas? The house looks amazing at that time of year, as Gloria really goes overboard with the decorations.' He grins.

'It sounds lovely,' I say, smiling, although I've been secretly dreading my first Christmas without Danny.

Greg drains his pint, picks his sunglasses up from the bar and puts them onto his handsome face. I'll miss him and, judging by the admiring glances from the females watching his departure, I'm sure I won't be the only one.

CHAPTER FIFTY-SEVEN

It's Friday afternoon and there's a stag do in the pub, with at least half of the lads already being the worse for wear.

The stag is approached by a sober-suited blonde, who suddenly unpins her tightly bound hair bun and shakes her flowing tresses over her shoulders.

Oh no, it's a bit early in the day for a stripper.

I steer them into a quiet alcove at the far end of the pub, thankful that it's not too busy, as the blonde unbuttons her white blouse to reveal her ample cleavage in a black lacy push-up bra. The rest of the stag party leer and jeer as the 'secretary' produces a can of squirty cream, which she invites the stag to spray onto her breasts. The stag pushes his head into her cream-filled cleavage, just as a grey-haired old bloke exits the gents' toilets and almost has a heart attack.

I'm going to have to put a stop to this soon. There's whipped cream flailing around everywhere and we only had the pub carpet steam-cleaned two weeks ago.

A short time later the floorshow has reached its conclusion and the stripper leaves the pub with a 'Ta-ra, love', dressed once more in a buttoned-up grey suit.

The stags have another vodka shot before they head off to Liverpool city centre. The groom has an inane grin on his face as he stumbles towards the taxi, and I wager he will be unconscious somewhere before 10 p.m., probably face down in a curry.

I am informed by the best man that this is only phase one of the celebrations. On Sunday, the group are flying from Liverpool to Benidorm for a four-day jaunt.

I don't know how people can afford it these days, I think to myself. Hen and stag celebrations have taken on a whole new level, with friends having to fork out more and more money, no doubt maxing out their credit cards.

I recall my own hen party – eight years ago in Blackpool – staying at a dodgy B & B and listening to 1980s music in a nightclub, with one of the group vomiting into a plastic bag all the way home on the train the next morning.

I'm coming to terms with the end of my marriage now and have begun to look for a house to rent, as I don't want to stay at the pub forever, despite its convenience. I'm realistic enough to realise that renting is the only solution, as it will take me forever to save another house deposit. Mum has told me I can go and live back home, to give me a chance to get some money together, which makes sense, I suppose, but I need my own space.

Joyce, the cleaner, is over in the alcove where the stags were, wiping down the tables and cleaning the cream off the carpet. She sprays Vanish foam onto a red-wine stain and tuts. 'Better clean this up before Brian notices it,' she says, with a flurry of a dry cloth on the foam. 'He'll go off his head; this carpet's only just been cleaned.'

'I know, I was thinking the same. I did tell Brian a patterned carpet would be far more practical, but he insisted on a plain one. He said something about patterned ones reminding him of old people's homes.'

'Well, if he wants to keep spending money on carpet cleaning, that's up to him. As long as it's not coming out of my wages.' She winks.

I do a quick stocktake, while it's quiet, and notice that we're short on Amaretto, as it's a base for a popular new cocktail. Gin has also made a comeback and some new flavoured ones have been a big hit, so I order some more. Liverpool gin is up there with some other well-known brands, and I feel a sense of pride every time I see it.

I have my back to the bar, refilling some optics, when I hear a familiar voice behind me.

'I don't suppose you sell ouzo, do you?'

I swing round and find to my astonishment that I am looking into the dark brown eyes of Costas.

CHAPTER FIFTY-EIGHT

'Costas! What are you doing here?' I say, coming down from the stepladder and leaning over the bar to hug him.

'Well, I always said I would come to Liverpool. You are right about the cheap flights. I was hoping you could show me the sights. You always talked so warmly about your city, I thought I would come and see it for myself,' he says, smiling.

I can't believe Costas is here in Liverpool. What a surprise! I'm so happy to see him! He looks so handsome and I notice some admiring glances from a couple of females at the bar.

In some respects, it's not the most ideal time for Costas to be here. It's full on at the pub over the next week and when I've finally finished my shift I tend to go and see my mum. But I want to welcome him to my city as warmly as he welcomed me to his village.

I think Mum's doing alright, actually, but you never know. Ever since I was a young child she has shielded me from anything that is upsetting. She hates anybody fussing over her and tells Dad and me that she's 'fine', even when she's been sleeping for half the day and clearly isn't.

It's late in the evening now, so after a meal of chilli con carne and rice, which Costas declares 'very good but not very English', I show him to one of the empty guest rooms at the pub. He was going to pay city prices at a hotel in town, but Brian was having none of it and invited Costas to stay at the pub for a fraction of the cost.

I feel a slight shiver of excitement, knowing that Costas will be staying in one of the bedrooms at the pub.

'I also came to invite you to my uncle's wedding in Paxos,' Costas tells me later over a shot of ouzo. 'It's going to be on the beach. I thought it would be nice for you to see a traditional Greek wedding,' he enthuses.

'Oh, Costas, I'm sorry. I'm so grateful that you have invited me, but I need to be here. For my mother.'

Costas twirls the cloudy ouzo around his glass. 'Forgive me. I should have spoken to you first. I have been insensitive,' he says softly.

'No, not at all, Costas,' I say, taking his hands and gripping them. 'You weren't to know. Every time you've asked about Mum I've told you she's fine. She's having her last lot of radiotherapy in ten days, so I'm going to speak to the doctor then and find out what's what.'

I realise I'm exhausted. I would like nothing more than to experience a Greek wedding and languish on a beach for a few days. I also know that my mother would insist that I go and tell me not to worry about her. But I would worry about her.

'Right,' I say brightly, 'I may not be able to come to your uncle's wedding, but you've come to my home city so the least I can do is make sure you have a good time. Tomorrow I will take you sightseeing.' I cross my fingers that Lyndsey will swap shifts with me as I tap out a text to her under the table.

A few seconds later a reply pings through.

OK but you owe me one. Ooh can't wait to see Costas X

'I would like that very much,' says my smiling Greek friend, as he raises his glass of ouzo. '*Yammas.*'

'*Yammas,*' I reply, feeling exhausted but exhilarated by the arrival of Costas.

CHAPTER FIFTY-NINE

It's difficult to know where to start in a city as wonderful as Liverpool. The modern architecture sits easily alongside its heritage buildings like two best friends.

I decide to take Costas on the Beatles Magical Mystery Tour as I know he is a big fan. The tour takes us to the birthplaces and childhood homes of the 'fab four', as well as places that inspired some of their greatest songs, such as 'Penny Lane' and 'Strawberry Fields'.

Costas is quiet as we stand outside the wrought-iron gates of the now-derelict children's home, Strawberry Field, as I tell him about John Lennon and how he would attend the summer fetes here with his Aunt Mimi, who raised him from the age of five.

'It must have been hard for him,' Costas says eventually. 'I was twenty-three years old when I lost my mother and that was bad enough.'

I explain that John's mum hadn't died, but was deemed unsuitable to raise him. She actually died when he was seventeen years old and he is quoted as saying it was like 'losing her twice'. So sad.

We finish off with a late lunch at a restaurant in Matthew Street before heading into the Cavern Club for a drink. A stag party is in full flow with the stags doing shots of Jäger Bombs. Costas is curious about the drink, so I buy him one. He spits it out.

'I am having a wonderful day today, thank you. Your city is so beautiful,' Costas says appreciatively, as he sips a cold beer to mask the taste of the Jäger Bomb.

'I'm glad you like it, but we haven't even scratched the surface really. There's so much to see. You'd need more than a few days here, but hopefully this won't be your last visit.'

'I hope not,' he says, looking at me with his dark brown eyes.

My eyes are almost closing on the train journey back to the pub, reminding me that I should forever abstain from drinking alcohol in the afternoon.

The following day, after a good night's sleep, I am taking Costas to the Maritime Museum, which outlines the history of Liverpool's nautical history, including the story of the Chinese immigrants, before I take him to Chinatown for lunch. Costas is silent as we peruse the section of the museum that looks at slavery.

'We are so lucky,' Costas says, thoughtfully. 'So free.'

His words make me reflect on a grand hotel in the Lake District that was entirely funded by profits from the slave trade. I turn my head the other way now every time I see it when I take a lake steamer across Windermere.

We spend the rest of the afternoon looking at the city's two cathedrals and I realise how much I am enjoying Costas's company. He prefers the Anglican cathedral, as do I. The newer Catholic Metropolitan Cathedral has a luminous beauty with its glass roof at the centre yet, for me, lacks soul.

The older Anglican cathedral is a stunning building with sandstone walls and huge, arched, Gothic windows. It looks old and atmospheric and it comes as a surprise to many people that the building work was only finished in 1978, having taken over seventy years to build. The cathedrals stand at either end of Hope Street and play an important part in the lives of the people of Liverpool and Merseyside.

We round off the afternoon with a ferry across the Mersey, which evokes strong childhood memories for me.

'I haven't done this for years,' I say, as a bracing wind on deck leaves me feeling exhilarated. The captain gives us a slightly crackly audio guide with the strains of Gerry Marsden's 'Ferry Cross the Mersey' playing in the background as we head across the river.

Costas is shivering. 'I like the boat, but I like the sun also,' he admits, as he zips his jacket up. He steps closer to me before putting his arm around my shoulders, and I find myself leaning into him comfortably.

On the return journey, I marvel at the sight of the buildings on the Liverpool waterfront. It's a sight I never tire of, particularly the Royal Liver Building with the two stone Liver birds perched at the top. Legend has it that if ever the birds fall from the rooftop, the city of Liverpool will crumble and disappear into the River Mersey.

'So, it's not just us Greeks that have myths and legends,' says Costas, grinning.

'I've never thought about it before, but I suppose you're right,' I muse.

✳

The next two days are filled with me trying to combine a shift at work and yet more sightseeing with Costas, who has fallen under the spell of the city. We're having a quick lunch with Gary and Hayley at Malmaison on the Albert Dock, when Gary casually invites Costas to Liverpool football stadium to have a look around and meet some of the players. Costas is speechless for a moment, and I realise Gary has just put the icing on his visit, with a cherry on the top.

To my surprise, I'm finding the thought of saying goodbye to Costas harder than I would have imagined, although I know I will see him again before too long. He is determined to return to England with Andreas to watch a Liverpool game, and of course there's the music festival again next year in Thakos. A lot can happen in a year. I wonder where we will all be in our lives twelve months from now?

I wave the plane into the wispy clouds, even though Costas can no longer see me. *Goodbye, my friend, I enjoyed our time here in my city. I hope it isn't too long before we meet again…*

CHAPTER SIXTY

It was the wedding of Costas' uncle in Paxos that changed everything. My mum absolutely insisted that I went – and for that I will be eternally grateful. I stayed for just three days. And in those three days something shifted. I sat next to Costas at the wedding feast at the beach restaurant, which was strung with fairy lights, and we talked until the party was long over.

I don't think I'd ever been to a more beautiful wedding. The bride and groom danced barefoot on the sand to the strains of music in the nearby restaurant, while the guests encircled them, clapping loudly. The one thing I remember was the laughter. The bride with her long dark hair and her handsome husband had happiness radiating from them.

Costas and I talked for hours until the sun went down. We talked about Liverpool and how much Costas had fallen under its spell. I said the same about Thakos. We sat there at a little table on the beach until the sun came up again over the horizon, and then he leaned in and kissed me. He kissed me gently at first but it soon built to a fiery passion. It was like all the clichés I'd ever read about. Sparks flew and time seemed to stand still. I never wanted to let go of him. They say that kind of magic is very rare. Costas told me that his heart had been stolen by a girl from Liverpool a long time ago. He never pursued me because he thought I wanted to mend my marriage, which made me love him even more.

We walked to the water's edge and listened to the gentle lapping of the waves, and Costas took my hand in his. 'I'm so glad you decided to come back to Greece. I have never met anybody like you,' he breathed, pulling me towards him and kissing my neck and sending shivers down my spine. 'I am sorry that your husband let you down. I will never let you down, Mandy.'

Something about the way he looked into my eyes as he said this, made me believe him. I feel so blessed to have found him. He is a beautiful man inside and out.

I'm glad I came back to Greece, too, I think to myself as I nuzzle into Costas's chest. My 'big Greek summer', as I like to think of it, has changed my life. Maybe it was written in the stars. The stars that shine so brightly in the Mediterranean sky…

EPILOGUE

FOUR YEARS LATER

I watch my husband playing with our two-year-old son in the sparkling Mediterranean Sea and remind myself how thankful I am for my life. I never imagined living here in Greece, but I think the Greek gods decided otherwise.

Mum recovered from her breast cancer treatment and, although not officially given the all clear for another twelve months, she's fully recovered now. She said it made her realise that we should grab hold of life with both hands and encouraged me to follow my heart, which I did, back to Thakos.

My parents have been regular visitors here, especially since their first grandson was born. They love to play with him in our garden as he splashes in his little pool, showering him with kisses and cuddles. The healthy food and climate have been a real tonic to my mum, who is looking wonderful, not to mention the joy of having a grandson whom she clearly adores.

Costas and I run a bar on the beach out here, which could only be called one thing – Christakis – which also happens to be the name of our son.

Gary Cooke decided he wanted to invest in some business projects for the future, for a time when he was no longer playing football, and purchased a gin bar in Liverpool's trendy Baltic Triangle district. At the same time, he had a beach bar built in Thakos, which is the one that we manage. He also built us an adjacent two-storey whitewashed villa as a wedding present. Yes, that's right. He bought us a home! I was initially reluctant to accept such a generous gift, but when Hayley informed me that it cost less than a week's footballing salary, it seemed ungracious not to accept. And, of course, they are regular visitors.

I love my home. I grow tomatoes in pots and they taste so different to anything back home. Everything does. Even the herbs in the small planters are super-sized. We have three chickens for our own eggs, too, but that's it. I have no desire to tend to vegetable beds every day in this heat.

Our beach wedding was the best day of my life. I entered into it wholeheartedly and unreservedly with a feeling of complete confidence that we would love and respect each other for the rest of our lives. I wore a simple cream silk shift dress, a far cry from my crystal-studded affair at my first wedding.

I was delighted that Leonard from the pub was among the guests at our wedding. He stayed on for an extra week to enjoy the sunshine and relax. It was lovely that he got to know some of my new Greek friends and he would chat to them, recalling fond memories of his previous visits to Greece when his wife was alive. He has also become rather good friends with my parents, which is lovely.

'Dinner's ready,' shouts Hayley from the step of our home as we arrive back from the beach. She's a regular visitor here so there's no chance of me missing her. Christakis adores her and, thankfully, so does Costas.

I'm so happy for Hayley. I think she has also found her 'happy ever after' in Gary Cooke. In fact, I'm certain of it. On their last visit here, we all dined in a swish restaurant on the harbour in Rhodes, where Gary got down on one knee and proposed. He presented Hayley with an enormous rock, which produced squeals of delight from her.

I must admit that I'd wondered if they would ever tie the knot, as they'd been together for over four years and Hayley always swore she'd never get married. I used to wonder if it was because her own parents' marriage had been so mundane. There seemed to be very little bond in the family unit, and when her brother quietly upped sticks and moved to Chester, they barely visited each other.

Gary kept the proposal a secret from everyone, including me and Costas, so we were just as surprised as Hayley. Champagne flowed and the whole restaurant cheered and applauded. Even a trio of Greek musicians serenaded the table with 'Love is All Around'. (I thought they had appeared out of nowhere, but Gary had managed to arrange that!) They are currently considering an offer from *OK!* magazine to cover the marriage, which will be in Bodellwydan Castle in north Wales next spring.

Oh, and Hayley is a model now, modelling ladies' fashions in magazines and catalogues, so they are quite the glamorous couple. She was scouted by a model agency in Liverpool when she was in Wetherspoons, of all places. Even wearing jeans and a T-shirt her model potential was obvious, they said. I'm only surprised she wasn't snapped up years ago.

I could never have imagined living my life in a Greek village, but now I find it hard to imagine being anywhere else. My friendship with Annis has really blossomed and I have also become friendly with Elyannia, the daughter of Joan from the Olive Garden Kitchen. We met at one of the Olive Garden barbecue nights and hit it off straight away. And I work with a lovely young woman called Nancy in Rhodes town.

Yes, I have an enjoyable part-time job in an estate agency owned by Stavros Papadopoulos. It seems one of his previous members of staff had no enthusiasm for the job and was quietly fired. I must admit I really enjoy it and I'm proud to say I helped to sell two villas in my first week. A young woman from the village called Elise helps out with Christakis when I am at work, if Costas is busy at the bar. She is generally regarded as the Mary Poppins of Thakos. She is the go-to childminder, adored by adults and children alike.

'Pork ofrito,' Hayley announces, proudly placing the pot of fragrant pork onto the table alongside a Greek salad and a mountain of rice. She has become rather an accomplished cook, has Hayley, and it all started with the Olive Garden Kitchen cookery lesson.

'Mmm, are you sure you are not Greek?' asks Costas, as he hungrily devours the tender pork.

'I'm proud to be a hundred per cent Liverpudlian, me,' declares Hayley. 'Although I must admit you Greeks are pretty cool.'

I have to agree. The Greek people are wonderful. I feel as though I will always have two homes.

Christakis jumps onto Hayley's knee and wraps his chubby little arms around her neck. She tickles him until he squeals with laughter.

We stroll back to the garden and sit down at the table, which is set with jugs of water and carafes of wine. (Still no afternoon alcohol for me.) I suddenly feel an immense feeling of contentment. My old life seems a million miles away now. I don't regret marrying Danny so young. I loved him then but it was never going to last. I wish Danny well and hope he finds true happiness eventually. Hayley sees him from time to time in Liverpool and it seems he is still enjoying the bachelor lifestyle.

We're spending Christmas in Liverpool this year, having accepted an invitation from Leonard. It will be good to see his family again. He's also invited my mum and dad along, so that will be lovely. Andreas has been invited, too, but he thinks he will stay here at the village and spend the day with friends and a widow he has been quietly dating.

I glance out to sea and notice a ship on the horizon, heading for the beautiful island of Symi. And, somewhere in the distance, I'm sure I hear the sound of a ship's horn on the Mersey…

A Letter from Sue

I want to say a huge thank you for choosing to read *My Big Greek Summer*. If you did enjoy it, and want to keep up-to-date with all my latest releases, just sign up at the following link. Your email address will never be shared and you can unsubscribe at any time.

www.bookouture.com/sue-roberts

I had a wonderful time writing Mandy's story and as the novel progressed I bonded with her more and more. I am lucky enough to be familiar with the wonderful settings in the story that are the city of Liverpool and Rhodes in Greece.

Part of the excitement of writing this story, was the opportunity of being able to share it with other readers who could join Mandy on her life changing journey.

I hope you loved *My Big Greek Summer* and if you did I would be very grateful if you could write a review. I'd love to hear what you think, and it makes such a difference helping new readers to discover my books for the first time.

I love hearing from my readers – you can get in touch through Twitter or on Goodreads.

Thanks,
Sue Roberts

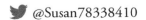 @Susan78338410

Acknowledgements

I would like to thank the following people for being involved in the journey of my debut novel: Firstly, Oliver Rhodes and his team for the fantastic concept that is Bookouture, providing writers a wonderful opportunity in the digital publishing world. My amazing editor Natasha Harding, for believing in the story and providing such wonderful editorial advice and support every step of the way. I am forever grateful. To my good friend Jackie Crispin for the hours spent on the initial proof read. To my daughters Rachel and Vicki and sister Lorraine for being so supportive and never doubting my ability to write a book. To my partner Derek for listening patiently as I threw plot ideas at him and for his unwavering support.

Finally, I would like to thank every one of my family, friends and colleagues for all their heartfelt good wishes when I received my book offer.

Much love to you all,
Sue x

Made in the USA
Middletown, DE
05 July 2021